D0402606

MISS SUBWAYS

MISS SUBWAYS

DAVID DUCHOVNY

FARRAR, STRAUS AND GIROUX : NEW YORK

Farrar, Straus and Giroux
175 Varick Street, New York 10014

Printed in the United States of America
First edition, 2018

Descriptions of the emu, emu constellation, and emu myth that appear on
pages 143–44 have been adapted from the following sources: https://en
.wikipedia.org/wiki/Emu; https://en.wikipedia.org/wiki/Australian_Aboriginal
_astronomy; http://www.sacred-texts.com/aus/mla/mla15.htm.

Library of Congress Cataloging-in-Publication Data
Names: Duchovny, David, author.
Title: Miss subways / David Duchovny.
Description: First edition. | New York : Farrar, Straus and Giroux, [2018]
Identifiers: LCCN 2017047951 | ISBN 9780374210403 (hardcover)
Subjects: LCSH: Romance fiction, American. | Paranormal fiction. | Fantasy
fiction, English. | GSAFD: Love stories.
Classification: LCC PS3604.U343 M57 2018 | DDC 813/.6—dc23
LC record available at https://lccn.loc.gov/2017047951

Designed by Abby Kagan

For my mother, who took me on those first subway rides to the Museum of Natural History—we hardly ever got exactly where we wanted to go, but who'd've known that we'd end up here? I guess that's the point. Our curiosity and incompetence taught us it's not the destination, it's the ride. To the dinosaur bones of T. rex—for being that dream/nightmare destination. For Madeleine West, and all former and future Miss Subways—stay on the train, the scenery will change. That goes for you too, Kyd Miller, who in some future may think about Uber the way I write of the underground. And to New York City, place of my birth. I will leave you one day, but not yet, not yet.

She has hurried from the Country-Under-Wave,
And dreamed herself into that shape that he
May glitter in her basket; for the Sidhe
Are fishers also and they fish for men
With dreams upon the hook.

—W. B. YEATS, *The Only Jealousy of Emer*

····PART

1

Even now, I can sit in the subway, and look up at the ads, and close my eyes, and there's Miss Subways. She wasn't the most beautiful girl in the world but she was ours.   —ED KOCH

EMER

ON MARCH 20, AT 6:37 P.M., Emer Gunnels sat on the Lexington Avenue IRT line subway deep below Manhattan hurtling toward the future, hopefully making a stop at Ninety-sixth Street as well. She tried to avert her gaze from any man. She didn't consider herself beautiful, but she had something some men sometimes liked. Some thing. Some times. Some men. Like she was in on the big joke. A blue-green refraction in her eyes of some charismatic, universal, lighthearted melancholy, like she saw things at a distance, a gently ironic remove. She dabbled in yoga; she could sometimes be found on a Stairmaster or a stationary bike; she was a New Yorker.

Here in the simulated captivity of a subway car, it seemed that the male imperative to gaze unapologetically at the female was a creepy game of chicken. The manspreading, lip licking, eye fucking—exhausting. These were men who would never act this way up in the disinfecting light of the street, but down in the subway, confined, these same males reverted to a kind of primal, almost prison-like dominance-testing behavior. It's like a big-game reserve underground, she thought. Every day down here was like a new Stanford experiment. Thanks be to Jobs for the iPhone, which seduced a good number of the underworld travelers into a zombified and harmless solipsistic reverie, though it also seemed to embolden others by adding a propulsive soundtrack to their passive ogling. It was as if they thought, like children, if they couldn't hear you, then you couldn't see them.

She laughed lightly at that thought, making inadvertent eye contact with a pin-striped homunculus across from her, who, taking this as a sign that Emer was into him, manspread his open lap over not one, not two, but almost three seats. This antisocial act of opening wide your legs to cover multiple seats, presumably to air out your impressive package, was a true urban media obsession for a couple months back in 2014 that had spawned its own word and six-day culture war.

She felt a cold bead of sweat liberate itself from her right armpit and track down her ribs to a latitude even with her belly button. The Manafort-looking manspreader in the pin-striped suit—could be a Wall Streeter, possibly a top one or ten percenter—arched his eyebrows and tilted his pelvis ever so slightly, subtly enough to maintain the wiggle room of plausible public deniability. He ran his tongue across his lips. Gross. And clichéd. Double whammy. She involuntarily winced and made a gagging motion, as one might wave a cross in front of Dracula.

It was rare that she was without a book—she favored nineteenth-century novelists: George Eliot, Jane Austen, Charles Dickens—but this was one of those times she lacked printed matter. She found that looking down at her smartphone or tablet as the train was moving made her dizzy and nauseated, and while she realized that some vomit might clear valuable space in this crowded car, she chose to pass the time by reading the signs and advertisements that lined the tops of the walls all around her. Ever since she could read, Emer had felt the compulsion to read and even reread—cereal boxes, toothpaste tubes, subway ads. She was a reader. It defined her. She fixed her gaze well above the lap of the manspreader and made out what she could.

The first ad that caught her eye was for the ambulance-chaser law firm of Washington, Liebowitz, and Gonzalez, offering lottery-type rewards for heartbreaking diagnoses—$5.3 million for lead poisoning, $6.3 million for rubella, $11.3 million for mesothelioma, and so on. The repetition of the .3 was slightly suspect. How could all the crappy tragedies that might befall you be worth a fortune point three hundred thousand? Emer did the dread math in her head that she was convinced we all do when faced with these types of Faustian lawsuit scenarios. 11.3 million for mesothelioma . . . uh, no, nope, pass, but 6.3 mill for a little rubella? Maybe, maybe. Beats working. What was rubella anyway?

Next to Washington, Liebowitz, and Gonzalez was a placard from a series the MTA had instituted called Trains of Thought, in which quotations from great literature and philosophy were randomly posted to entertain the masses in the midst of mass transit.

One morning as Gregor Samsa was waking from an anxious dream, he discovered that in his bed, he had been changed into a monstrous, verminous bug.　　　—FRANZ KAFKA

"The Metamorphosis" was one of her favorite stories. She'd read somewhere that Kafka couldn't get through a reading of his own work without collapsing into fits of laughter. A deadpan humor

DAVID DUCHOVNY

born of incomprehensible horror. The literary equivalent of her favorite comedian/actor—Buster Keaton. Kafka was a dark fantasist whose unadorned prose read like newspaper accounts from hell on earth. She wondered at the wisdom of bringing the specter of the cockroach, which was really the official anti-mascot of New York City, into the minds of subway riders trapped belowground, a place arguably more hospitable to vermin than people. She had seen roaches the size of New Jersey and rats you could throw a saddle on play on the tracks like they owned the place, like a postapocalyptic Disney movie.

She did not like to kill anything and had been an on-and-off, semi-strict, nondogmatic, occasional vegetarian since college when she'd read *Diet for a New America*, but she made an exception for cockroaches, flies, and mosquitoes. (And really good sushi.) Some insects deserved to die. She thought briefly of the Zika virus and its sad crop of pin-skulled, brain-damaged infants. She had no children. She was forty-one years old.

She quickly glanced down to see what el manspreader was doing, and shit goddammit, she met his eyes, and, having failed to hide a jittery and guilty flinch, she flailed around for something else to read. As she cast her eyes nervously about the car, she was surprised at the violent and vindictive fantasies of revenge that visited her. Her inner judge never had rehabilitation in mind— Hammurabian, very eye for an eye, and leaning heavily toward poetic justice. Vengeance would be taken from the man's offending organs. A ball for an eyeball. An image flashed into her mind unbidden—of the offender's junk stretched across the third rail as a train barreled down. She felt bad for visualizing that. A tad harsh, perhaps. Maybe the draconian Giuliani had recommended something like that. She shook her head, remembering the days of that lispy, hissy, death's head of a mayor.

She readjusted her gaze to the next placard, which, she was warmed to see, featured a new Miss Subways competition. Miss Subways? Really? She happened to know all about that bygone "pageant."

It was a real thing. She'd read about it in an Urban Studies program she'd taken a few years ago at Hunter College, where she'd decided to take a course every now and then, because, to paraphrase Dylan, if she wasn't busy learning or being born, she was busy dying. The qualifications for entering the contest were both lax and touchingly parochial: she "had to be eligible, a NYC resident, and herself use the subway." This was 1941, mind you. And yet as quaint as those strictures may seem, the contest itself was progressive, opening up to races and ethnicities that no other American pageant of the time would consider for decades. The clownish but deep former mayor Ed Koch had once said, "Even now, I can sit in the subway, and look up at the ads, and close my eyes, and there's Miss Subways. She wasn't the most beautiful girl in the world but she was ours."

Thinking about a seemingly more innocent past, when the messiness of private life was no doubt the same, but the façade, how one spoke of the inside in public, was much simpler and the codes more easily figured, made her sleepy and warm. The lights flashed on and off like the staccato announcement of an epileptic seizure. "Dostoyevsky," she muttered to herself, like an omen, another underground man. The subway itself was womb-like, dark, and humming—Emer, who could have trouble falling asleep in her bed at night, often dozed sitting straight up on her commute. Sleeping amid strangers on a crowded subway car in New York City—an act of trust to make any saint weep with joy.

The train shuddered to an unscheduled stop between stations and the lights went out. Everyone groaned en masse. Perfect, Emer fretted, I'm already late. Con wants me there. He wants me there, but then he wants to ignore me. Like a child, a man-child. But that's okay. This is his time, his time to shine, and she still had her secret wish, her secret plan within herself. A type of plan hatched in the infancy of civilization and the more primitive parts of a superstitious brain stem that lay underneath a rational modern forebrain, like water flowing under rock. A hope more than a plan, a wish she shared with no one for fear she'd be ridiculed as an old-fashioned gal.

She wouldn't even form the words in her mind right now. She thought only of Miss Subways. July 1946 was one Enid Berkowitz, whose bio next to a fetching photo of the dark-haired Jewess read, "Art student at Hunter College—interested in advertising and costume design—plugging for B.A. but would settle for M.R.S."

One step forward, one half step back. In April '48, thirty-five years before the first black Miss America was crowned, meet caramel Miss Subways Thelma Porter, who "sings in a choral group and is a Gershwin devotee." Of course she is. One step forward, and, oh well.

By the mid-'70s, the old girl, Miss Subways, quietly faded away, a necessary casualty of raised feminist consciousness, but she was nostalgically reinstituted for one year by the *New York Post* in 2004. And it now appeared the whole thing was making another postironic run again in 2017. Emer felt a little out of step with the times, and thought sometimes of the days of Miss Subways when it could be said without irony of a woman like Rita Rogers of March 1955 fame, "A sparkling, dark brunette, Rita was graduated cum laude last June from Notre Dame College of Staten Island. Works for a magazine. Likes fencing. Knits Argyle socks expertly." Well, touché then, what man can resist a gal who can crochet up some Argyle? (Was it misogynistic? Was it pure nostalgia and therefore obviating questions of misogyny—like her uncle collecting Negro League baseball cards was not considered racist? But more important, was she too old to apply?)

The lights came back on and the train started up again. To save time, she was going to get off at Eighty-sixth and run the six blocks to the 92nd Street Y rather than going on to Ninety-sixth. Even in these heels. Her right hand wandered up to trace a scar hidden beneath her hair, by her left ear, a remnant of surgery to remove a benign tumor from her temporal lobe almost ten years ago now. She was beginning to realize that this had become a habit, and was less and less surprised when she caught herself in a reflective surface with her hand to her head.

When she thought about the significance of this tic, she figured it was grounding, reminding her, unconsciously, of who she was, her history, bumps overcome, and of mortality. She had been having some very mild, imperceptible seizures and ever-so-fleeting hallucinations, which ended with the removal of the tumor. She was supposed to get checked at least yearly, but for the past couple of years she'd been delinquent, telling herself that she would feel with her own hand if there were any changes that needed attention. It was her secret, kept from her mother when she was alive and her father now and all her friends, even her boyfriend, that she sometimes felt under the power of hallucinatory thought, of dreamlike late-night states in the middle of the day. If she were honest with herself, she might admit she liked the hallucinations.

They were infrequent and often beautiful, and afterward, she felt a spent calm that many epileptics report feeling after a seizure. But, yes, she would make an appointment with the doctor. Just not this week.

The only outward sign of anything amiss was the difference in the size of her pupils. One black circle in the green was more dilated, larger than the other, as a stroke victim will sometimes present, but Emer had never had a stroke. It was merely a consequence of the operation the doctors could not explain and Emer, after crying for a week that her symmetry had been ruined (as it turns out, no one ever even noticed), started delighting in the fact that now she looked like David Bowie, and that it represented to her a certain rebellious, schizy nonconformity—as if one eye, with the smaller pupil, was focused on the light of day, while the other, the larger, the right one, was always trained on darkness and night.

Removing her hand from the ridge on her scalp, she returned her eyes to the manspreader, and thought of Con, and how they had made love last night. She liked the phrase "making love," as if the act itself brought something new into the world, created something—made more of love itself. Con was very good at that. They had been together years, and sometimes she did feel that the consequent steps of their lovemaking were as predictable as Christ's stations of the cross—as they lay in bed, Con's hand would brush up against her thigh, he would turn her to him, they would kiss for thirty seconds, while his fingers explored her and opened her up, followed by a couple minutes of obligatory but still blissful oral pleasures, and then onto ten or fifteen minutes of fairly vigorous coupling in two or three positions, culminating in simultaneous, mutually assured orgasm.

As she put these clinical words on their still nightly ritual—it felt rote in retrospect, in the telling, like a how-to-assemble-an-orgasm manual, but it never felt rote in the doing. In their bed, Con was most present through his touch, and his presence conjured her own call to a full presence. Maybe it wasn't fireworks, but it worked. She loved making daily, end-of-day love with Con, and the sameness of their moves felt to her not as the boredom of puppets going through the motions, but like being known—known by her man, and in turn, knowing, and pleasing, that same man. She could weep at the prospect of not making love to Con anymore. So she banished that thought.

Her man, not this hedge-fund simulacrum of masculinity across from her. She decided on behalf of all former and future Miss Subways to confront the Wall Street manspreader. She resolved to mouth the words "Fuck you, asshole" at him as she left the train car in minor triumph. She would confuse the offender, stun him, divert his attention, paralyze a retort. That would show his entitled smug jerk face. The douche bag probably worked for Lehman Brothers and caused the recession. I'd like to shove the whole subprime-mortgage crisis up his ass. She started to feel righteous. She took a deep breath and leveled her eyes at Lehmanschpreader, her upper teeth already pinched on her bottom lip to form a very capital "F" . . .

But the man had dozed off, his mouth open dreamily, like a little boy. His once widespread lap was pulled up into a childlike fetal position. Emer's shoulders fell. "Aw . . ." she heard herself say involuntarily, then recoiled and wondered, What the fuck is wrong with me? before someone who saw her not as an object, but an obstacle, pushed her from behind making for the opening subway doors.

CUCHULAIN CONSTANCE

THE BIG SHIPS brought exotic cargo. Plums, pea-
cocks, bamboo, people with almond eyes, black
skin, brown skin, blue-veined yellow-white skin. All
this was aboveboard, commerce, accounted by meticulous hand in
parallel ledgers marked debit, marked credit.

But there are always stowaways.

Not everybody pays for a ticket. Take the rats in the holds of
trading ships to Hawaii. Rats and snakes are not indigenous to the
islands. No prey has evolved learning to deal with them. Those
stowaway predators greedily feasted on defenseless songbirds. No
more songbirds in Hawaii. Stowaways, illegal aliens, if you will,
write the unwritten history, history's story. Say goodbye to the
Hawaiian honeycreeper. {slide}

This is called evolution. Or unintelligent design, if you will, with
the understudy, Man, playing the role of God tonight. Some will
say that God has abdicated his iron fist in favor of Adam Smith's

invisible hand. They say God is angry, with good reason, perhaps bored with this particular part and looking for new challenges, Mars perhaps? {slide of Elon Musk} Or one of a number of Goldilocks planets? {slides of Kepler 442b, 452b, Proxima Centauri b, etc.} Or maybe to spend more time with his family? {slide of the Kardashians, raise eyebrow à la Belushi, wait for big laugh}

But it's not just Hawaii. Stowaways colonized the world, introducing new flora, fauna, and pestilence to places where they had not existed. Half a century ago, there went most of our indigenous elm trees to misnamed "Dutch" elm disease, which was in actuality a fungus from China caused by beetles laying infected eggs beneath the bark. So goes sudden oak death, beech wilt, and sweet chestnut blight.

Smallpox took a ride on oceangoing, ecosystem-hopping ships and decimated unprepared native immune systems. {slides} Cockroaches, another New York City icon, got to feast on the Big Apple by hitching a ride on slave ships from Africa.

Like Malcolm Gladwell before me—and Steven Levitt and Michael Lewis—I am hoping to make sense of your lives by marrying statistics to simplicity. Statistics will be your new god and probability will become Fate. If Twitter mated with Malcolm Gladwell {slide of Gladwell kissing the Twitter bird} and moved a little to the right—that's me.

I posit to you that those ships that brought immigrants and rats, slaves and cockroaches, to the New World also brought gods and customs, folktales and superstitions. America is the theological melting pot, the universal stew, gumbo of the gods. You already know that history is appropriation. That our Roman gods first had Greek names. That Jove became Jupiter and Aphrodite, Venus. Issur

Danielovitch {slide of Kirk Douglas} became Kirk Douglas became Spartacus. Roberto {slide of baseball card} became Bob Clemente. Albert Einstein became Albert Brooks. {slide/slide, laugh}

To the victors go the nomenclature.

You know that Christ was born on December 25 because the Christian bigwigs were trying to make the pagans' enforced slide into monotheism as painless as possible, right? And December 25 or thereabouts was already a big holiday throughout organized human society as a winter solstice celebration? {slide of Stonehenge—maybe from Spinal Tap *Stonehenge scene? Cheap laugh? Why not?}*

And how the Jesus resurrection Easter myth co-opts so many returns from the underworld before it. Osiris, Beowulf, Persephone. {slides} While we're on the subject of December 25—it's a perfect example of a foreign god mutating to survive. St. Nicholas or Sinter Claus/Sinter Klass {slide} was a stowaway with the Dutch, who were the first in charge here in Manhattan; well, after the natives, that is.

In 1773, after the Boston Tea Party, old St. Nick was resurrected as a symbol of New York's non-English past; he was a Dutch middle finger to the British and the patron saint of pre-Revolutionary societies that sprang up calling themselves the sons of St. Nicholas. So St. Nick got up off his deathbed, first to symbolize a non-English identity for the fledgling revolutionaries and then, in an even bolder move, to make himself virtually indistinguishable from Jesus Christ and Christmastime. {slide of Jesus in a red Christmas hat} Arguably, it is the free-spending, gift-giving St. Nick who enabled Christ to assume the mantle of American capitalism and, with the help of Calvinism, confer his holy blessing upon the almighty dollar. You might even argue that St. Nick helped Jesus more than Jesus helped him, since some, and I say some, may still be offended at the sight of Jesus Christ himself enjoying an ice-cold Coca-Cola. {slide}

The return from the underworld, resurrection, was a tune the world's people already knew, a tune they loved—so St. Paul and the early fathers were just tossing new names around, new lyrics on an old melody. Saul became Paul, solstice became Christmas, the many became the only. It was a brutal, effective, and glorious re-structuring of the soul. The first downsizing. A corporate raid on the spirit to make Jack Welch proud and Oliver Stone angry. {slide, laugh} The pantheon became the one. As an aside, ask yourself— what are the myriad saints that are added as objects of worship, to say nothing of the Cult of Mary, except a sop to those depressed converted pagans who missed a bunch of gods, especially the females, missed Baal or Zeus or Mother Nature, after the downsizing? It's a form of winking, plus ça change, plus c'est la même chose, my brothers and sisters.

And I posit to you tonight that this shrinking from the chattering discord of many gods to the one Jehovah played out again in min-iature and in fast motion in New York City roughly between the years 1800 and 1935. I'm being specific with dates for a reason, and that reason is to make you think I'm being scientific.

That as our immigrant ancestors came through Ellis Island, they were smuggling beliefs, smuggling local gods into the New Ordered World, hopelessly scrambling the smooth gleaming surface of official WASP monotheistic America. Forced to wait in detention to screen out smallpox or other infectious diseases from the decadent continent {slide of young Vito Corleone waiting on Ellis Island in The Godfather}, *there was no detention long enough to cure them of the spiritual infestation of their local customs and beliefs. Gods are immortal and therefore patient. Their gods waited with them.*

See, the only American religion, the only religion to have sprouted on American soil—and I am willfully excluding Scientology, not even I can stomach Old Mother Hubbard's moronic Buddhist sci-fi mélange {slide of Tom Cruise or Travolta}—is Mormonism, or the Church of Latter Day Saints. {slide of Mitt Romney} The genius of Joseph Smith was in the "Latter" of Latter Day—the time of miracles ain't over, we are not belated. 'Cause isn't there something depressing about old-world Christianity constantly looking back to the good old miracle days of water to wine? Why did the men of the past get proof and all you get is faith? Joe Smith figured that out. No, Joe said, that crazy shit is still happening.

We see a Darwinian struggle in species, we see it in ideas, and, I am suggesting to you, we see it in gods as well. And what if the native gods and the gods of different countries went underground, or intermingled and interbred, just like the peoples of their countries? Imagine what new gods came into the world, hybrids with unforeseen wacky combinations of old powers—how badass would Superman be with Batman's gadgets? {slide}

And what if those old gods interbred with humans in a template struck by those randy Greek deities—Leda and the swan? Let me quote you Yeats—"A terrible beauty is born." What other terrible beauties are out there now? Some hybrid Greek Hermes with Beats in both ears instead of wings? {slide of Mercury wearing headphones}

And here's where you get to boo me, you secular, liberal relativists. I'm telling you this unreal struggle is real. And it has consequences. It's not "just debate." I'm telling you that it is possible to judge systems of belief as being better or worse than one another. Just as there has been an evolution of man, there has been an evolution of gods; just as we are superior to the apes, the new god is superior to the old. The old gods are good entertainment {slide from Twilight}, *good box office, but inferior soul sustenance. I stand before you tonight, a relativist come to slay relativism, to tell you the Qu'ran is a lesser work than the New Testament, and that all the Greek gods and African folklores that were improved morally and subsumed into the Christ story—that that rewrite was an advancement.*

I want to talk about our country now. I want to tell you that there is a separation of church and state, yes, but also that Christianity, the shared belief in the system, was the key to the assimilation of all the poor huddled masses and made it possible for America to be great. And I want to declaim that the deconstruction of that core system into the fragments of our educational and social approach is a real and present, and not just literary, danger.

Because ye olde gods are not dead. They walk among us still, with their pagan ideas and habits, waiting for reanimation. They are lonely. They are bored. And very, very pissed off. They grow tired of waiting, and they sense another historical moment is imminent. There is no wall high enough to keep them out, pace Donald. I'm afraid their time has come again.

GIVE US THIS DAY OUR DAILY PAIN

S SHE RAN FOR THE Y, Emer slowed by a Pain Quotidien and eyed the pastries in the window. She always marveled that the owners of this particular franchise seemed unaware of their hawking a daily dose of caffeine, bread, and sadness to passersby—their quotidian pain. She settled down with a hot cocoa and a scone, knowing full well Con's speech was about to begin. Yes, there was resistance in her dillydallying, but the hot chocolate made her feel cozy. She could get on the Versaclimber and work it off tomorrow.

She walked into the Y when Con had about five minutes to go, basically missing the speech. She knew it by heart anyway, had done a lot of research for it, but still. She thought she'd wanted to be there for Con's moment. The small auditorium was about half full, and half of that half seemed asleep. The applause at the end was not exactly rapturous, it sounded more like fifteen elderly people were testing the efficacy of the famous Clapper gadget.

She felt bad for Con. Even this tepid reception had been a

long time coming. Con had been working full-time on his opus for more than ten years, bringing in very little income, maybe penning the occasional ad hominem book review for a few bucks. And even though Con had dreams of his work "crossing over" (to what? she wondered), how much would a somewhat right-wing treatise on New World pre-Christian deities and folklore ("J. K. Rowling meets Michael Lewis in a London pub, they fuck and have a baby that William Buckley raises") bring to the coffers?

But really, there seemed to be no way for Con to gain traction in the fractious, attention-deprived intellectual marketplace. He had been unable to score an interview with pre-disgraced, pre-MeToo-ed Charlie Rose, even though he knew one of the producers well and used the pretentious "Joseph Campbell angle" as bait. Feelers sent out to "Jimmy Fallon's people" at *The Tonight Show* fell short, as did scattershot flailing to get to Kelly Ripa (Emer had tutored the child of a woman who claimed to be close to the popular morning-show hostess). Con's work seemed destined to be that lonely tree falling in the forest; he himself said, "I'm afraid now we're finally going to get the answer to what is the sound of one hand clapping."

She felt bad for her man because so much of worldly success seemed like timing—in Con's case, bad timing. The ascension of Trump had made politics the only so-called intellectual entertainment around. Whereas five years ago, Con's diligent, years-long work might've been seen as predicting and prefiguring a hybrid monstrosity like the current president, in the actual age of Trump, Con's warnings felt belated, coded, impotent. Wine from sour grapes. And this made her feel bad for him as a mind and as a man. Timing. Did it all come down to that? She felt that in another era, maybe a pre-Christian one, Con might've been a king, a king like his namesake, even, Yeats's Cuchulain (Coo-cul-lan)—he had potential heroic qualities of mind and body: he yearned for battle, but he had missed his worthy opponent by a few years, or a few thousand years.

In today's world he was a nobody. Deprived of his enemy, shrugged to a standstill, still his character needed the fight. And with no worthy opponent, no masculine outlet for his heroism, his kingliness came out sideways in wrong ambitions and seething frustration. His need for that fight warped his soul rightward more than was his nature, she knew. She was afraid that what she loved in him might very well end up being the thing that, unharvested by the world, would pervert and even kill him, or at the very least, take him away from her bed. Such was the fate, she mused, of latter-day kings.

So Emer had worked harder the last handful of years, almost invisibly, to shore up Con as a man and make him appear, to the outside eye, successful and thriving. She herself had always harbored barely conscious ambitions of being a writer, which she neatly silenced and folded into being an unpaid research assistant for Con's project. And, in addition to teaching first grade at St. Margaret's School in lower Manhattan, so that Con could spend all his time working on his books, she had supplemented her income by tutoring the kids of wealthy New Yorkers on how to ace the ACT and SAT tests. You could make a living at it. Every year there was a new crop of nervous and coddled offspring of the previous generation's nervous and coddled looking to jump through the standardized hoops that the Ivies and Near-Ivies required.

Emer's twenty to forty extra hours a week were enough to eke out a livable existence for the two of them in their rent-controlled apartment on the Upper West Side. It was obscene what she charged for her services, less obscene when you thought of whom she was charging. When she was ushered into bright, sprawling Fifth Avenue apartments to hold the hand of some third-generation Brearley girl and admired the David Salles, Basquiats, and Schnabels on the walls, the chef in the kitchen, the maid in the hall, and the mom at Pilates, she saw where much of the runoff from the 2008 financial turndown had been smelted and recast. As she sat in these homes of the half percent, chewing on carrot sticks or a delicious gluten-free madeleine, she felt a not unpleasant, disenfranchised resentment.

She was in touch with a hollowness at the center of this second "job," not because she harbored any great yearning to achieve other glory, and even as she genuinely liked some of the kids she tutored, but because ultimately she was teaching them a useless skill—how to take a test was not far from showing them tips for crossword puzzles or Rubik's cubes or video games. Still, it was the kids she worked with, even as she accepted the parents' blood money, and, with none of her own, Emer loved kids, many of them anyway, even these privileged ones.

As she munched on the madeleine, watching her young charge assay her umpteenth practice ACT, Emer kept returning to Con's thwarted ambitions. He felt that movies could be made of his work. Movies that dressed old folktales and myths in new clothes for a forgetful and fickle generation uninterested in the morality of plagiarism and attribution, and maybe he was right. They got their music for free—is that why they didn't care about a creator's ownership? Was this what rap had done? Emer wondered. With its endless sampling having enacted finally the death of the argument over originality? Aside from the occasional multimillion-dollar lawsuit, who cares where that undeniable hook came from when it's repurposed by Kanye, Kendrick, or Jay-Z? Wasn't it stolen from the black man to begin with? Doesn't everything belong to everyone? Isn't that a positive, democratic trend? Could you write a check to the man who invented the blues?

No, she remained old school on the issue. She liked attribution and accountability. It seemed unfair that something like *The Hunger Games*, a shameless feminist-TV-era reworking of Shirley Jackson's *The Lottery*, came off unscathed on its leisurely stroll into pop consciousness and to the zillionaire's bank. Or those *Twilight* movies that were so important for a couple of years a while back. Just old vampire schtick with beautiful, pouty high school outcasts. Brilliant, yes. Disheartening, yes.

"I don't wanna be famous, I don't have the clothes for it," she joked, protesting while humoring her man with the thought that these fantasies might be within his grasp. He had kissed her and said, "This is my big idea. I don't know how many I have in me. Maybe this is it. I'm not Thomas Edison, I'm not gonna create the lightbulb AND the phonograph AND the motion picture camera . . . but the work, the message is legit. Maybe I'm a right-wing George Lucas and this is my *Star Wars* moment, and we're gonna ride it as far as I can."

When she would sometimes interject that his worldview seemed intolerant, he would take her aside, put his arms around her, and say, "Then think of it like professional wrestling. I'm playing a role. Maybe I'm a bad guy, maybe not, but I have to stay on message. You have to be able to sum me up in one sentence. My identity can't be longer than a tweet. I read somewhere Alice Cooper, né Vincent Furnier, said he and his band got to LA in the late '60s and they were doing okay, you know, playing the

Strip, opening for the Doors, but they weren't making it *big*. He looked around and saw it was all peace and love everywhere, hippy dippy, and there were no bad guys on the scene, so he perceived an opening in the market and decided to be the bad guy—and the rest is VH-1 shock-rock music history. So think of us like Alice Cooper. That feel better?"

"It does, actually, a little. Thanks, Alice. But you're not gonna start biting the heads off of live bats, are you?"

"That was Ozzy, I think."

"Oh, good."

She loved it when he said "us" or "we"; she was as alert to his use of pronouns as a drug dog at the airport, her ears pricking and gratified by any use of the first-person plural. At those moments, her one wish rose up: to be acknowledged and spoken of, but she merely sshed it, patted it on its head, and swallowed it like indigestion.

Cuchulain Constance Powers was a good man with a comic-book name; no, what did "good" mean after all anyway? Con was a man, her man. If he was maybe a little weak and insecure, she was no comic-book heroine either. They were well suited. She wanted a victory for him and wanted to feel a part of this victory, part of him; she felt he was part of her. But the thought sometimes occurred to her: Was the corollary true? Did he feel she was a part of him? She didn't know. Sometimes yes, maybe, sometimes no. Did that mean no? She washed the last of her madeleine down with some green tea almond milk latte.

ANANSI

AFTER CON HAD LEFT THE AUDITORIUM, Emer caught up with him in the backstage "greenroom," which was really just somebody's office rechristened for the speaking series. She walked into a space sparsely filled with people she had never met before, wolfing down toast points, scavenging off the obligatory cheese plate, and drinking wine out of plastic cups.

She spied Con speaking with a couple of very tan men in dark suits and fresh haircuts, and a striking young African American woman she had never seen before. The cheese plate wafted by her like a lactose apparition on the outstretched arms of one tuxedo-clad server. The waste at these shindigs, Emer thought, the terrible waste of good food, and she made a note to maybe grab a jagged hunk of forlorn Brie and stuff it in her bag before she left so she and Con could live off it for a couple of days like sharks feeding off a whale carcass. The impulse to stuff food in her bag had blossomed in her after her parents had divorced.

Her mother, always concerned with money, fiscally paranoid

as a single mom, would hold her big purse under the lip of the plastic tables at McDonald's and slip tiny packets of ketchup and mayonnaise off in the crook of her arm. Emer remembered thinking they looked like lemmings falling into the black abyss of her mother's bag—imagined them screaming as they plunged to their deaths among the gum and keys and loose change.

Years later, going through her mom's apartment after her death, reaching high into a pantry, Emer, surprised by the weight of an open cardboard box on a top shelf, brought the mother lode of stolen tiny red ketchups, yellow mustards, green relishes, and white mayonnaises crashing down on herself. It was true, then: you can't take it with you, not even the condiments. When Emer had recognized this forgotten stash, the years of mini-stealing and hoarding, the huge hope and fear it represented packed into neat little rectangles, she fell to her knees keening, as if this was all that was left of her mother's poor grasping soul, the pretty little packets skittering about her on the kitchen linoleum like bait fish spilling out of a net. There had been enough after all— enough money, love, mayonnaise. She needn't have worried so hard and so long.

Emer elbowed and weaved her way to Con's side. "Hey, Alice," she said, using a secret endearment in public the way people who are suddenly feeling insecure about their place at the table will stake out territory. She noticed the African American woman pull the hand closest to Con back with more speed than one would think was needed, as if she'd been caught in the cookie jar, or more precisely as if she wanted Emer to think she'd been caught touching Con's hand.

Con winced microscopically at "Alice," and planted a terse kiss on Emer's mouth. He tasted of cheap red wine and smelled of the stale, spent adrenalized fear of public speaking. "I prefer 'Dr. Cooper.'"

They all laughed overhard, not because they understood the gag, but because they knew it was supposed to be funny—hahaha.

"Emer, I want you to meet Alexander Stevens and Steven Alexander from CAA." He pointed to the two suits, who dutifully extended their soft palms. One ID'd himself as Steven and one as Alexander, and she immediately forgot which was which. Con now waved his hand toward the beautiful black woman. "And this is Nancy. I'm sorry, I didn't get your last name."

The woman seemed gravely insulted, but then smiled brilliantly and said, "Anansi. Not Nancy. Just Anansi. No last name."

"Like Cher?" Emer helpfully supplied, adding lamely, "Or Oprah."

"No," the woman said firmly. "Like Anansi."

Con jumped in. "Anansi is interested in getting us seed money to develop the movie."

"What movie?" asked Emer.

"Exactly," said Alex or Steve.

"Seed money? Is that like magic beans?" No one laughed at Emer's attempt at humor.

"I represent certain African interests that are interested in Hollywood, and telling indigenous and representative and affirming stories vis-à-vis other cultures while still remaining firmly in the Judeo-Christian tradition of Christianity." Emer thought that Anansi's word salad seemed to contain information and intent, but didn't really. She replayed it in her head; it was devoid of specific meaning.

Anansi had an accent that Emer thought might be African and wanted to ask her where she was from, but somehow knew better. She wore her hair in thick dreadlocks haphazardly framing her smooth, makeup-less face, reminding Emer of renderings of Medusa's head from some of her grade school mythology books, only hot. A hot Medusa. Emer looked closely and determined that it was all real hair, no extensions. Dammit. Like Medusa, Anansi was mesmerizing, too. Con was enthralled; Emer felt him pull imperceptibly away from her as a moon might be captured by a larger planet. It wasn't humiliating. Yet. Con was beaming, high on his own lecture and attention, however scant, but generally so, not necessarily high on this one riveting younger woman.

"Steve and Alex want to take us all down to Nobu, to get the ball rolling."

"The movie ball? Git it rollin', git that ol' movie ball a-rollin' . . ."

Emer was surprised that her anger and unease were leaking out as irony and a sudden halfhearted cowboy accent, but the haircuts didn't seem to notice. Their Hollywood duds had been sprayed with sarcasm retardant.

"Exactly," said Steve. Or Alex. One of them said, "The left has had their run in Hollywood since forever."

"Don't know about that," said Emer.

"Well, since the '70s," countered Steve, or Alex. "There's a lot of money floating around to make movies that walk on the other side of that street. The Koch brothers want to buy a studio and make films—there's money to make films on a *Star Wars* scale with a more fundamental Christian message. Clint to direct, maybe. Mel is in the middle of another comeback. This action Christian stuff is right in his wheelhouse. The window is wide open now. And your man has the goods. We feel like he's the Joe

Campbell of the moment . . . J. K. Rowling, that New Olympians thing—maybe even set some kind of supernatural war of the gods between the English and Americans, we've just been spit-balling here, at the time of the Revolution, you know, English gods versus homegrown gods, just claim it and full-on *Hamilton* that bad boy, right, Con? But without so much politics."

Ding-a-ding-ding—a "Joe Campbell moment." Ding-a-ding-dong—"Tea Party Harry Potter." And ca-ching—"*Hamilton.*" Emer felt that she was a contestant on the old Groucho Marx game show when she heard certain buzzwords. She looked up at the ceiling to see if maybe there was a duck descending. No such duck. This must be what Con meant when he said, "I have to cre-ate the vocabulary by which I will be discussed." He had thrown the buzzwords out like a demagogue, and the agents were more than happy to snap at them like trout at flies. Emer realized her mouth had dropped open during that dissertation. She looked over at Con. He was grinning like a fool.

"May I have a sidebar, counselor?" Emer swallowed the re-maining half glass of her third vinegary red. She took Con's elbow and led him a few feet away for privacy.

"Have we just entered Penceville? . . . Population—a fuck of a lot more than you ever thought."

"What?"

"Nothing. Nobu? Really, Nobu? Who are you?"

"What do you mean? Why can't I eat at Nobu?"

"Of course you can eat at Nobu, that's not, it's not Nobu, Nobu is . . . Nobu . . ." And she started to laugh uncontrollably; Con squinted at her impatiently as she tried to gather herself. "I'm sorry, it was just saying Nobu so many times in a row, started to sound ridiculous . . . you know, like nonsense Dr. Seuss—

Nobunobunobu . . . hooo . . . hoooooooohoooohoooo . . ."
She lost herself to another fit.

Con waited her out and then said, "I would like for once in my life to eat at—"

She raised a pleading finger and cut him off. "Don't say it."

"Emer."

"Please don't say it, I can't, just say you wanna . . . eat insanely overpriced, pretentious, raw, misidentified fish, even though I've never seen a pretentious fish, that's besides the point, just don't say . . ."

"Fuck Nobu. It's not about No-fucking-bu."

She laughed hard enough so that part of the room took notice and even Con, who was pissed and a little embarrassed, was halfway charmed by the tears that were now rolling down his longtime, long-suffering girlfriend's face.

Con said, "Now, Emer, dear, I have to go to . . . you know where, and you're welcome to join Steve and Alex and Anansi and me at . . ."

"Please don't. Not again. Have pity, I'm an infant."

"At the . . . Japanese restaurant that shall not be named."

Con was making a peace offering of sorts. She knew he kind of wanted to be alone, at least to be perceived as being alone tonight, by the Hollywood guys, by Anansi, by the world at large. Though it gave her a twinge, she chalked it up to simple human frailty. She knew who Con was, knew what he was, and loved him in spite of his weakness, maybe in part loved him on account of it even, because she knew how vulnerable a king without a throne feels. And she thought she knew what she was, neither heroine nor doormat, not a queen, but something in between—a hero-mat. A modern-day Miss Subways, it occurred to her.

A new woman in an old mold. Another woman might be terrified of sudden success for her man, but Emer had her plan; she was playing a long game.

She smirked and gave Con a proprietary kiss on the lips. "No, you go, alone, to Nobu . . . see, I can say it: you go alone to Noooooo"—she almost lost it there but held, the last syllable a forceless whimper—"bu . . . and come back with Kristen Stewart's personal e-mail and a three-picture deal, that's what they say, right? And an action figure."

"Okay. Haha, okay."

"And maybe a spicy tuna roll?"

Con kissed her and said, "Will do. See you later. I love you, Alice."

"Love you too, Alice."

Emer turned and curtsied, she wasn't sure why, and waved goodbye to CAA and the beautiful, one-named Anansi, her eyes coming to rest on the floating cheese plate. She took a breath and expelled her impulse to hold on to Con's reins tonight. She would not be her mother. Or his. She left without stuffing any Brie in her purse.

JESUS, AND OTHER FAMILIAR STRANGERS

I T WAS A WARM EVENING for the first day of spring, so Emer was inspired to walk home through Central Park. She loved the park; it retained magic for her even though Con always bad-mouthed it as the "world's largest prison yard" or a "giant wee-wee pad for the canine one percent" or "Jewrassic Park." It's true that, if you focused on it, the stench of dog urine could reach you at almost any point on a midsummer's journey. But why focus on that? The park itself was a man-made miracle. The wild green heart of a vertical urban sprawl. She knew it wasn't really un-tamed, but it sustained a sense of primordial nature to her—as if it had its own hierarchy apart from the city at large, Rousseauian laws, an earlier world unto itself. The park was the city's vernal atonement for its endless commercialism, hustle, and concrete.

Manhattan was a rectangular, numbing numbered grid, but once in the park, numbers evaporated. You might say you're "around Ninety-second Street," but it was always an approxima-tion; more often you just said, "I'm in the park," using landmarks like "just south of Sheep Meadow," "northeast of the Reservoir," or "I see tennis courts" rather than the digits of streets and avenues. You were figuratively, if not literally, "lost."

You would flip from the intensely vertical consciousness of the streets into some kind of spread-out horizontality, emphasis on horizon. And in this vein, Emer felt like she was entering church when she took those first steps off Fifth Avenue. And as you might in a confessional, the park was the only place in the city, outside of your apartment, where you might truly feel alone, in communion with, and even afraid of, not humans, as you might be in the streets, but something else less corporeal. Emer could experience an almost primitive, spiritual fear that she half enjoyed. It expressed for her a yearning she couldn't quite pinpoint. An emptiness inside her broached and became shadowed, if not filled. She breathed deeply the cut grass and canine ammonia, and felt almost free.

Exiting the park at Ninety-second Street, but before heading straight home, she stopped at a bodega on Amsterdam Avenue to get some ice cream. She was feeling revved up and jangly, figured maybe she'd watch Fallon or Colbert, and wanted a little treat for herself. She'd been buying ice cream, cereal, milk, unripe bananas, and the occasional lottery ticket from the old Dominican man, Jesus, behind the counter for years. They never spoke, she knew his name only because she'd heard another man call him that, and they barely nodded at each other when she reached up to place her salted caramel gelato on the counter.

A couple of years ago, riding the subway, she'd seen Jesus get on the train, and was sure she knew him, but didn't know where from. She felt a strange joy at seeing him, and driven by some impulse, had gone up, smiling, hugged him, and exclaimed, "Hi!

How are you?" as if he were an old and intimate friend. He had reacted politely, if a little embarrassed at her intensity, and she backed off slowly as she realized they had nothing at all to say to each other, that he was actually just the dude from the bodega.

Out of their context, she had behaved out of character. It made one wonder at the independence of character from place and from there to the strange, malleable liquidity of character itself. Now, when she settled her account at the bodega, she always had a small shudder, recoiling at the memory of the hug-mugging and how happy she'd been to see Jesus on the subway that day. She tried not to appear like a jilted lover. She was quite sure that Jesus was aware of none of these gymnastics.

IZZY

EMER WAS STILL TROUBLED by Anansi so, a few blocks from home, just off Columbus, she called her good friend Izzy, who worked as a child psychologist. They had met through school connections, Emer the test tutor, Izzy the hand holder, truth teller, discoverer, and assuager of trauma. "We missed you at the Y tonight," she said.

"Is this a telephone call? You're calling me? What are you, a hundred and three years old?"

"I'm old school."

"What up, Guns . . ."

"The Y?"

"Was that tonight?" Izzy lied badly. "I completely spaced. Either that or watching three hours of *The Bachelor* has broken my brain. Will you accept this rose?"

Emer laughed. "Well, Con kind of left with a bunch of people."

"Kind of?"

"Kinda sorta yeah."

"A bunch?"

"Kind of a bunch. Bunch-ish."

"I guess it went well? For him, at least?"

"Kind of."

"So he was all high on his own self-actualization and thus felt more secure about not satisfying the needs of others. That'll be two hundred and fifty dollars, please."

Emer laughed. "Is that how you would diagnose a kid?"

"No, that's how I diagnose Con, as a mild narcissist. On the scale somewhere between Ted and George."

"Ted and George?"

"Bundy and Clooney."

"Closer to George, I hope."

"Yes, dear, closer to George. Where most men are, on the spectrum, which is why I am where I am, pitching for the girls' team."

"So is that your professional opinion, then?"

"Well, I'd also recommend he repeat the second grade."

Emer laughed again. It wasn't exactly what she wanted to hear, but it seemed like the truth, and while it was sharp and annoying, it wasn't horrendous. Emer defended her man. "You have to understand Con thinks outside the box."

"Does he?"

"Yeah, he's an outlier."

"I'm sorry, the connection is bad. Did you say 'liar'?"

"Come on, you know what I mean, he's kind of a rebel."

"I see him more as an Imperial Stormtrooper."

"What?"

"Sorry. *Star Wars* reference. If you work with little boys you have to know their Bible. Look, Inersh . . ." Izzy sometimes called Emer "Inersh," short for "Inertia," 'cause she thought it sounded like a Hindu goddess, like Ganesh. Inersh—the goddess of no change, the goddess of doing nothing. Izzy continued—

"It's not that he's hitched his considerable intellect to this right-wing nonsense that bothers me so much . . ."

"Easy . . ."

"Well, it bothers me a little, but not as much as the hypocrisy of these types of guys who espouse this so-called morality and then go to Cipriani with . . ."

"Nobu."

"Right, Nobu, with a bunch of good-looking women on a corporate expense account. Jesus would not go to Nobu!"

"I don't know. He was a fisherman, he probably liked the fish."

"I see Jesus ordering in, though, avoid the paparazzi."

"Think they would charge a corking fee for turning water into wine?"

"Of course, it's fucking Nobu. Big tipper, I'm thinking, Jesus . . ."

"Big tipper."

Emer was happy Izzy was airily airing this shit. Emer thought it, and she knew Izzy thought it, but Emer could not say it, so she inspired Izzy to, and Izzy, as a friend, provided. Emer could hear it, and hearing it somehow made it all less deadly, out in the open—it was just some sort of goblin, not a big lethal monster. Izzy continued her attempted ventriloquism for her partially mute and selectively blind friend—

"I get it. I don't mind Con thinking outside the box, I just don't like him thinking outside your box. That sound you just heard was a microphone hitting the ground."

"Good one, but I don't *know* anything for a fact. It's not really about sex for him."

"No? Okay. It's about sex for me. What about you?"

"You know—me and sex, we're friends."

"Oh? You and sex are, like, texting buddies?"

"Yeah, text, e-mail. The occasional dirty phone call." Emer didn't really like to talk about sex, even with good friends. It felt private, and maybe she was a bit old-fashioned like those '50s Miss Subways, but Izzy would light up around the subject.

"You sext with sex? So meta. That's probably the future right there."

"You know," said Emer, trying to steer Izzy away, "it's not even about some other girl, that's not really his thing."

"Not 'really' his thing? But kind of his thing?"

"I don't know, really. Our sex is fine, it's great. I don't really wanna talk about it anymore. It's making me sad. Saying the word *sex* so much is making me sad."

"I won't argue, but it's more that this book, this success is, like, half yours in my estimation—you did so much research, and I'm not sure which ideas were yours and which were Con's. I'm not sure it wasn't your idea in the first place and he ran with it, and twisted it in a certain direction to make it worth more or appeal to a niche that would bring him fame or money. For you, it was wisdom, but for him, it was calculation."

"It doesn't matter. It's hard to be a man."

"It's harder to be a woman. And this other part does matter. Don't be surprised that he pushes you away like some goddammed medieval amanuensis. When you're around, people see the little woman behind the curtain. No man likes that."

"So what am I supposed to do?"

"Either lie down completely or stand the fuck up. It's gonna kill you in the middle. You being like this is allowing him to be the worst version of himself; I'm not just blaming him, I'm blaming you, too."

Emer laughed; she laughed, but she got it.

"You sound like Oprah, except mean. Maybe I should 'lean in'?"

"Whatever you do, do NOT 'lean in.' Lean way the fuck out, if you have to."

"Thanks, Izzy."

"You okay?"

"Yeah, I'm okay. I feel better now."

"That was not my intention."

"Haha. Thanks."

"Anytime. So what you gonna do?"

"Eat ice cream?"

"Emer . . ."

"I'm gonna do me."

"Queen! Mean Oprah approves. Night-night, Guns."

JUNO

PAPA WAS THE DOORMAN on duty tonight as Emer entered her building. An immigrant from Haiti, he'd been in the boxy, bland brown, vaguely militaristic uniform, as if conscripted into an unknown army of doormen, for as long as Emer had lived there. He'd been a tall man once, but was old and stooped now, and Emer instinctively helped push the heavy metal door open as Papa pulled it. Papa's legs were noticeably different lengths, and he walked with a pronounced limp that he did his best to transform into a '70s pimp roll. She could tell that her attempt at teamwork was an affront to his professionalism and manhood, so she stopped, but now, having anticipated her help, he had trouble opening the door, and he silently and unjustly blamed her for this fresh reminder of his diminished manliness. You had to walk on eggshells in this crowded world of men, she thought, with its invisible lines and slights real and imagined. It just never ends.

She smiled and offered, "How you doing, Papa?" like they

were on the same softball team, like she might just pat him on the ass next. Papa nodded a grumpy "Miss" at her as he barely impeded the heavy door from closing and crushing both of them. The thing was mostly brass and weighed a ton. Emer offered her clenched fist to Papa to bump. She had seen him doing this with the kids in the building and had envied the ease of this social maneuver. She had been taught this "hip" move by one of her tutorees back in 2010, and even though she sensed the world had moved on, she was going to ride this particular greeting past irony, through nostalgia, and into the sunset. They bumped fists and then Emer made the blowing-up gesture. "Blow it up," she said. Papa bumped but he didn't blow it up. Emer made her way to the elevator.

It was 11:30 by the time Emer settled into her bed with her ice cream to flip between Fallon and Colbert, an ADD act that she called "watching Fallbear." She checked her phone to see how many tutoring hours she had scheduled for tomorrow, and there was a text from Con with a photo of a piece of sushi that read "$45/piece!!! wish you were her"—ugh, "her," not "here," what an unfortunate typo. Couldn't he have just proofread before hitting send? Her chest tightened, and then she breathed it out, the sudden image of Anansi's exotic dreads. It meant nothing, close to nothing.

She checked her e-mail and her voice mail. She looked through *The New York Times* on her phone. As Fallbear began their monologue in their eternally boyish, slightly too ingratiating way, she started reading an archived article about the spacecraft *Juno*, which had flown 1.7 billion miles toward Jupiter and had taken some amazing photos. She guessed 1.7 billion miles was close if you were Jupiter. You could clearly see Jupiter's moons Europa and Ganymede. She thought of all the gods' names in Con's speech and how we endlessly recycle these personifications—this Greek goddess was now a spacecraft; what was once the anthropomorphizing female embodiment of all we didn't know was now the anthropomorphizing agent of all we did know.

Thinking on Juno, Emer was surprised to feel a tear on her cheek—daughter of Saturn, sister/wife of Jupiter, mother of Mars and Vulcan—all forgotten now or morphed so many times into meaninglessness. The forgotten Greek goddess, among the legion of discarded deities of Con's book, but also of this man-made spacecraft. This spectacular contraption made by human hands was now billions of miles away from the place of its conception. So, so far away. Like the goddess, also abandoned by the humans that worshipped her. And like the goddess, destined to get not much closer than 1.7 billion miles from her husband-planet as she dutifully took pictures of other bodies orbiting him. Fucking Ganymede. A boy? A boy! Oh well. And fuck you, Europa: you enthralled Galileo first, true enough, but you're just the sixth-largest moon in Jupiter's orbit, bee-yotch.

Emer laughed off her own catty inner dialogue between planets, moons, goddesses, and spacecraft. But really, how scared must *Juno* be? How disconnected, lonely? Surely the hands that made her unwittingly encoded DNA through sweat, feeling, and attention into the malleable materials, and surely *Juno* must feel cold and afraid tumbling through space, snapping photos like a homesick tourist. It was just too much for Emer at the moment, and she gave herself permission to ascribe all her own feelings of orbiting abandonment to this dead goddess machine and allowed herself to fall apart by proxy. She was surprised at the vehemence of her sadness, her tears making jangly counterpoint to the obligatory laughter of Fallbear's studio audience.

Though it felt bottomless at first, her fellow feeling for the intrepid *Juno* was soon spent, and she dozed off.

When she was awakened by a knock on her door, the uneaten ice cream had completely melted; she glanced at her phone and saw it was 3:37. She'd missed Fallbear and Con still wasn't home.

SIDHE

ON?" Emer called out as she shook off the drowse and headed to the front door. He'd probably gotten drunk on Nobu sake and lost his keys. She rubbed her face in her hands, trying to disappear the telltale signs of weeping. She opened the door and saw no one, then sensed something at her feet, and dropped her eyes, realizing this was a child here, no, not a child, a very short man, in a doorman's uniform.

"May I enter?" the small doorman asked. Emer was still stupid from sleep. "You have to ask me in. Those are the rules," he said in a bored tone. This pint-sized doorman.

"Oh, I'm sorry," Emer recovered. "Come on in. It's late." She squelched an urge to lift him up like a baby, he was that small.

The little man scowled at her as if he'd read her mind. He stepped into the apartment, keeping his eyes fixed up at her, pissed, it seemed.

"Is there a problem?" Emer asked. "In the building? It's very late."

"No, no problem in the building. The building is not the problem."

"So, what's the deal, then?"

"I'm Sid," the little man said. "Pronounced 'seed' actually, but Americans call me 'Sid.'"

A strange little man, he had an accent. Was it Scottish? Irish? South African? Australian? One of those.

"You're a doorman in this building?"

Sid nodded, looking around.

"I've never seen you before," Emer said as pleasantly as she could.

"Sure you have."

"No, I think I'd remember."

"Oh yeah? Why is that?"

Shit.

"Because I remember things."

"Oh. Oh, good. I thought you might say 'cause I'm a smidge shorter than average."

"Are you? I hadn't . . ."

"I thought you might say because I'm a wee midget. An un-forgettable mini-me in a monkey suit."

Emer laughed. "Can I laugh at that?" she asked, as she flashed on an image of anyone trying to break into the building picking Sid up and carrying him off like a fumbled football.

"Fuckin' well hope so, you giant woman, you," Sid said. "I came on at two a.m., replaced Papa Legba, that shifty, limping interloper."

They stood there. She thought about calling the front desk, but she felt more curiosity than danger.

"Would you like something to drink? Water? Sprite?" she asked, half apologizing.

"Sprite? Is that a joke?"

"Oh god, no, I'm sorry . . ."

"I'll take an Irish whiskey, if you have it."

Emer nodded and walked over to the bar, still in a bit of a sleepy trance.

"I have some Dewar's scotch." She knew a few of the doormen drank a bit on duty; she didn't blame them. She would.

"Scottish shite."

"And I have some Bushmills."

"Bless you, my child."

"How do you take it?"

"The way they make it." Emer poured a drink neat, brought it over, handed it down to him.

"So . . ." she said. He downed the whiskey like a champ and offered the glass back to her.

"More?"

"It'd be rude to decline."

She poured him another. He savored it this time.

"Where's Con?" he asked, startling Emer.

"What?"

"Con. Your beloved. Your inamorato. Where he be?"

"Um, that's a strange question."

"Only if the answer is strange, my dear."

As so often in her life, she decided on politeness over confrontation, until absolutely necessary.

"Well, he went out to Nobu."

The word no longer seemed funny coming out of her mouth. She felt the air around her change, like a temperature drop, and suddenly the little man seemed full of menace. He had a face "like a map of Ireland," her father might have said—thick black hair, a prominent craggy nose, and eyes as turbulent and blue as the North Sea. Depending on how the light hit him, he was alternately handsome or troll-like. She felt like she couldn't fully wake up, the oddness of the situation dawning on her as if from behind a screen; up and down and left and right felt wonky, like watching a sunset in a rearview mirror. She took a step back.

"Business. He should be back any minute. Why?"

"Business?"

"Yes, with some associates."

"Associates." He made the word sound like it smelled bad.

"Well, do you want to tell me what you came here to tell me, 'cause he'll be back any second, he texted me he was in an Uber about fifteen minutes ago."

"Uber. Fancy."

Sid went to the door and shut it. He tried to lock it, but couldn't reach the dead bolt. Up on his tiptoes, he could only scratch the bottom of the brass cylinder. He jumped up, grabbed the lock box with one hand like a monkey on a jungle gym, and did a pull-up, reaching and turning the lock successfully with his free hand. He landed hard and wagged his head.

"Still got it." He turned back to Emer, out of breath. "I came to return your phone. We found your phone."

"I didn't lose my phone. I was just using my phone. Reading an article."

She looked back into the bedroom where she'd fallen asleep, but it wasn't there. She checked her pockets, nothing. Sid reached into his doorman's uniform; Emer gasped like he might be pulling out a weapon, but he produced a phone, one that looked like it could be hers, replete with a familiar crack in the screen and the ironic Hello Kitty sleeve.

"When did you grab that?"

"I didn't grab it. It was found in the lobby. You must've dropped it."

"I don't think so."

"Do you know everything about your phone?"

"What?"

"Your phone, all these crazy new apps. Did you know there's a spouse-tracker app called iSpy. You might want to think about that."

Emer had had enough. She was about to toss the little man out the door, when he offered her the phone. Clearly playing on the screen was a video of Con in what must have been Nobu yukking it up with the CAA boys and Anansi.

"How did you . . . ? That makes no sense."

Con and Emer never took pictures with their phones. It was their stand against modernity. They were committed to living their lives rather than documenting them on Facebook, Instagram, and Snapchat. The one concession they had made as a couple to stashing memories was the purchase of an old Polaroid camera. So they had hundreds of little Polaroids taken over the years that Emer would toss in her "'roid drawer." So, to see photos or a video of Con on a phone was strange, sacrilegious in the institution of their relationship.

Sid replied, "Sense? No, there's no sense to be had here anymore. We're past all sense of sense." She looked down at Sid. She was sure he reminded her of someone.

"You're not a doorman here."

Sid shrugged. "You caught me out. Was it the uniform?"

"Who are you?"

"I told you. I am Sidhe."

"Sid, yeah. Sid who? What's your last name?"

"No. Bean Sidhe. One of the Bean Sidhe."

Emer was nonplussed, though that term kind of rang a bell. Maybe through Con's work? Maybe through some of the research she did for Con?

"Bean Sidhe," she repeated, trying to jog herself.

"It's a race. Well, it's a type of Celtic fairy."

Emer took in a long, slow stunned breath and as she exhaled said, "You're saying you're a kind of . . . leprechaun?"

"I am not a leprechaun! Fecking shoemakers!"

"Elf?"

"Watch yourself, Giantess! Sod Will Ferrell, fuck Keebler, and bum-fuck Christmas! Bean Sidhe, you gargantuan freak, Bean Sidhe!"

"Okay, okay—Bean Sidhe, I'm sorry."

"Two thousand years ago, we were everywhere; now nobody's heard of us. Do you know how hard it is to have to sit back and watch the vampires and the werewolves and the mutherfecking *Game of Thrones* Dinklages get all the tail? Maybe we need a publicist, haven't had one since Yeats."

Emer found herself unable not to engage in this. If she accepted some of what he was saying as true, she might have to accept it all. Was this just a crazy person, a volatile, crazy little person in her apartment with the door locked behind him? Or was he something else entirely, something not quite human, or something a bit more than human? She made a real effort to remain calm as she surreptitiously found Con's contact on the phone screen and pressed it to redial. Whatever would happen to her over the next few minutes, Con would hear, or it would be recorded on his phone.

She relaxed just a bit. Some of the unpaid and unattributed research she had done for Con started coming back to her.

"Bean Sidhe," she mused. "Bean Sidhe . . . sounds like 'banshee,' and is associated with the banshee—spirits—usually of mothers who died in childbirth . . ."

"I am neither banshee, though I know a few, nor am I a woman, clearly, I hope. I told you we need a publicist."

"Wailing spirits, omens of death—omens of death, right?"

"There you go."

Emer started laughing like people do when they give in to a roller coaster. "You've come to kill me?"

"Bite your tongue."

"You've come to tell me I'm gonna die?"

"Now you're back in the game, but no, not you."

"Where did you get that video?"

She was still scared, but felt a sudden calm spreading like cherry-flavored Nyquil—her drug of choice did not exactly walk on the wild side—like whatever was going to happen, she was somehow ready for it, had somehow been preparing for it. And then she thought, This is probably the way a lot of people feel right before they're murdered.

"Where I got the video is unimportant, what is important is how you answer my question. Because I know about your wish."

"What wish?"

"Your only wish. But first, here, look at this app. It's called iRemember."

Sid took the phone from Emer and played with it, turning it horizontal to maximize the screen. She saw images of her and Con from when they met, but it was videoized like a Ken Burns doc—pushing in and out of static close-ups, stately local music to give a sense of history to their little story, a sense of sweep, as if someone had been filming them as they fell in love. It was surprisingly moving.

"That's . . . who . . . I don't . . . that was right after college . . ."

Sid took the phone back and swiped at it a few times. "That's history. This, as I showed you earlier, is happening right now." Back on the screen came Con and Anansi. Now they were out of Nobu, but still somewhere downtown on a deserted street, walking arm in arm.

"I don't understand," Emer said.

"Of course you do. Fast forward."

"What?"

"On the phone, fast forward." Though she didn't really want to, Emer felt herself compelled to tap the two right-facing arrows. The figures of Con and Anansi sped up cartoonishly as they entered another bar alone and shared some more drinks and comfortable postures. She was hurt, but she knew Sid was trying to get a rise, so she played it off.

"You don't feel it because of your wish. Your wish is prophylactic, a condom on the soul."

"Gross."

"I know you, Emer, with your old Irish name. I knew your ancestors before they came here and abandoned me. I know your mind and I ken your heart as I ken Cuchulain, too. You will indulge him in his wandering, saying to yourself, Aye, that's a man—a man in search of his kingdom; you will indulge him tonight, saying to yourself, Let him have his day and let him find his way—he needs her, you say to yourself, he needs her money and influence and protection, and she needs his soul, and perhaps more than his soul, and so he may lead her on, hell, he may even lie with her. Oh, you sigh, he will come back to me, and after all, this is a sticky world and a man will do what a man must do."

It was as if he had spied into her soul, but more than that, had penetrated into the shadows of her soul, where she was most the small dark self she shared with no one. She felt exposed, violated.

"No."

"No? You lie to yourself and you lie to me, and you shield yourself from the pain by wrapping yourself in the wish, the hope that in time the king will outgrow his wandering eye, outgrow his ambition, and you two will have an old age together. Look at this app now—iWish."

Sid manipulated the phone, and now Emer saw an old couple walking the beach hand in hand, some perfect-looking, fine white sand, blue water beach, two old people hand in hand in the stiff syncopation of easy, well-worn love, her and Con. She welled up.

"There's your fantasy, your endgame."

"How do you know that?"

"How do I know anything?" Sid took the phone and tapped at it again. "Everybody's a fucking wizard with these things. It's all in the cloud. The cloud. There used to be gods in the clouds. The cloud is now the god. I was taken unawares. I did not see phones screaming across the sky the way the dinosaurs saw asteroids, I assure you. But I digress. Where was I?"

"I have no idea." Emer suddenly felt so tired.

"Ah yes, look again."

He held out the phone and the scene changed from the beach back to the street: Con and Anansi walking in the rain downtown. Anansi stumbled on her high stilettos, and Con steadied her as they laughed at her clumsiness. But Anansi held on to his arm after she'd regained her balance, and Con had not yet released her. Emer went to the window and looked out. It was raining. Sid said, "Keep watching."

"I don't wanna see."

"You should keep watching because in less than a minute, Con is going to die."

"What?"

"Oh yes, that Anansi is a spider, she's right death itself, and she's gonna walk Con in front of a car."

"Why?"

"Does a spider need a reason to catch a fly? She's hungry. Her bite is her kiss and it kills. And maybe she's angry about the book. It's hard to tell with those people."

"What people?"

"The gods of Africa. We came willingly, they were forced. They retain an attitude. I don't agree, but I can relate. Or I agree, but don't relate. This man wrote a book about gods purporting to know their whereabouts and desires—I'd say he threw down the gauntlet, wouldn't you? It's a pretty classic case of hubris, or over-reaching, no? As well as his right-wing-spin shenanigans, that might anger gods of color. She means to silence him one way or another. She is no doubt making her own offer to him at this very moment, and she and I are not necessarily on the same page or timetable. I'd say you have about thirty seconds to make up your mind."

"Make up my mind about what?"

"You can save him. You can save Con from death, from Anansi. Death is only one version amongst an infinite number of possible outcomes."

"Well, then yes, of course I want to save him. Save him! Stop it!"

"There's no sport in that, no pathos, no justice, no juice. There is a balance. A quantum of wantum that does not vary. To save something, something must be sacrificed. That's the way it goes, and the way it goes pleases me."

"What, what must be sacrificed?"

"Can't you tell by now?"

Emer sat down. "My wish."

"Smart lass, I knew you'd be fun to play with. You have about fifteen seconds. Give up your secret wish to spend an old age with Con and he will live."

"That's ridiculous."

"He will live, but here's the kicker, he will not know you. That's the deal."

On the phone screen, Con and Anansi were walking up the middle of a dark wet street. Emer could see a car turn the corner ahead, its lights hitting the couple.

"There's the car now. Here it comes. You can save him, but from here on out, you will be strangers. To prove your love for him, you have to let go of your love. That has a kind of delicious symmetry, you have to admit. That's one scenario, where he lives and you live on, knowing he is the love of your life, but unknown to him. The pain is only yours."

Emer saw inside the car. The footage on the phone was cut like a movie, switching back and forth between Con and Anansi and the interior of the car, where the driver was nearsightedly texting through pince-nez and glancing up at the road.

"And if you can't, then just close your eyes and do nothing.

You're good at that. And when you wake up, it will be like he never existed. That's another scenario. You live and Con is erased."

"But I don't want to kill him."

"Why is he with that spider?"

"He's trying to make a future."

"A future with you?"

"Why? Why me? Why am I getting this deal?"

"Because your love is lukewarm and your wish is half-assed and prideful. I'm from another time and place, my dear, when love made the cup run over and love killed. That's what I stand for. When gods and men wrestled, fought, and fucked; and the offspring of their union was sometimes hideous, sometimes wondrous. Sometimes the Minotaur, sometimes Hercules. Win some, lose some, get mauled, raped, and eaten by some. Your love is the holding of hands, the peck on the cheek, the Cialis couple in matching tubs. Your love is the tepid treacle left on Oprah's hanky."

"What the fuck?"

"When was the last time your knickers got wet just because your man walked into a room?"

"I don't know. I don't think like that."

"Why not? Where are your lady balls? You need to remember why you fell in love in the first place."

"I remember . . ."

Emer opened her mouth to speak, but nothing emerged.

Sid laughed scornfully. "You won't let him be a man and you won't let yourself be a woman. Perhaps you're right. Perhaps I am grinding an ax—I am on the short side, and I suppose that comes with its own issues—but admit it, this is the best conversation you've ever had with a doorman. And the truth remains that you humans have become muted, and we gods have become bored. You're boring! You're an animal, lass, fucking well live like one. I am not punishing you, I am punishing your life-negating rationality, and your deification of Lord Mediocrity. Nature will not be denied forever, nature will exact her revenge."

Emer felt off balance. She looked outside at the rain falling hard, a spring rain scrubbing the city streets for a moment of clarity.

She said, after a while, "But I do love him."

Sid took a deep breath and nodded, then finished what was left of his drink.

"So watch what your love does to him."

On the phone screen, the driver of the car looks up from texting, but it's too late. He turns hard, tires squealing on wet pavement, missing Anansi but plowing over Con with a sickening noise at impact. Sid grinned like a teenager at an action flick—

"Ooohhhhhhh . . . that's gotta sting."

"No! Omigod! No!"

"Don't fret. I've made this offer dozens of times, you're neither bad nor good."

"You've done this to others? Other women?"

"And men, too. Don't be sexist. Yes, in New York City, people disappear into the gray. This is one way they disappear—love. Love and money. Reality will always be the favorite reality show of the gods. Past century, though, I did a lot of my deals on Wall Street. Lotta gamblers down there. The whole subprime-mortgage thing? That was mostly my minions dangling carrots and benjamins. Ponzi was an Italian Sidhe back in the day. You're welcome."

Emer was now crying. Sid reached up and put his hand on her shoulder and said, "Or. You could press rewind."

"What?"

"Rewind. Rewind time itself—can't do that on a Samsung."

"Yes, yes, press rewind."

"You have to press, I can't—rules."

Emer pressed the left-facing arrows and the car came careening backward, death in reverse.

"Cool," Sid said. "Let's watch that again, that was an epic hit."

Sid pressed PLAY again, and the little figures on the screen took up where Emer had seen them before, the driver texting, Con and Anansi walking and laughing, arm in arm, as if they were fated to. It played right to a few moments before impact. Emer pressed PAUSE, the equal sign, two parallel lines that will not touch unto infinity.

Sid saw Emer perched between Scylla and Charybdis. He spoke to nudge her this way or that: "Hey, doormat, he's feeling like a king and making his deal with the spider, with the devil, with death, with success, whatever—he's taken her arm and who knows how much more, he's selling his soul and not consulting you." She heard the words, she saw her man joined to another woman, she knew the terms. She spoke:

"Fuck his ambition. And fuck him."

"You'll be a stranger to him, you understand? And a stranger you must remain. An absolute stranger."

"Right. Will we still live together?"

"What is wrong with you, woman?"

"I mean, will it be like he wakes up in bed tomorrow and

doesn't recognize me like a movie where the guy gets amnesia and I get to nurse him back to health and he ends up loving me even more than he did before?"

"What fecking god-awful movie is that? No, that's not how this one goes. He ain't waking up in your bed. Ever. You'll never know him. He will be alive somewhere on the planet, and his life with you will be a poorly remembered dream, and you have to stay away from him or he dies all over again."

"Okay, okay—you don't have to be so impatient. The rules aren't all that clear but, okay, I understand now. I think."

"You give up your claim on his heart and soul and body in the past, present, and future?" He poised his finger threateningly over the PLAY icon.

"Yes."

"Then press 'stop,'" he said dejectedly.

Emer pressed STOP.

"Now press 'delete.'"

Emer pressed again, but hit PLAY instead. "Shit, that's 'play'!"

"Whoopee, he's a goner!"

"No! Where's 'delete'?"

"It's your phone. How the fuck should I know?"

Emer moved her finger over the screen like a child speed finger painting; she found the trash icon.

"Delete!" she kept pressing and saying, "Delete! Delete! Delete!"

"You don't have to keep saying it. Just the finger is enough."

"Delete!"

"Deleted."

"Deleted?"

"In the trash. He lives."

A video on the screen showed the car swerving mightily to avoid hitting Con and Anansi. The headlights illuminated the startled but safe couple and moved off, leaving them in darkness. Then the screen went black.

"Cuchulain lives," Emer said.

Sid nodded. "The man lives. Love dies."

⋯PART
2

[The walrus came] from "The Walrus and the Carpenter." "Alice in Wonderland." To me, it was a beautiful poem . . . Later, I . . . realized that the walrus was the bad guy in the story and the carpenter was the good guy. I thought, Oh, shit, I picked the wrong guy. I should have said, "I am the carpenter." But that wouldn't have been the same, would it?   —JOHN LENNON

EMER II

SAAC HAYES'S EASY LISTENING, masochistic soul classic "Walk on By," not the less lethal, better-known Dionne Warwick cover, jostled Emer from deep sleep like a hot buttered two by four. Emer grabbed for the phone on her bedside table at 6:46 a.m. on March 21 to swipe-silence the alarm, but then leaned her head back on her pillow. Not to doze, but to recall a dream, and the song was helping.

Never a sound sleeper, Emer had slumbered hard last night; she felt an indentation on the mattress, as if she hadn't stirred for hours. It felt almost like the deep sleep after surgery or a seizure, which she used to get as a kid, but hardly experienced at all as an adult.

It reminded her of a time in college when she had smoked so much weed and got so paranoid that all she wanted was to black out, then wake up no longer high. She had closed her eyes on her dorm room single mattress and had a sensation of falling through blackness, descending through different levels of consciousness, like an anchor sinking through a pitch ocean of lethe. It was pleasant, but she felt she was picking up too much speed as she fell, as a body must through space, and she intuited that just below the last, deepest, most forgetful level of sleep was death, beyond the pleasure principle, from which there was no return, and if she kept falling like this, she would break on through to the other side of sleep and die. She willed herself to jump out of bed that night in college, convinced in her stoned way that she had saved her own life.

But Emer had been altered by the experience; she felt she now knew there were dimensions we were normally barred from, where different laws applied, physical and spiritual. That's the type of sleep she felt she had had last night. One that allowed disparate worlds—dreams, waking, somewhere in between—to touch for a moment. The sleep of the dead.

What had she dreamed? There was a bowl of melted ice cream on the nightstand. She remembered that she'd wanted to watch Fallon for some reason, but must've dozed off. She recalled a midget and a wager; though she knew *midget* wasn't a word she was supposed to utter out loud, she felt okay speaking it silently in her head. The midget had had an Irish accent and a magic phone. She picked up her own phone to check it. Looked through her pictures—her dad, some friends, work photos, a series of "keep calm and fill in the blank" slogan/stickers. Nothing strange. Isaac Hayes sang "walk on by" but he meant "please, please stay" . . . ah yes, in the dream, she'd had a boyfriend. Was it the midget? No. The little man was something else. A boyfriend— that's how she knew it was a dream.

She grabbed her computer, opened a new file, called it "Big

Dream" and jotted some recollections, though, as the dream itself faded, some images might have been free association or after-the-fact glosses—*midget* (this time she wrote the word on the screen and felt less good about it—but it was a dream, and we can't police our dreams, she thought, don't judge, keep at it), magic midget phone, spiders, there were spiders, or a spider, death, somebody might have died, love, Nobu (Nobu?), yes, Nobu (and it was fading, fading, now she couldn't be sure she wasn't making the rest up)—car accident, seeds of some sort, seeds—and . . . and . . . it was gone.

All the images from last night receded and fled from any sort of specificity, replaced now by a deep, pervasive feeling of ambient loss, of being bereft. Bereft of what, she did not know, but the intensity of the loss feeling shocked her. Felt like a death. Now she was fully awake, barred off from that world; she could not get back or get it back. Emer was back. Time to work. Time to make the doughnuts. Walk on by.

As she waited for her coffee, she picked up her ukulele and began strumming Pearl Jam's "Even Flow," which sounded castrated, hysterically funny, and bad-ass on the uke. She'd taught herself to play a few years back, and had been horrified to find it listed so often on the dating sites she sometimes observed without participating in. Playing the ukulele was the new ironic hipster thing to do, like artisanal beer and this and that from Brooklyn. She hated the hipness, but loved the uke, its plucky, ballsy innocence and inescapable association with Hawaii and its white sand beaches.

She drank her coffee out of her "Shrinks do it for 50 minutes" mug, a gift from her friend Izzy that was chipped on the rim so she always had to rotate it or risk a cut lip. She should have thrown it away long ago, it was a health hazard, but Emer had trouble parting with things she liked, and if she owned a thing long enough she would start to ascribe feelings to it—"Poor old mug," she thought, you shouldn't toss something in the garbage just 'cause it's old and not what it used to be. Even if it cut you sometimes.

SAINT MARGARET (OF ANTIOCH)

EMER TAUGHT FIRST GRADE at St. Margaret's Catholic School on the Lower East Side. Every morning, if the subway gods were smiling on her, she'd find a seat on the train and look about for reading material. There was the ad for Miss Subways again. She wondered what her entry bio might sound like: "Meet Emer Gunnels. 'Guns' is a first-grade teacher who lives alone. Weep for her." No. "Emer is reasonably happy, thinks Twitter is the end of the world, hasn't seen *Hamilton* but lies about it; she also 'worries about the environment.'" That sucked. "Meet Guns, that's what her millions of Facebook friends call our newest Miss Subways—she enjoys Harry Potter fan fiction, artisanal fruit ciders, and stand-up 69—"

She laughed—she had no idea where that came from. She didn't even like Harry Potter. Oh, she was on a roll now—no, it was stand-up 69 she didn't like, or she didn't know if she liked it as she'd never tried, and didn't really know what it was, though she could hazard a pretty good guess given the precise numerical terminology. It seemed . . . strenuous? It had been a while since she'd had sex at all. With another person corporeally present. "Meet Emer Gunnels—it's been a while since she's had sex . . ." She imagined doing one of those stripper moves on the pole in the middle of the subway car and shook her head so hard the dude sitting next to her glanced over with genuine concern.

No creepers, manspreaders, or Lehmanschpreaders today— thank God. She found a Train of Thought to occupy her need to read—

> Be not afeared: the isle is full of noises,
> Sounds and sweet airs that give delight and hurt not.
> That if I then had waked after long sleep,
> Will make me sleep again; and then in dreaming,
> The clouds methought would open and show riches
> Ready to drop upon me that when I waked
> I cried to dream again.
> —WILLIAM SHAKESPEARE, *The Yempest*

That was how she had felt this morning, awaking from that dream, that she would cry, like Caliban, to go back and dream it some more. Oh, that Billy Shakespeare, he got everywhere first, didn't he? He took the virginity of the language itself, after Chaucer had bought her a few drinks. She noticed a misprint, courtesy of the MTA, *Yempest* for *Tempest*. So good. She liked *The Yempest* almost as much as *Yakbeth*, the dark and bloody tale of an overly ambitious moose, or *Yamlet* or *A Yidsummer Night's Dream*, which would kind of write itself, she thought.

She closed her eyes, listened to the rumble of the train, and fought back the latent claustrophobia of a packed car. Be not afeared, she thought, this isle of Manhattan is full of noises. So many noises could become an overwhelming din, so she mindfully separated the sounds out—the tracks, the hum, the human voices, sound of feet, opening and closing doors—but it was even too much one by one, and as the sounds mixed with scents, synesthesia took over, the perspiration and halitosis merged with feelings and interpretation—a general, unquiet desperation. She oscillated between the separateness and the oneness—the individual players in the orchestra and the whole. And then she gave up, and let it all wash over her. A sweet little subway doze she half hoped would gain her reentry to her big dream. It did not.

Ms. Emer Gunnels's classroom was on the third floor of the old building that stood near where Brevoort's orchard once had. When they were expanding Broadway, circa 1815, they were aiming straight through his orchard but Brevoort didn't want to sell. That's why Broadway hooks west between what is now Tenth and Fourteenth Streets. Emer knew a lot about Manhattan history because of an abandoned project she'd worked on for years about foreign gods in New York City assimilating with their assimilating immigrant communities. She had begun to write a sort of quasi-fictional or semi-factional spiritual history of the city, and then decided she didn't have the goods; she was a reader, not a writer. That subject matter, though, reminded her of the dream. Yes, her dream seemed to outline hazily all that old research she had done. Funny that. The brain, like an attic, has only so much room, the poet John Ashbery had written, and yet it accommodates everything.

"Good morning, Ms. Emer!" the children called out in ragged unison. She was the type of woman who wanted her kids to call her "Emer," but St. Margaret's was the type of school that wanted the kids to call her "Ms. Gunnels," so they had struck a compromise.

Ms. Emer was a master teacher, treasured at the school and in the neighborhood, with graduates, now grown, often coming back to thank her; or ones that she ran into on the street. It was weird to see a former first grader, now in her early twenties, pushing a stroller and calling out, "Oh my god, Ms. Emer!" The former pupil had a baby and a husband and had been transformed into an adult, a parent, while Ms. Emer was essentially the same, merely older. These occurrences, which happened infrequently, but often enough to be a thing, Emer would have to gird herself for, would induce a kind of time-warp vertigo on her. She didn't feel pressure to marry and have a baby, but when she saw the pride in a former student, the transformation—it was just weirdly unsettling. She was happy for the kid, it wasn't that, and she wasn't jealous, it was more like identities had been so rearranged, there was no time to adjust—that twenty-two-year-old six-year-old girl had had sex and given birth, that child was a mother. Trippy thoughts like that jumbled her head.

Emer had been pregnant a couple of times with an old boyfriend, and the second abortion had left her so badly scarred from the D&C that she was told it would be "very hard" to get pregnant again. So that wasn't going to happen, at least in this life even if she did find a suitable partner under the wire, and besides, Emer had plenty of kids to "mother" at the school. She taught them how to read. She gave the kids her favorite thing to do in life.

And it all began with the "Vowel Song." Emer began to sing

it: "Ah Eh Ee Oh Eu, Ah Eh Ee Oh Eu—now we say our vowels, now we sing our vowels." Emer had made the little tune up when she found that the written way of teaching reading was counter-intuitive to the way it sounded to the kids phonetically. She didn't sing "A E I O U (And sometimes Y)," she sang "Ah Eh Ee Oh Eu," as spoken, not written. Over the years, she had found the phonetic approach, not to mention the little ditty, very effective. When a child started to read aloud for the first time, Emer still cried. It was like she had enabled the child to enter the human race and the life of the mind, stamped their passport to grown-up humanity.

Even though, last year finally, in a belated concession to the times, she had delivered a "rap" version of the "Vowel Song," the memory of which still made the back of her neck hot with shame. Had she really sung "Ah Eh Ee Oh Eu, and sometimes Yo Yo Yo"? She had. Good lord, she had. A debacle in her own mind. But the kids had loved it.

She began to sing the "Vowel Song," and noticed immediately that a recent transfer, a pale little blond girl named Lucy, was grimacing and squirming in a telltale expression of needing to go pee. Emer paused a moment and asked her, "Lucy, would you like to use the restroom?" Lucy bit her lip and shook her head no. Emer nodded and they went ahead with the song. About twenty minutes later, as the kids were splitting into groups and working on their projects, Emer again asked Lucy, seeing her continuing to shift in her seat, if she needed the bathroom. Lucy again said no. It was then she saw the puddle of pee beneath Lucy's seat and the yellowish urine dripping down her pale white legs to the floor, her blue uniform socks and Mary Janes darkened. Emer smiled, walked over, and took Lucy's hand. "C'mon," she whispered, "let's get you cleaned up, okay?" The child, wet eyed and mortified, silently nodded, took Emer's hand, and allowed herself to be led down the hall.

Once in the bathroom, Emer helped the girl remove her soiled underwear, and asked her to stay put as she ran to the lost-and-found to get a fresh brown uniform jumper. On the way back to the bathroom, she popped her head into her classroom to make sure hell wasn't breaking loose. What she saw stunned her.

The children must have sprung into action as soon as teacher and student left. They had cleaned the floor and desk, dried it with paper towels from the art section of the classroom. They were still so busy eradicating any evidence of the accident that they didn't see Emer in the doorway. They worked wordlessly and separately, but in utter harmony, like a hive. Emer took a step back into the hallway so the kids didn't hear her gasp and then stifle a sudden sob. She was so moved by the generosity of these little people, their natural empathy. Sure, these kids were often brats, too, but this moment of undirected compassion broke Emer's heart in two.

When she got back to the bathroom, the little girl had forlornly balled up her dirty uniform. Emer simply reassured her that all was okay. "That's okay, Lucy," she said, "I used to do that sometimes myself, everyone does." The little girl changed into the clean jumper and they went back to the classroom like nothing had happened, and by the looks of things, nothing had.

At lunch, Emer told her good friend Izzy Morgenstern, the school psychologist, what had happened, and Izzy, harder than Emer, saw less the compassion and more the collective shame. Izzy called it a "cover-up":

"You see the little programmed robots' advanced sense of shame already instinctive—horrible—you had a teaching moment there, Mrs. Chips, and you blew it."

"Come on, Izzy, it was a thing of beauty—a beautiful, communal act."

"It was them acting like body-hating, repressed bourgeois adults, sweeping ugliness, the real, under the carpet, looking the other way."

"It was sweet."

"Airbrush dicks and cunts and piss and shit."

"I'm eating."

"They lost their innocence today."

"I feel like they grew up a little, in a healthy way."

"And what of this girl, who pees herself and then sees it miraculously disappear? What of her shame, her silence?"

Emer pointed to another table in the lunchroom where little Lucy was eating with a nice group of friends, all of them laughing and talking over one another, not a hint of what had happened this morning.

"She does look miserable, doesn't she?"

"I hate it when bourgeois values win. Nice job, by the way. Can we talk about *Girls* now?"

Izzy was serious in her condemnation, but only by half. She liked to play at being the Marxist firebrand, but it was more like a role she enjoyed because she knew how good at it she was. She knew Emer enjoyed the performance. Emer felt brave around Izzy, or she felt in touch with her own ability to transgress and break rules in her presence, even though she never followed through with any actual transgressions.

"Hey, listen, Izzy," Emer asked, "did I call you last night?"

"Like on the phone?"

"Yeah."

"Don't think so."

"Huh."

"Huh?"

"I had the most lucid dream—where it wasn't just that the world was changed or obeyed different laws, but that I was changed, I was a different person with a different life. I've never had a dream like that."

"Alert the media."

"What's your problem?"

"I'm sorry, but there's nothing more deathly boring than having to listen to someone else's dream. Let me guess, there was a unicorn, what, vomited a rainbow and shat Starburst? Fascinating . . ."

They laughed.

"I had a boyfriend in the dream."

"Do you mind if I kill myself right now?"

"You know, you're not a very good psychologist."

"I can be a good shrink or a good friend. Not both. Choose."

Emer chose. "Friend."

JIMMY GUNNELS

O N THE WAY HOME FROM WORK, Emer stopped by to see her eighty-one-year-old father. The old man was suffering from incipient dementia and in an assisted-living home on Riverside and Eighty-sixth. It was pretty damn nice there, with views of the river and twenty-four-hour nursing, paid for mostly by insurance and her dad's dwindling savings, but it was still depressing. The staff tried to keep the shuffling, doddering occupants occupied as much as possible, scheduling movies, walks, trips to the museums, performances by grade school orchestras. The sloth-like frenzy of activity in the place had the opposite effect on Emer of hammering home the fact that these people had nothing, absolutely nothing to do. When she walked in the doors, the world felt like it ran down into slow motion. Eighty-sixth Street was the last stop on the mortality train, the Oblivion Express.

She found her father lying in bed as usual, watching Fox News with his Filipino nurse, Ging-ging (Evangelina). Emer said in mock anger, "Fox? Ging . . . why?"

"He like," said Ging-ging. "He can follow." And this was true, the old man liked to watch Fox and professional wrestling. Emer thought there wasn't much difference between the two, you knew who the good guys and bad guys were at all times.

Emer preferred to read to her dad, as he used to read to her when she was a child. She had spoken to doctors who dealt with aging about how activities like music or dancing, deeply encoded in muscle memory and sheathed in the myelin of youth, were more easily retrieved than other knowledge, and that participating in these activities momentarily and intermittently made them young again. Like in an Oliver Sacks book. A *Flowers for Algernon* moment. A woman whose mind and personality seems gone dances a waltz in perfect form and timing and suddenly returns to herself for an instant while she moves, while she dances, while she sings. She hoped for that as she read to her dad. But most often his response was to turn the hectoring Fox volume up further.

The other alternative to Fox News was a Ging-ging monologue, which consisted of a hallucinogenic combo of *General Hospital* and other soaps with a healthy dose of Filipino folklore thrown in from Little Manila in Woodside, Queens. She remembered once walking in on a discussion of the Manananggal between her father and Ging, her father taking part and animated like he rarely was anymore. It was doubly strange because James Gunnels had been a devout Catholic for most of his adult life. It was to Jim Gunnels that an eight-year-old Emer announced one night at dinner that she was going to become a priest. Her mother got up from the table, leaving it to her dad to tell her that was a job avenue closed to women.

"You can become a nun," he had said.

She then researched and realized that, indeed, the priesthood could not be for her, so she decided to become a Presbyterian minister. Her father had not laughed at that. "Over my fucking dead body," he had said.

And that's what had injured Emer deep in her soul, this rupture with her dad, in the black and white of her young mind, where she was not good enough for him or God because she was a girl, and she had turned against God in some private, irrevocable, obstinate way. She would not serve, and her *non serviam* took the form of her dog-eared, yellowing paperback of Edith Hamilton's *Mythology: Timeless Tales of Gods and Heroes*, which replaced her Bible.

It was this same dogmatic Jim Gunnels who would rather die than see his daughter embrace Protestantism, who was now aflame with Ging-ging's pagan folklore. It appears the Manananggal is an evil, man-eating monster capable of severing its own torso and sprouting huge bat wings to then go fly in search of victims in the night. Its prey is mostly sleeping, pregnant women, using a proboscis-like tongue to suck out the heart of the fetus. Emer was gratified to learn that the Manananggal, like the Balkan vampire, was vulnerable to garlic and sunlight. Hence the cloves dangling above her father's headboard.

She bent down to kiss her father and said, "Hey, Pops." He craned around her head as if there were something urgent happening on TV, not just that pinched-faced thumb in a real-hair toupee, Sean Hannity. She browsed through her Kindle library to see what she might read him, hoping to catch her dad out before some dreaded inflated talking head appeared.

Without acknowledging Emer, her dad said, "I can't remember. I can't . . ."

"Can't remember what, Pops?"

"I can't remember the last time I got laid."

"Whoa, hey, Pops."

Ging-ging giggled like a debutant. "Oh, Mr. Gunnels."

"Don't be such a pussy, Bill."

"I'm a woman, Pops."

"Of course you are, Bill, whatever turns you on. That's the end of America right there. Bruce Jenner. I refuse to say 'Caitlyn.'"

"That's okay, Pops, you don't have to say 'Caitlyn.'"

Ging giggled again. She giggled a lot, but was tough as nails. Sometimes Emer would cry at a back-and-forth like this and sometimes she would laugh, and then reprimand herself for laughing.

But everything out of her father's mouth could be a clue to some lack she felt; she would hang on to her dad's few words and worry them like a dog trying to lick the marrow out of a broken bone, trying to tease out the significance, to find the man she once knew in the mostly wayward garbage that came out of his mouth. She hadn't gotten enough of him when she was a child; she wasn't done with him, she wanted more, and this want brought an uneasiness between them, even as he was now. He did not want to be asked for something. He did not want to feel like he was coming up short. Sometimes she would try to lead him somewhere.

"Hey, Pops, do you have a daughter?"

"Yes, I do."

"What's her name?" Out of the corner of her eye, Emer saw Ging-ging raise her hand like an eager kid at school.

"Ging! Don't help him, now . . ." Kindhearted Ging-ging would often supply the answers from the other side of the room like this might be a game show where you could ask a friend for help.

Her father said, "Emer." Ging-ging clapped and looked like she expected confetti and balloons to descend from the ceiling.

"Am I her?"

"Don't be stupid."

"Where is she?" Emer had his attention now. This happened less and less frequently, so she pressed on.

"I don't know, brother, she's missing in action."

"I'm Emer."

"Bill, this is no time to come out of the closet."

"So what about this Emer? What's she like?"

"What are you getting at, Bill?"

"I don't know . . . was she a failure? A disappointment to you?"

Emer didn't know where that came from. Ging-ging sighed.

Her father focused on her and said, "No, but she thinks she is."

This brought a sob from Emer. She wasn't expecting that. She'd been going for Alzheimer-lite and got hit with Alzheimer-heavy.

Her father had often been her champion. A floaty child, Emer had sometimes mistaken her dreams for real when she was young. Her mother hated this, as if it threatened her own tenuous grasp on the real, and had even brought Emer to a psychologist at the age of seven so she would "stop dreaming." Like it was something she was doing on purpose to annoy her mother. Emer enjoyed talking to the psychologist and liked doing the Rorschach tests that he laid out in front of her, but even then she knew that this dreaminess made her a little different.

They ran needless tests. Emer kept on her lucid dreaming and even had a couple of seizures late at night in bed that she never told her mother about. She continued having these mild mini-seizures to this day, and privately referred to them as "my time-outs."

Little Emer was shown an X-ray of her brain, her mother pointing at it, and saying, "Look, perfect, beautiful." But then the doctor had said, "Actually, no," and had gone on to point to a tiny shadow on her temporal lobe by the left ear that he wasn't overly concerned with, but that they would need to biopsy nonetheless. Emer had been fascinated by the photos, the black-and-white symmetry of the organ, like a halved honeydew melon, the left and the right hemispheres, and she had asked what that connective tissue was between them. She focused on that. The connection. Told it was the corpus callosum, Emer diagnosed herself to her mother, saying, "The left part is awake and the right part is for sleep and dreams, and in most people this bridge is closed usually, but mine is open. So few people walk back and forth. My bridge is open." Even though there might be something terribly wrong with her, she watched her mother cry in gratitude at this wondrous little self-diagnosis.

And biopsy they did, finding nothing, but leaving Emer with a lifelong scar that was soon covered by her hair growing back. The "fits," the visions, stopped for a while after the removal of the shadow, but over the years, they returned, though no shadow was ever caught by the doctors again. There must be a shadow of a shadow, that's how Emer thought of it, as a child, and she thought of it as hers, moreover, as the part of her that made her her and made her see the way she saw. She took to fingering the hidden scar in times of duress as someone else might twirl hair. To touch the shadow of the shadow was to bring her back to herself.

She got up to pour herself a drink. She opened a fridge stocked with wine coolers. In his prime, her father had liked his Johnnie Walker Black and his Peter Luger steak, on those special occasions for a lower-middle-class man of that time, bloody, but in his present state was reverting to the taste buds of a child and preferred the sweetest, cheapest wines and Chef Boyardee cold from a can. Which was the "real" him? Guinness and salted almonds or Hard Lemonade and Oreos? Which version did she prefer? She took a sip from the attached straw. It tasted like an alcoholic's chilled piss with a lemon squeeze. Her father called out from his bed.

"I need to tell Emer something."

"What?"

"For her ears only."

"Tell me, and I'll tell her."

He motioned her close so he could whisper. Emer shivered when she felt his dry lips and stale breath on her ear. "Git some, Bill."

"Get some? Get some what?"

"Git some, whilst you can."

CORVUS CORVIDAE

E MER WANTED TO WALK HOME through Riverside Park. Poor
Riverside Park, the redheaded stepchild to Central Park, the
silver medalist, the Chrysler Building to the Park's Empire
State. Just as she stepped out of her dad's building, a downpour
announced itself in fat, dime-sized drops. Like sub-Saharan
flowers that open at the merest hint of rain, the African sellers of
umbrellas seemed to sprout up out of the barren asphalt when
any sort of deluge hit, offering their knock-off wares. At a moment's notice, as dark clouds blocked the sun, the fake high-end
items, the faux-Prada bags and faux-Hermès scarves, were pushed
aside and kept dry, exchanged for a seemingly infinite display of
umbrellas.

Emer approached a dark man in the colorful scarf wraps of
his country behind a cardboard display upon which he was
scrawling "10$" in black Sharpie. She knew these cheap things
were good for only a couple blocks before they turned inside out

at the slightest gust, but it was something of a New York tradition, buying a cheap umbrella. She offered the man a ten and he made eye contact as he extended his own hand and stopped, smiling broadly but weirdly, almost laughing.

She hoped he wouldn't haggle. She didn't like that part of street sales. Her father, the Christian half of her parents, used to delight at December haggling with the sellers of Christmas trees. It was a New York City tradition the devout man adhered to religiously. He used to bundle Emer up and tell her what their mission was—to celebrate the birth of Christ by getting the best deal possible on a dead tree. He would coach Emer in his casual, breezy, unabashed New York anti-Semitism—to her mother's begrudging amusement. He liked to call Jews "noses" or "hats" or "bagels"—and yet his prejudice was completely impractical and inert, like he'd been inoculated with a dead strain of the disease. His best friend, in fact, was "Matty the Hat."

"What are we gonna do, Emer darling?"

"We're gonna get a tree."

"How we gonna do it?"

"We're gonna 'Jew them down,' Pops."

"Shut your mouth, Emer. Never repeat that," her mother admonished from the kitchen.

"Correct," her father elaborated, laughing. "We only haggle when the Savior is involved." Her mom would scowl, and her dad would say, "Come on, baby, it's Christmas."

Emer had no desire to negotiate this African down. And he seemed to have no desire to even take her money. Instead, the young man went off in some serious consultation with a coworker. Eavesdropping, Emer thought she caught the word *announce* or something like that, and she distinctly heard the word *shango* as they looked up in the sky. When the men realized she was listening, they moved a few more feet away.

Finally, the first man came back and pushed the umbrella toward Emer, almost, it seemed, afraid to have his skin touch hers. "Announce," he seemed to say again.

"Announce? Announce what? What? How much?"

"Shango," he said, pointing up to the darkening sky. "Free. Friend Anansi. Free."

Emer wasn't sure if this was a scam of some sort that she was slowly being ushered into, like those bogus African e-mails from the addresses of friends who had lost wallets and needed cash, and was afraid if she took the umbrella without paying that these men might pull something shady, but she was getting wet.

"Thank you?" she said quizzically, and clicked open the umbrella, realizing immediately that the spring-loaded mechanism had imploded on its maiden voyage, and that this was the first and last time this umbrella would open or close. She turned and walked toward Riverside Park.

It was raining harder by the time she got to the park, a proper spring rain, and the sound of the big fecund drops on her umbrella effectively and pleasantly drowned out the traffic. She marveled at how so many activities city dwellers seemed to prize were ones that made you forget you were in New York—strolling in Central Park, having a weekend getaway upstate, a rainstorm or a snowstorm blanketing the city sounds and bringing it to a muffled halt. She found it odd that so many people expressed their love for this metropolis by seeking and valuing experiences that negated it, either physically or psychically. As if what made the city great was directly correlated to your ability to leave it, in your mind or in your car.

As she walked, she became aware of an undersound, a clicking or chirping. She stopped to locate it. She zeroed in on a fat tree trunk a few yards away. At its base, something was barely moving, or struggling to move. Approaching, she could see it was a tiny jet-black bird, a chick really, that must have fallen from the nest, and was drenched now, struggling to disengage from the mud.

She knelt down to get a better look at the tiny creature, extending the shelter of her umbrella. She looked into the dark, wet, blinking eyes. If she wanted to, she could see dinosaur malevolence and power in the black hooded orbs or she could project the uncomprehending baby terror of a defenseless thing. She could not decide whether she was looking "at" the bird's eyes or "into" them, whether the shiny dark surfaces were reflective barriers or receptive pools. We share the planet with such ancient beings, she thought, even in this city, as far from nature as man could get. There was still natural Mannahatta magic and horror if you listened closely. There are still tiny dinosaurs falling from trees.

She looked up for any signs of adult birds in a nest and wondered if she should help this Jurassic avatar. Would that act of compassion be subverting nature?

She reached out to see how "she" would react to her hand (she called the bird a "she" in her mind, though she had no idea what sex it was), but was stopped short of touching her by the secondhand knowledge (and here she wondered just how much of her city dweller's wisdom was secondhand, especially of the natural world—and what a tenuous, once-removed hold we have on things we think we know, anyway . . .) that maybe some animals will reject one of their own once it had the smell of a human on it.

Were we that feared and hated in the natural world now? she asked herself. Probably so, and probably with reason, as we humans were gods of destruction, we were Shiva, destroyer of worlds, bringing death and extinction wherever we went, she considered, as she looked up in the tree again to see if there was any concern or love at all up there. Mankind. Man not kind. Womankind. Woman kind. She did not come to destroy. Decisively, she scooped the baby bird up in one hand and gently slid it into her jacket pocket like a slick thief, and hurried on home.

BIRDIE NUM NUM

EMER GOT BACK TO HER BUILDING as fast as she could walk without jostling the bird too much in her coat. She put some old soft dish towels and shredded paper in a big salad bowl for a makeshift nest. She emptied and washed a bottle of Visine and then filled it with milk, and squeezed a droplet or two onto its beak, but the little bird didn't seem to be hungry. She just lay sideways on the towels breathing so fast and shallow that Emer thought she couldn't possibly continue long in that panic. She put the tip of her index finger against the bird's breast and could feel the barest suggestion of a racing heartbeat. The bird made no concessions to kindness and no protests. She half covered her with the paper towel like you might tuck a small child into bed.

Emer went to the kitchen to see if there was any solid food fit for the bird. She grabbed some grapes. She found some almonds and even some sunflower seeds for some reason, so she cut all of them up as finely as she could, using a Cuisinart, added milk, and smeared a knife's-tip worth of the goo on a small coffee saucer that she balanced near the bird. She swiped her fingertip in the mixture and touched it to the bird's beak. Again no acceptance and no protest from her visitor. She thought about googling the number for some sort of wildlife rescue, but then figured she could handle it for now. She decided to call her Birdie Num Num generically, in homage to the immortal Peter Sellers, and by not naming, hoping to remain unattached.

She curled up next to the salad bowl on the floor and started humming a tune. First, the Jackson Five's cover of "Rockin' Robin," which she didn't make it through, figuring almost immediately it was too on the nose, or even insulting since this clearly was not a robin. She grabbed her uke and essayed the Beatles' "Blackbird." Too sad. She went on to a verse and chorus of Pearl Jam's "Black" before embarking happily, she didn't know why, on a severely unplugged version of Led Zeppelin's "No Quarter." Its haunting melody, possible menace, and nonsense shadowing of Norse mythology seemed more or less on the money for this rainy evening.

She fell asleep this way for a few hours and dreamed of the midget again, and of the boyfriend—Con was his name, she now remembered. And she had a clear picture in her mind of what Con looked like and was just as sure that she'd never met this person. Her dad was in the dream too, young and handsome and at the top of his game.

When she awoke, her neck was stiff from sleeping on the floor. She went to the kitchen and ate a few grapes, followed by a handful of almonds and sunflower seeds. She realized she hadn't eaten dinner. She took a few slugs of milk. She dozed and dreamed some more by the bird, and woke up again. The midget and the man named Con. It was as if that one dream was now playing continuously in her head and whenever she went to sleep, she reentered it; as if she had two lives—the conscious one and the dream one playing in separate movie theaters in her mind, showtimes conflicting, but screens never overlapping.

It was 2:50 a.m. when she squatted again to check on the bird, and the chick seemed to crane forward and up in a spastic motion as she might hector a parent for food. Emer felt a primitive rising in her gut and swallowed it back, but then placed two fingers deeply down her gullet, and promptly barfed a little into her other hand. Surprised at herself, she held her open palm, the partly digested mixture of milk, seeds, and bile—toward the baby bird, the black orbs blinking. The bird tilted its eye to Emer and to the slop, to Emer and to the slop, then moved its head forward and began, miraculously, to wet its beak. Emer saw the world go blurry and then clear, as a tear from her own eye grew heavy then dropped into her palm. The bird ate that, too.

THE CORVSTER

EMER MASTICATED AND REGURGITATED AGAIN for Birdie
Num Num in the morning, all the while thinking, No way
am I gonna tell Izzy about this. She'd make fun of me, but at
least I'm not one of those cat people. Over coffee, she googled
blackbirds, crows, and ravens to see what the chances of domestication and survival might be, medical care, etc. From the descriptions, she decided that this was a crow, a baby crow, *Corvus* in
the family Corvidae. She read that they were omnivores. At four
weeks they were able to leave the nest, though their parents still
fed them until they were sixty days old. So Birdie Num Num was
a crow no older than sixty days and living in an apartment on the
Upper West Side. It remained to be seen whether that was very
lucky or unlucky.

Ever the teacher, Emer reveled in the Latinate poetry of the
taxonomical classifications—kingdom/Animalia, subkingdom/
Bilateria, infrakingdom/Deuterostomia. What the hell was an in-
frakingdom? Phylum/Chordata, subphylum/Vertebrata, infraphy-

lum/Gnathostomata, class/Aves, order/Passeriformes, family/Corvidae, genus/*Corvus*. There. Well, at least we know what we are. She spoke to the bird, "Hello, *Corvus brachyrhynchos*, I am *Homo sapiens*, we share kingdoms—Animalia and the Bilateria superphylum as well as the Vertebrata subphylum, obviously, and interestingly the infraphylum Gnathostomata—and I have no fucking clue what that is. Don't worry, there won't be a quiz."

As she double- and triple-checked that all her windows were closed, she wondered if she should buy a birdcage. "That's all the knowledge for now. All I'm sayin' is that we have much in common, much to build on. I'm gonna bilateriate myself on out of here and I'll see you after school. I'll call you Corvus, 'cause that's what you are and it sounds cool to me, like a male Corvette, a Corvette with balls. Later, Corvus. The Corvster." And just like that, the little bird changed sexes.

On the way out of her building, the young Serbian on duty, Novak, opened the door for her. She thought about asking him if he might check on the bird now and then, but decided not to. She wasn't sure of the crow-owning rules in this tight-assed building.

"Morning, Novak," she said, and wondered if she sounded guilty of something.

She started down the street and then doubled back to the building entrance.

"Hey, Novak, listen, is there a doorman that works here who's like . . ." She held her hand at about waist height.

"A child, you mean?" asked Novak incredulously.

"No, a little person."

"A little child person?"

"Not a little child person . . ."

"A child door man?" He paused between each noun like it was a sentence unto itself. Child. Door. Man. That staccato rhythm made Emer laugh. She realized she was in a buoyant mood. A. Buoyant. Mood.

"No." Once again, Emer held her turned-down palm around waist height. A sunflower seed was stuck to one of her fingers and she brushed it off.

"Oh, a midget."

"Sssh, yes, named Sid or something."

"Yes, we have no midgets doormen."

"Yes, we have no bananas?"

"Excuse me?"

Emer half sang, "We have no midget doormen today."

"I'm sorry for that," Novak replied solemnly.

Emer smiled wide. Even this series of non sequiturs filled her with a sense of blissful order this morning. The little bird, something to care for, had made her giddy.

KIJILAMUH KA'ONG

DURING SCHOOL, Emer found herself thinking and worrying about Corvus. In the afternoon, at story time, she settled the kids into their seats, and to honor Corvus, began to tell them a Lenape legend she knew. "So you guys know the Lenape were a people that lived here on Mannahatta before the Europeans, right? We studied this. Indigenous is the word." The kids nodded somberly, like they were going to get some medicine. Gliding past that genocidal minefield for another day, she soldiered on. "So the Lenape would tell themselves stories about how things came to be the way they are. So to explain winter, they said a Snow Spirit appeared and made the world cold. But before that, in prehistoric times, even before Mr. Crotty was your age . . ." The kids laughed, she had them.

"Back then, the world was warm, and the crow had all the feathers of the rainbow and a voice like Adele, a beautiful singing voice. But after the Snow Spirit showed up, everyone was cold and grumpy, so all the animals needed a messenger to go talk to their god, who they called Kijilamuh Ka'ong—which means 'the creator who creates by thinking what will be.' So the other creatures chose Rainbow Crow to go up to the Creator and ask him to take the cold away.

"Rainbow Crow flew up, straight up, for three days, and he got Kijilimuh Ka'ong's attention by singing a beautiful song. But the Creator said that because he had already thought of Cold with a capital C, he could not now unthink it—cold was here to stay, he said. But he saw how sad that made Rainbow Crow, so he jabbed a stick into the sun and created Fire with a capital F, and he gave the burning stick to Rainbow Crow to bring back to earth.

"On the long flight back down, the burning stick in his mouth charred all his feathers black and made his voice raw and hoarse. Rough grumbles and *ca-caw* are the only sounds he makes now. But Rainbow Crow made it back down; he brought fire to all the creatures so they could be warm again, and because of that, he is revered—which means loved and respected—by everyone. And it's also true that if you see a crow in the sunlight and look closely at his feathers, you can still see many, many colors highlighted there, shining in the black."

"Crows are cool," said Liam Rosenthal.

"Crows are black and scary," added Eckhart Jones-Tillerson.

"Don't say 'black'—my mother says that's racial." This from Brooklyn Spicer, whose mother worked for Merrill Lynch.

Emer jumped in. "Okay, first of all, we say 'racist,' not 'racial.'"

"Told you."

"Wait, I'm not agreeing with you."

Some of the boys in the class, attuned to any kind of show of dominance, snickered as Emer continued, "No, not like that, 'black' in this story is merely a description of color, and as it's said later in the story, the black of the crow actually contains all the colors of the rainbow. Right?" (Not technically, but the kids didn't need to know that.) "And sometimes black things are scary, like the dark, just as some white things are scary, like ghosts—but that is not to say the black skin or the white skin of a person is scary."

Emer was troubled at how all interpretation now devolved into matters of race or gender or religion. There was no art anymore, even in children's stories. Why wasn't the crow female? Why was the Creator a 'He'? Wasn't Bald Eagle insensitive to men with hair loss? This is how we spend our time now.

Yes, these were legitimate questions and deep, worthwhile historical concerns, but she was reminded of Wordsworth and how we "murder to dissect." Everyone bending over backward to not cross any lines, like a huge game of gender-race-neutral mental Twister. "I want you guys to think of something, something weird that doesn't exist, maybe."

"How can I think of it if it doesn't exist?"

"Imagine."

"A unicorn pooping rainbow sherbet."

"Excellent."

"Rainbow sherbet pooping a unicorn."

That brought down the house. Even Emer had to laugh at that bit of homegrown surrealism. "Okay, these are all great. So now, what did the Creator say about the cold? Anyone?"

"He said he couldn't make it go away."

"The Creator says that, even though he'd like to take away cold, he can't because once he's had a thought, and he thought of cold, he can't unthink it, which means, I think it means that we are all creators, creators of thoughts, and the things we think cannot be made to disappear, cannot be unthought—which means what?"

A quiet child raised her hand. "It's a busy, busy world, and crowded."

"Yes." Emer smiled at that precise locution. "It's a busy world and it also means that rainbow-pooping unicorns and rainbow sherbet unicorns all exist as of five minutes ago."

"No, they don't."

"Oh, no? Then try to unthink those things. Everybody unthink the pooping unicorn."

She waited a few moments.

"Is it gone?"

"No!"

"I can't get it out of my head. I'm naming him Ray 'cause he won't go away."

"Nope, he never will. Exactly—that's what part of the story is saying about the power of your mind, it can think things that never were, and once thought, those things are here forever."

A child said, "It's a busy, busy world."

TRAIN IN VAIN

THE SUBWAY HOME WOULD NOT MOVE fast enough. Emer was pondering Corvus, worrying. She kind of weirdly looked forward to barfing for him again tonight. She remained standing, as if that could speed things up. She found a Train of Thought to occupy her mind.

> When an inner situation is not made conscious, it appears outside as fate.   —CARL JUNG

Wow, that was some heavy shit for the subway. Emer wondered if they had a Jungian conductor today. The quote seemed to make sense, to have truth, but Emer couldn't quite pin it down, so she reserved final judgment. She thought it might be a good antidote to one of her least-favorite sayings of all time—"it was meant to be." She hated when people said that. "Oh, I guess it was just meant to be." Obviously, whatever happened was "meant to be." It was such a cop-out. But Jung was saying, it seemed to her, that if you didn't know yourself, shit would happen that appeared "meant to be," but was really you making it happen unconsciously.

Your unconscious was fate, or God. If you didn't do your homework and get to know yourself, you would be buffeted by fate, by your own shadow. The world would seem to lack free will, but it was really your own self-ignorance that made you powerless. Or something like that. Freud said character is destiny. That was similar, but not the same. Young Jung was rebelling against his master. It started to make her brain cramp.

Like the thing she recently heard about time, likening it to a guitar string between two points, the past and the future—but the weird thing to her was that a fixed point in this theory was the future, and the present is always vibrating, tuning, and moving to get a fixed past in line with a fixed future. So the past is unchangeable, though somewhat knowable, and the future unknown but set. It was like Schrödinger's cat—the cyanide vial is always both broken and unbroken, the cat is always alive and dead until we open the box and look, the looking, knowing itself, being the end of the experiment, the end of life: life is the experiment. The future was as random and fated as the past. She liked that, though it blew her mind, and didn't make a lot of human sense.

What little she knew of science made her feel stupid. She thought of taking up the guitar. Or the drums. She thought Schrödinger and Heisenberg should have opened up a law firm, or a bake shop. Not a pet shop. You wouldn't want Heisenberg to babysit your kid any more than you'd want Schrödinger cat-sitting. Sometimes Heisenberg is watching the kid, sometimes he's not. It's uncertainty at ten bucks an hour. She chuckled. Another limited version of free will. Her future was fixed, she just had to get in line with it. Cool. Okay, how?

The train passed through a "ghost station" at Eighteenth Street, an abandoned stop. Emer stared at the retired platform, wondering if it missed all the feet it used to support. There she was again, ascribing feelings to things. She also wondered if the ghost station was like one of those ghost planets—invisible to us except for the power they wield over the orbits of planets we can actually see. We know of the existence of such ghost planets exerting the influence of gravity only because of the inexplicable, erratic orbital behavior of the affected planets. Does the ghost station wield that type of power over the trains and the bodies of citizens? she mused. When we become erratic as people, she thought— okay, when I become erratic, she specified—could it be a ghost exerting influence on me? A ghost planet? A ghost station? The ghost of an idea?

No, she guessed the station was not nostalgic for busier days, when she saw something moving and a pair of eyes transfixed her. There was a guy standing there on the empty platform, looking homeless or something—big guy, hulking, menacing, even. And it reminded her of those occasional stories in *The New York Times* about bands of homeless seeking shelter from the winter in the warmth and privacy of disused subway tunnels and abandoned stations. It could be another one of those apocryphal New York stories, like the baby alligator craze that ended with fearful owners flushing their growing gators down the toilet and, over time, unwittingly creating a race of blind crocs in the sewers, alligators that had never seen the light of day. Like the stories of phantom limbs where amputees could feel cramps in muscles that no longer existed, the city was full of ghosts and phantoms. Alligators and stations. The phantom limbs of the city.

But the eyes holding her from the platform were real. She

maintained eye contact with the blurry man as she quickly sped away; he held up something like a coin or a piece of jewelry on a string or length of leather, in the way a hypnotist might present a coin to a willing mark. He seemed to her like he was specifically looking for her, for Emer, not just anyone. The object caught the light momentarily, she saw it gleam, and with that flash, the man's head seemed to take on the form of a crocodile, like Sobek, the ancient Egyptian deity.

Emer knew her fluid mind was projecting associations—hadn't she just been thinking of toilet-flushed alligators? Egyptian society and religion was part of the first-grade curriculum—near infants studying the infancy of civilization. So she knew Sobek. Isis. The underworld. She blinked and Sobek was gone; she saw the human face again, and then both the man and the shiny thing were gone, strobed behind metal stanchions and lost in darkness, the train having hurtled past.

What was the homeless guy's story? Why did she have to give him a story? So she could blame him, make him deserving of his fate. Could she empathize without poetic inflation? Why couldn't she just help? Just jump in and help. So much of life in New York City necessitated looking away—from pain and disaster, other people's suffering, the sheer amount of possible stories that came your way every day. You could open up and empathize with all of it, and thereby explode your soul into smithereens and paralysis, or you could look the other way and think of the baby crow in your apartment. Why was it easier for Emer to extend her heart to a crow and not a lover, to a crow and not a homeless man on an abandoned platform? Why did she have to turn this homeless man into a mythological deity? Was her heart infinite or was it just a certain size?

Was it her heart or a phantom heart that obsessed about Corvus, her boy, now as she looked up, trying to shake/shiver like a wet dog, to vibrate these sticky ideas off her, derail this particular train of thought; she saw a man across from her, a nice-looking man who seemed familiar. Another familiar stranger? She'd never noticed him on this line before, she was sure.

And then it hit her.

He was the man of her dreams—well, not that, but the man from her recurring dream, the one her mind called Con. She didn't know that for a fact, but she knew, she knew it as what she might call a "soul fact"—her gut. She had a picture of the man in her mind from the dream. It, or he, had been dreamed, he had been thought, and once thought, could not be unthought.

Maybe, more likely, she'd seen this dude before, on the subway, or somewhere else, and for some reason, he'd made an impression, and then she dreamed about him. Yeah, that was way more probable. But it was super weird anyway. She whispered the name aloud to herself as a question—"Con?"

Just then, the man looked up. And smiled.

MY DEAREST FELLATIO

THE NEXT COUPLE WEEKS PASSED with Corvus growing and apparently thriving. She no longer had to regurgitate for him, and he ate a medley of seeds and berries she tossed in the blender. One Thursday, Emer was called to sub for sixth-grade English class. It was actually one that Izzy taught, in addition to her duties as school psychologist. Izzy was sick and called in the favor. So while her own teaching assistant babysat her younger kids, Emer rode herd on the middle schoolers.

The assignment had been to compose a letter from one character in *Romeo and Juliet* to another. It was a good idea—giving minor characters a voice, a density and dimensionality they might not have access to over the course of the story, something of what Stoppard had in mind for his *Rosencrantz & Guildenstern Are Dead*—that pawns have the dreams and fears of rooks and bishops, queens and kings. That Izzy was a clever teacher.

One student read her letter from the Nurse to the Apothecary, making sure to give them names—Mary and Steve—and then going on to place an extensive sixteenth-century Shakespearean stream-of-consciousness pharmaceutical order while complaining about her own aching feet (all the while adding the abbreviations that texting has generously given the language)—"Oy, my dogs are barkin' fml (Steve-o!) . . . how are your newts? Are they fresh? My mistress has full on RBF and FOMO at the mo, but please set aside four newt eyes ttyl."

When she was done, and it was time for the next missive, a boy rose from the back row and announced, in all innocence and seriousness, that he was going to read a letter written by Mercutio. Emer nodded. She shared the English major's general love for the witty Mercutio, and wished he had lived to have his own vehicle written for him. She saw in Shakespeare's in-depth creation of a minor character who dies so early one of the deepest wisdoms of the play, in all of Shakespeare, actually; the fact that the best and the brightest do not necessarily mature into greatness, that there is random tragedy and random fate, and that the quickest, funniest, smartest character in this play, and by extension the world, could be murdered during a stupid family quarrel stoked by a couple of stupid, horny teenagers.

It was a profound and heartbreaking truth—not only the good die young, but also the best and brightest, bravest, most charismatic. Emer was hoping that the assignment would touch upon some of these issues when the boy announced that the letter was "from Mercutio to his cousin Fellatio."

That blow was so unexpected that Emer barked a seal-like laugh, and collapsed into convulsive giggles. It was a good ten seconds before she relaxed her diaphragm enough to draw a cautious breath, which unfortunately fueled another run of laughter. She looked up through tears at the class, which seemed mostly nonplussed at her mirth, and at the boy, who she could see had not intended to make this joke, and in fact was looking a little hurt.

"Do you want me to start over?" the boy asked. "This is a letter written from Mercutio to his cousin Fellatio—"

"No! Don't start over!" Emer managed to yell at the kid. "Okay, okay—just pick up where you were . . ."

The boy swallowed and blinked, confused, and cleared his throat. "Okay—'My Dearest Fellatio . . .'"

Emer literally doubled over. This time, though, she found the "Dearest" funny. "Wait, no, stop, please . . . oh my, look at the time . . ." There were a good twenty minutes left in the class. "Why don't we take the rest of the period as a 'study'—okay? Get a jump on tonight's homework." She managed to get to the door and out into the hallway, where she could give in to a couple more giggle fits. On some level, she would forever be a five-year-old. Jesus. She thought about how she would laugh again when she told the story to Izzy.

She looked up at the sound of heavy feet coming down the hallway and saw the not always welcome face of St. Margaret's headmaster, Sidney Crotty, a very short man. The clumping that preceded Sidney was caused by the heavy lifts he wore in his shoes, which was like the open secret/joke of the school. By fourth grade, most of the kids could see eye to eye with their headmaster. No one, absolutely no one, had ever seen Sidney in bare feet or out of his heavy black shoes with the two-inch heels and three-inch lifts.

Sidney was a pocket-sized Jesuit priest who had taken the school through the transition from strict Catholic education to Ivy League prep. Despite his stature, before the advent of cell phone cameras, say before the mid-'70s at least, Sidney had been known to drop a truant high schooler twice his size with a clipping left hook on more than one occasion. He had the reputation as "pound for pound the baddest Catholic on the Lower East Side." You got the feeling he would fight like a wild animal, clawing and biting, and you'd have to kill him to make him quit; and if you did kill him, as he was dying, he would find a way to clamp on to you with his teeth so you would eventually die of exhaustion carrying this attached dead priest around.

Those "good old days," as he called them, when you could slap a child for insolence and not see your world come crashing down as a result, were long gone, but there was still a sense of flashing, righteous hostility with Sidney Crotty, and his being handcuffed over time by the tide of political correctness and enlightened pedagogy had channeled all that potential violence into a colorful vocabulary and a well-honed passive aggression.

Even as it was part of Greenwich Village, St. Margaret's had sat out the '60s, keeping the boys' hair short and the girls in bland brown jumpers. But as the Village changed and was overrun by moneyed folks, and the bankers and hedge-fund cowboys chased out the gays and the artists, the mission and position of the school changed. Sidney oversaw this questionable regime makeover with an expert hand and a winning, constant air of incredulity and be-musement underneath a small man's terrier toughness. Having traded Keds for Cole Haans, both feet of the school were now firmly in the new city—both big-heeled, high-lifted, size-six boy's feet.

"There you are, slumming it up here in the middle school. May I have a word?"

"Of course. Here or . . . ?"

"Here is fine. Have you been crying?" He offered her a hanky from his jacket pocket. He still carried a pocket square. His clothes were custom made; they had to be. She'd never seen him in leisure wear, but she wondered if he could shop at Gap Kids or had bid on any outfits from the Prince estate. She dabbed at her eyes with the hanky.

"Thank you. One of the kids, oh god, it was funny. It just hit my funny bone."

"Diving right in . . . I've been having to deal with some parents this week, last couple weeks actually, parents in your class, both sides of the culture wars, really. Not a big deal, but I think you need to be aware. Yes, we are a liberal school and yes, most of our parents would contort themselves to circumlocute any tinge of racism on the one hand or association with the Christian right on the other."

"I'm not following."

"That was a bit of a preamble, wasn't it? A little birdy told me—did you serve watermelon as a snack a couple weeks ago?"

"Maybe, probably—I sometimes bring a watermelon in for the kids. They love it."

"Their parents don't love it."

"What the hell, Sidney, sugar?"

"Sugar? Ha, no, it's not sugar. An African American kid, Obama Johansson, well, not the kid, but his mother, his white mother—she said that watermelon made her and her child uncomfortable and could you find a less-offensive fruit."

"A less-offensive fruit?"

"Yes, a less-offensive fruit. I'm quoting. Or snack."

"What's a less-offensive snack? Not a banana, I'm thinking. Too cisgender a fruit?"

"Banana seems fine to me. As long as they're not too big. People get uncomfortable around those."

"No graham crackers—crackers will make white kids uneasy. No white bread—well, white bread does kinda suck."

"I'm not the enemy here."

"I know, Sidney, I'm sorry. I don't envy your position. Is that all? No more watermelon?"

"Did you read your kids a story that could be interpreted as arguing against Darwinism?"

"Darwinism? I don't think so."

"Advocating Creationism? Some blessed Indian thing?"

"Oh god, yes, maybe, the story of Rainbow Crow."

"Okay, well, that has some parents up in arms that you're back-dooring Creationism into the young hearts and minds of their privileged progeny."

"I'll have to go back and read it, but I don't think so."

"I have Molly Hager's mother crawling up my ass that she's okay with teaching creation myths of Indians as long as you give equal time now to Genesis and some Hindu shit. Our curriculum, as you know, is Post-Christian Christian but de-emphatic—though we do lean slightly on our Bible, we maintain a separation of church and curriculum, and we can't be seen to be teaching any one body of belief too much at the expense of another. Everything is a story placed in its de-phallocentrized sociopolitical context." His tone was so arch, she couldn't tell if he was a true believer, a half believer, or taking the piss out of the whole thing.

Emer defended herself. "I was teaching it as a story. Hell, I wasn't teaching it, I read it as an exercise in imagination, I didn't post it as scientific fact."

"Well then, what the fuck happened with a trigger warning?"

"I forgot my trigger warning."

"You can't forget the trigger warning. The (trigger warning) fucking trigger warning is our (trigger warning) fucking insurance (trigger warning) fucking policy. I don't like the (trigger warning) cunting thing any more than you, I feel like my (trigger warning) balls have been cut off, but I (micro-aggression) bloody well have to do it." He took a small bow after that virtuouso performance.

Sometimes she loved Sidney. He scared her, but she loved him. Sidney turned around and offered Emer a view of his ass. "Would you like to speak to Mrs. Hager yourself? If you look up there I'm sure you'll see her head peeping out. Say hi to Mrs. Hager. Have you ever had a middle-aged Wasp take up residence in your ass?"

"Your (trigger warning) ass?"

"My (trigger warning) ass."

"Can't say that I have, Sidney." Emer absentmindedly fingered the scar on her scalp.

In the middle of all this, it dawned on Emer that the Sidney in front of her had been the prototype for the little doorman in her dreams, who, it came to her, was called Sid. It took her right out of the conversation, and she actually said aloud, "You're Sid. You're Sidhe!"

Sidney took a step back, nodded, and said, "What?"

"Nothing. It's just I remembered something."

"You remembered my name."

"It's nothing, Sid, just something I thought of."

They stared at each other. Emer felt like she was challenging him, but she had not meant to.

"Just a dream I had."

"You dreamt about me?"

"You were in a dream I had."

She felt suddenly like she wanted to choose her words very carefully. He paused and looked away, seemed to smile or grimace, Emer couldn't quite tell.

"I'm flattered." He turned back to her now. "Anyway, Emer, you might have to do some damage control. A couple of the parents now feel 'unsafe.' Maybe take a couple of parent-teacher conferences. As a palliative and prophylactic. Might take some extra time, but I think it's worth it. To me, anyway."

"Whatever you want, Sid."

"What I want has very little to do with any of this. Anyway, please don't stray from the approved curriculum. You're a valued teacher here, but these parents are rabid, entitled freaks. I had one ask me yesterday if third grade was too early to put in a week in Costa Rica for Habitat for Humanity—as in, would it still count on the college application if she 'gets it out of the way now.'"

"I hear what you're saying, Sid."

"Good. Now would you like to say goodbye to Mrs. Hager?" He turned to show his rear again. "'Cause if not, we'll be on our way." He made it to the exit, and then turned back to Emer, stopping her just before she went back into the classroom. "And Emer . . ."

She turned. He was now backlit by the bright sun coming through the stairwell window; there were dust motes swirling about his head in the slanting light like a halo or particulate heavy smoke from a strange fire. His whole aspect seemed changed, or rather felt changed, because, lit like this, she couldn't really make out his features to gauge expression or intent. He was glowing, otherworldly. She couldn't see his lips move, but she heard what he said. Before he turned and walked away down the stairs, he called out, with no trigger warning:

"Watch your ass."

CORVUS FUGIT

EMER DIDN'T CLIP THE BIRD'S WINGS. The mere phrase itself bothered her, and she didn't know how to do it, and the procedure she saw online looked tricky, and she didn't want to risk taking the bird out of the building to a pet store to get it done. The bird was thriving and flying around the small apartment. She was afraid that he would fly too hard into a mirror or a closed window so she had draped blankets over reflective surfaces. Her apartment began to have a humidity of its own, like a jungle ecosystem, and Emer thought of it as an oasis.

It crossed her mind that she might appear crazy to a stranger, or even a friend. Not the cat lady, but the bird lady. But it was only one bird, after all. How crazy is that? Not very. She worried that Corvus's cawing, which was getting more full throated and confident by the day, and the varied assortment of grunts, clicks, and guttural shout-outs that sounded to her as differentiated as a secret language, would slice through the old walls, alerting nosey neighbors to her secret world within.

Corvus was extremely intelligent. He already knew his name and, adorably, like a dog, would follow her from room to room, waddle-hopping as she went about her day. This waddle-walk lent Corvus an old-fashioned, gentlemanly, fussy air that was quite winning. There was something so satisfying in this domestication of a wild animal that was of a different order from the bond between man and dog. Though Corvus felt trainable, he also felt wild and unattainable. Kind of what you'd want in a man, she thought.

If you want to catch a bird, Jim Gunnels always said, become a tree. So she looked around the fetid apartment, and at Corvus, and decided to open some windows. When she lifted the pane, it felt momentous in a minor key, like a graduation for the bird, the opening of one world to another, the inside meeting the outside. She went out for coffee. She felt as free as she wanted Corvus to feel.

A few days ago, Izzy had called, and called her out. "Okay, something is up with you. You've gone underground."

"Not really."

"Just tell me about the man and spare me the faux shame."

"Well . . ."

"I knew it."

She would tell someone. She had to. She didn't mind secrets. The density of secrets would sometimes lend her dimension, make her visible and vibrate in the way she had to conceal, and that density placed her more firmly on planet Earth, in less danger of floating away. But she liked having a confidant too, a co-conspirator. It was about a bird.

"A bird! As in English-speak for 'girl'? You're one of us now? Welcome to the team!"

"No, a bird bird."

"Oh, like Polly Wanna Cracker?"

"More like that, yeah. A baby crow I rescued from the street."

"So are we talking about sex? At all?"

"Nope. Bird. Corvus, I call him."

"Well, that's pretentious."

"C'est moi."

"I'm pretty sure this is the wrong direction. But at least he's black."

Walking to Pain Quotidien, Emer almost wanted to cry. She realized that these were child-centric feelings she was having about the bird, and that this was a moment, like a first day of school or a graduation, when the offspring stakes out some independence from progenitors. So she was doubly sad, sad about Corvus growing up and possibly "leaving the nest," and sad that she was having these feelings about a bird and not her own child.

The sun was setting. Summer was coming, and she felt a little unstable, flashing hot and cold, like the seasons. She couldn't decide on a hot or iced mocha frappé/latte (she always sang this in her mind as the song "Lady Marmalade"—"mocha chocolata ya ya"). What a fucking mess I am, she thought.

She went with iced, as a nod to the future summer, not the past spring, though she couldn't seem to locate a bounce in her step. She walked with her eyes on the ground, but she was still aware of the sheer numbers of couples with young babies out for an early evening stroll in the nicening weather. Some kind of tyranny of normalcy was taking over the Upper West Side, at once consoling and horrifying.

She watched as a father paid for a syrup over shaved ice for his son from a Latino vendor, knowing they viewed this transaction as exotic and archetypal, almost like a touristy pocket in their own safe world. She was reminded of something Izzy had told her about the Village in the mid-'90s when, as a just-out lesbian, she lived there on Christopher Street, a ground zero capital of Gay America; Izzy had seen a young man in a purple NYU T-shirt unpack a set of golf clubs from a Range Rover. Golf clubs! In Greenwich Village! The Village of Dylan Thomas and Stonewall. "That's when I knew it was over," Izzy said. "That golf bag was the Trojan Horse that all these little straight hedge-fund fucks spilled out of under cover of night. They won. We lost. No sleep till Brooklyn." As Emer was laughing about this, she felt someone tap her shoulder kind of hard. She turned around while pulling back to see who would be so forward. No one there.

She turned homeward again. The sun had disappeared for the day behind the taller buildings, but she hadn't made three steps when she was tapped again. Harder this time. She wheeled around, saying "Hey!" and again, no one and nothing there. As she circled around looking, something glinting and wet on her shoulder caught her eye. Matte white, creamy, and lumpy—bird shit. "Oh, fuck me," she said. "Gross."

Realizing she had only her bare hand to wipe it off, she headed to a trash can to see if there was a thrown-away napkin or something, when a cawing stopped her. She felt she recognized that voice, as it occurred to her as more voice than sound. She looked up, and there, perched on the intersection of signs, 92ND ST/ COLUMBUS, was a crow. She walked out into the middle of the avenue, almost getting hit by a procession of deliverymen on bicycles heading the wrong way. The cyclists, maybe eight of them, weaved around the scared-stiff Emer with the impassive confidence and precision of circus performers, blowing her hair back but leaving her unscathed. The riders had the aspect of a presidential motorcade for some hungry dignitary. She could read on the side of their plastic bags the name of their restaurant, Dragon King. Maybe she'd complain to the management. But maybe not—no harm, no foul, Emer thought.

The black bird, which she was sure was Corvus flown the coop, rose up and veered eastward. Emer gave chase, toward the park.

GO ASK ALICE

MER WAS GIDDY from following her overhead bird, and Corvus waited for her, sitting in the branches of a big tree on the east side of Central Park West. When Emer caught up, she could see that Corvus had been joined by a murder of other crows, though she felt she could pick him out of that lineup, the way a parent of twins always knows who's who. The crows made an arrow formation, Corvus the point, and headed deeper into the park. Night was falling.

She followed the crows as one follows logic in a dream. She pushed through some shrubs and low-hanging branches to an opening by the model boat pond. There she watched the crows alight on the statue of Alice in Wonderland at the north end. Curiouser and curiouser, Emer thought. There were a couple of elderly folks sitting at the base of the sculpture.

Emer took a seat on one of the benches that ring the oval pond. She watched as more elderly people materialized out of the night, like slow-walking zombies, and congregated around

Alice, touching the bronze sculpture as one might a religious relic. The moon was bright tonight, nestled in a high ceiling of windblown clouds that gave it a type of strobe effect. The old people huddled together as the crows had done. Emer tried counting them—twenty, now thirty. She looked around. There were a few other pedestrians, but no one seemed to notice this eerie assembly at the foot of Alice.

A hand landed on Emer's shoulder. It scared the shit out of her, she was so focused forward. A man brushed by her in the direction of Alice. Emer recognized the stained chinos and the shuffling gait.

"Pops?" she said.

The old man stopped, his back to Emer, then turned to face her. It was Jim Gunnels, all right. He seemed in a trance. The man's eyes shifted, as if he had trained his focus from a great distance, from eternity itself, then onto Emer. He smiled and tipped an imaginary hat to her. "Lough Derg," he said, and then, seeing her confusion, added, "The Red Lake." He resumed shuffling toward Alice.

Emer looked around for Ging, but the nurse was nowhere in sight. She wondered if she was losing her mind for real—but how could you know when you'd gone 'round the bend? Wasn't being pretty sure you weren't crazy kind of a possible sign that you were? She'd had an episode in college where she'd stayed in the school infirmary over Christmas holidays junior year. Did that give her a "history of mental illness"? Was this like that?

That episode was over a breakup with an unfaithful boyfriend and an uncharacteristic spate of B's, and therefore "situational," and understandable in the land of cause and effect, "healthy" even. That had been the takeaway back then. The exception that proved the rule. But when do the exceptions pile up and make a new rule for which the old rule becomes the new exception? This recent, constant dreaming, the unspecific, lingering sense of regret—barfing for a baby crow, for fuck's sake—felt more mysterious and systemic. When was the moment that the scales tipped you into Crazyville and you stopped interrogating yourself and your weirdness and rescued five or six cats and a raccoon to go with your pet crow?

But her senses were too acute to be failing: she could feel everything around her, smell the grass and the musky standing water of the pond, see the moon and make out the face that always looked aghast to her—as if the moon, in its slow orbit, were watching Earth the way drivers slow down at the scene of an accident. Each long night was a new, slowly unfolding catastrophe.

Maybe she was lonely, maybe she was deeply unfulfilled, maybe she was looking too hard for magic, but she was not nuts. Not yet. And she had just watched her father, in the throes of dementia, walk into the park at night alone. She had better keep her shit together.

The elderly group was milling about the statue, haltingly, stiff in the motions of the aged. She heard Corvus caw and fly up. The black bird headed north and the murder fell in behind him. Slowly, like ancient ducklings, so the old followed. And dutifully, almost reverently, so did Emer.

THE DRAGON KING DELIVERS

THE GROUP OF ELDERLY MOVED, a cohesive mass beneath the murder of crows, with the slowness of a monster jellyfish, pulsating vaguely north through the park. The amoebic organism got to the Bridle Path and climbed up along small bridges and riskier embankments to the runners' path around the reservoir.

Emer maintained a discreet distance. She watched Corvus land on the steel-and-cast-iron six-foot fence that rings the water. Behind the bird, she watched as the fountain emerging from the southern end of the reservoir intensified, reaching all the way, like a rainstorm, to the elderly huddling on the runners' path.

The water seemed to have an immediate, salutary effect on the old. Like wild animals, they began to scamper up the fence and dive into the reservoir. Emer had never seen any living thing in that water, beyond the tough urban mallards and the never-been-to-sea gulls. Her own father scaled the fence and scrambled down the twenty-foot-high earthen berm and dived, with the grace of a man fifty years younger, into the black water.

She took a few more steps forward. She was maybe fifty yards away now, but a big fat crow cawed evilly at her, and she stopped. It seemed like the birds didn't want her any closer. She looked around to see if anyone else was witnessing this, but the crows were dive-bombing stray pedestrians away from the scene, like avian bodyguards.

The reservoir had been dug from the schist by about a thousand Irish immigrants in the 1860s. The old people were now swimming in its stagnant waters like withered, gray Olympians. Yet they made no noise; it was like watching one of those old musicals with the water ballet interludes on mute in the black and white of night. The spray from the fountain, built in 1917, and capable of spewing water sixty feet high, grew ever higher and thicker, casting shapes now, similar to when fireworks displays outline forms with light.

The old men and women in the water began to reconfigure and cohere and make love as one—a roiling, rolling, moonlit mass of time-slackened bodies sliding over one another like a bucket of gray eels, the image occurred to Emer, but sweeter, if not sexier. She couldn't find her father within the orgasmic organism. For that, she may have been thankful, 'cause she didn't know if she was ready to see her demented old dad, working-class Catholic Jimmy Gunnels, doing the AARP nasty with some stranger(s) in a Busby Berkeley–redux water orgy.

The spray above the swimmers/lovers, backlit by the moon, took on the shape of a dragon. The lovemaking mass of supplicants began moaning at the beast. "Dragon King," they chanted. And "Lough Derg," the name her father had used.

Allowed in by the bouncer-like crows, the same procession of Asian deliverymen on bikes that had nearly taken Emer out earlier in the evening made a reappearance on the runners' path. In unison, they donned garbage-bag raincoats against the spray and began throwing their cardboard cartons of food and goodies toward the liquid mouth of the Dragon King, currying its primitive favor with burnt offerings and fried rice. Pounds and pounds of chicken lo mein, moo goo gai pan, and fortune cookies went flying over the fence and into the water.

The Dragon King, its mouth of spray salivating, shook its mammoth head in pleasure, water flying off in all directions. A droplet landed by Emer's feet. She bent to touch it. It dried instantly. She picked it up. It was shiny and hard, like a guitar pick, catching rainbow colors like a fish scale. It smelled disgusting—like dead fish, monosodium glutamate, and raw innards. She looked up again. The Dragon King seemed pleased, its undulating translucent gullet moving the food down to its underwater cave. The seagulls, ducks, and crows were feasting on his floating scraps, and the old folks, for now, remained young.

THE DAY BREAKS, HER MIND ACHES

ONCE AGAIN, THE ALARM COMES TOO SOON. Emer has a snippet of Nirvana's "Smells Like Teen Spirit" on her phone that does the trick most days. Kurt Cobain howling, "a mulatto, an albino, a mosquito, my libido, a denial." She'd like to take the ukulele to it, but her head is heavy on her pillow today, her hair matted again with sweat from fitful dreams. She waited to come back to herself, to feel fully within her body again. Images from the night before flashed at her, like she was in a car speeding by. Corvus. Alice. The reservoir. Her father. The dragon. All so real. But not possible. Well, some of it possible, but surely not. She fingered the scar on her scalp, but it had no answers, or even comfort.

She dressed in a kind of trance. She thought of her childhood diagnosis of her "bridge," her corpus callosum, failing to demarcate waking from dreaming. We change so, and do not change, she thought.

Corvus was gone, so there was less to do this morning. No

feeding. She would miss that little dude. She reached for a sock on her dresser and knocked it off, down the back against the wall. She had to get on her knees and reach blindly underneath. As she felt around for the sock, she touched something sharp and flat and pulled that out. Not a sock, but a photo, an old-fashioned Polaroid, of her, her and a man. Emer's face was lined up with the man's face so you couldn't see him, only his dark hair. Emer was smiling in the photo. The man's hand was caressing her hair. She thought she'd never looked this happy.

She didn't know where the picture was from or who the man might be. Curiouser and curiouser. She reached her hand under the dresser again, but came up empty. She put the photo in a drawer.

PASCAL WAS A GAMBLAHOLIC

THE DAY ITSELF PASSED like a dream. There was an unreal quality to it that could not be shaken off, and it was not lost on Emer that as her dreams became more real, her reality became less so. She was looking forward to checking in with Izzy at lunch. She found Izzy in her office.

"Not you again," Izzy joked.

"I think I'm having a crisis of faith."

"Uh, I'm the token Jew in the citadel here. Perhaps you want to talk to Sidney?"

Emer held up a paper bag. "I come bearing vegetable panini."

"In that case, welcome to my office."

Izzy motioned to a tiny chair, made for a small child. Emer sat, her knees pushing up nearly under her chin.

"Can you just not argue with me about God for a moment?" Emer asked.

"No, that's not possible."

"Let's just put that aside, like, okay, I agree that your atheism is legit and I won't assail it and you agree that my faith is legit and you don't assail it, and then we can talk."

"No," Izzy protested, "that's like saying, okay, you get to be bat-shit crazy for a second and say there are virgin births and a handsome blue-eyed straight-haired dude from Palestine turns water into wine, but for the rest of the time, you'll be sane? I can't do that. I can't get beyond your a priori."

"But to deal with my crisis of faith, you have to accept my faith."

"Okay, to acknowledge that you're having a sudden flash of sanity, I'll allow that you're insane."

"Plenty of geniuses believed or came to believe—Shakespeare, Eliot, Einstein, even Wallace Stevens had a deathbed conversion."

"It was the air they breathed. It was the water they drank. You've come later, you have a better shot. You know I had a little first grader in here an hour ago who was mourning the death of his imaginary friend, too."

"What about if it's as tepid a belief as Pascal's wager? What if we have nothing to lose? If we believe in God, and there's a heaven, we win; if we believe in God, and there's nothing—so what—we all lose, and we were no worse off for believing in him. That's like faith as a free insurance policy."

"But you were worse off. You had to abide by his laws, and do the nasty shit he says to do, and hate yourself and your body in just the way he says to hate yourself and your body."

"You think I hate myself?"

"I think you have your moments. Like anyone."

"Maybe there's something more."

"More than God? I'm hoping maybe there's something less."

"More than just the one God, you know, like many gods.

Maybe I was right to believe in a System, but maybe it was the wrong System."

"Why do you need a System?"

"A System feels good. I've always been a good student. I like structure. I like to know I've done the homework, that the teacher likes me, maybe get a gold star at the end of it."

"Maybe that's just nostalgia. For safety. A nostalgia for the order of childhood."

"Maybe not."

"What about love as a System?"

"That's what Jesus brought. He brought love. He replaced vengeance with love. He turned the other cheek."

"Too many strings attached with that guy. Pauline strings."

"Maybe we need the strings. Maybe without the strings we float away."

"Okay, so now you're saying, a priori, you're not just a little crazy, you're lots of crazy, a big steaming bowl of crazy. You want the Baby Jesus and a whole host of other phenomena."

"I ain't crazy, I'm just waking up. I'm woke."

"Are you gonna start speaking in country songs?"

"My Jesus is not like that; he's not the walks-with-me-and-talks-with-me kind."

"How about the Jesus-that-makes-you-rich kind? Where's that cat? Dial that fucker up."

"Mine's more like your Yahweh, I imagine: a tough, unreasonable mother."

"My Yahweh? Did you just call me a Jew, you mackerel snapper?"

"You are a Jew, Jew."

"Of course, but being a Jew is not a religion in this city, it's a culture. We Jews like to leave God out and the cream cheese in. There's this ultra-Orthodox group, the Satmar sect, right now, that wants to ban girls from higher education. Clearly I'm not down with that retro-madness—I'm an agnostic, Netflix-addicted lesbo with two advanced degrees working in a school run by Jesuits—they're not inviting me to their big beard and payess party, and I don't wanna go. But don't take away my fucking bagels, the Sunday *New York Times*, and the two-week August time-share in Cherry Grove."

"You can't judge a religion by its extremes."

"That may, in fact, be the best way to judge, like blossoms on the branches."

Izzy took a bite of the veggie panini and sipped iced coffee. "Can we talk about *Game of Thrones* now? *The Bachelor*? Remember when we used to talk about Trump all the time? He gave our lives focus, like cancer. But funnier. Then it got real. And no longer remotely funny."

"I'm having visions," Emer confessed. "Visions and dreams."

"Good," said Izzy. "Good, I think."

"What do you really think?"

"I think you need to get laid."

"That's such a guy thing to say."

"Thou shalt get some sexy time."

Emer secretly dived back into the imagery of her dream last night. The Dragon King. Her father making love in the reservoir with strangers. What the fuck? There was no way to process that—either as a dream or as reality. As a dream, what did it say about her? As reality, what did it say about everything else? There was nowhere to put it but aside, in a dark corner maybe. Locked away in the house like a gun in a box in a safe on a shelf in a closet. The bell rang for class.

Emer rose from her seat, her knees stiff from the extreme angle of the little chair. Izzy rose and took her friend's face in her hands.

"You're gonna be okay, okay?"

Izzy's baseline kindness made Emer want to cry.

"I think your father is fading and you're heartbroken. Those are the words, the rest is bullshit. But you're gonna sail on through. I know this."

Emer nodded. "Okay."

Izzy kissed her on the cheek. Emer hugged her and whispered in her ear, "I need to find someone like you."

"With a penis."

"That would be a bonus."

"The holy grail. Now get back to work and mold some young minds. As-salaam alaikum."

FEAR AND TREMBLING

ZZY'S WORDS made Emer want to check in on her dad before heading home. Most days, after school, she spent a couple hours with him. But with Corvus around, she'd been somewhat delinquent. She felt guilty. But Corvus was gone now and she could get back into the lulling rhythm of her days: home, subway, school, subway, dad, home. On the subway, she looked around for the mystery man. Nope. But she did land upon a Train of Thought that caught her eye:

> When one has circumnavigated existence, it will appear whether one has courage to understand that life is a repetition, and to delight in that very fact. Repetition is reality, and it is the seriousness of life. —SØREN KIERKEGAARD

Yeah, tell that to the assembly-line worker or the zombie-eyed barista at her Starbucks. She remembered the Camus story where

Sisyphus, pushing his rock up that hill day after day, was ultimately deemed "happy." Doing the same thing over and over again, without hope of completion or victory. "Shoulder to the boulder," as that other Irishman in her life, Sidney, liked to say to buck up the troops. Were we all characters in a Beckett play directed by Sartre? And if so, looking around, she wondered why more people didn't seem delighted by their serious lives of repetition.

She wondered if some omniscient MTA honcho had posted Kierkegaard as a sop to the riders who did the same thing every day. And wondered further if such existentialism was more of a palliative than the idea of heaven that she still clung to somewhere deep in her childhood mind that curated her doomed desire to become a priest.

Her reverie was broken by one of those spooky half-human, half-automated announcements that had run like a horror-movie theme beneath the sounds of the subway ever since 9/11—warning that people should be aware of any unattended bags and to report suspicious packages blah blah blah. It was like the safety instructions on an airplane. The scary stuff inevitably merged into the voice of Charlie Brown's parents. For your safety wah wah wah . . . tighten the buckle wah wah wah . . . always put on your mask first before helping with someone else's wah wah wah. But the fact remained that there were people willing to kill for their tiny corner of God, and that left her in awe and terrified and wasn't it the same one God we worshipped and wah wah wah.

Opening the door to her father's apartment, she half expected to see her dad up and about, dancing around his room with Ging-ging, but no such luck. The old man was asleep and Ging was perturbed. "He no sleep good," she said. "And look . . . he up eat in middle of the night. Chef Boyardee." Ging pointed at the kitchen counter, where no fewer than eight cans of Spaghetti and Meatballs stood open and at attention, their still-attached jagged lids forming some sort of ironic salute.

"He ate all that himself?"

"I no eat it." Ging seemed insulted at the insinuation, which Emer had not meant to make.

"Let me ask you, Ging, and please, this is not an accusation, but is it possible he's sleepwalking?"

"Sleepwalking?"

"Yes, where a person gets up and does things—walks, eats"— she didn't say "takes part in a mass aqua-orgy in Central Park"— "but is still asleep."

"I know what is sleepwalking, miss."

Emer checked the old man's gray New Balance sneakers. They were caked with mud.

"It rained yesterday," Ging-ging said, and then giggled strangely.

Emer did not know what to make of the giggle, and didn't want to provoke the woman further. Ging took the sneakers from Emer's hand.

"I clean."

Two words that sounded more like "fuck you" to Emer. Ging-ging left with the sneakers and, moments later, before she could protest further, Emer heard the tub running. Ging was going to get the New York City filth, shit, whatever it was on her dad's shoes in the tub? She let it go. She didn't want a fight; she needed Ging too much. And that made her feel all the more guilty for not being a better, full-service daughter. Hadn't this man changed her diapers? Why couldn't she clean him? Why was she too busy for that?

"Well," Emer called out, extending an apology to the Filipina in the bathroom, "eating is better than not eating."

Her father opened his eyes and said her name. Then, raising himself up slowly, he whispered as if he didn't want Ging to overhear. "I have to go to confession."

Remembering the night of the Dragon King, Emer nodded.

THE SACRED HEART

EMER COULDN'T REMEMBER the last time she'd been to church with her father. She had to use Google to find Holy Trinity Roman Catholic Church on West Eighty-second Street, just a few blocks from her dad's place. They could walk there easily. She was encouraged that the church was averaging 4.6 stars out of 5 in its reviews. Most movies, books, and gods would take that.

They entered the building in silence. She made a bee line to the confession booths, ushering her father inside one. She figured that was enough, that the priests are used to dealing with crazy shit all the time. Emer found an empty pew and hit her knees. She didn't know what to pray for; she wasn't without, she wasn't unhappy really. It had been so long since she imagined herself talking to Christ.

She had once visited the Sacré-Coeur in Paris where traditionally there is always someone or many anonymous someones praying twenty-four hours a day, not for themselves, but for others.

It was like a version of the Buddhist monks who live on alms because their "work" is of the spirit. These Parisian mendicants prayed for the world at large, not personally but universally. She liked that idea, and decided that she would import her own minor-key version of the Sacré-Coeur to New York City. Nobody would know.

She closed her eyes and began to pray. "I pray for all the Bobs in distress"—that made her laugh, but she soldiered on—"and all the Janes in pain, and Franks, and African and Asian names I don't yet know. And all these poor babies with Zika. And Thalidomide before them. And the children, all of them. And my father. And Corvus—can I pray for a bird?" She decided she could. "And all the children being taught terrorist ideology"—sometimes it was as if someone else were speaking inside her head; no matter—"and the brokenhearted, and everyone named Jones . . ."

She looked up and saw another man, middle-aged and listless, on his knees. "And that guy, let him feel peace before death. And the horses that trot around Central Park. They don't look happy to me, no matter what Liam Neeson says. But let Liam Neeson be happy too, please."

She began to sob. Almost to the point of losing control. Once you opened up so wide, how could you ever close up again? It wasn't like a zipper on her heart. Her heart suddenly felt like a suitcase into which she was trying to repack the unfolded world. It couldn't fit, could it? There was so much pain, everywhere. Where could she start, and once started, where would she end? She felt a part of everything, this big feeling world; she lost herself in the vast ocean of souls, an image of endless space, and stars, and a cold airless wind. Reeling, she put on the brakes, dug in her heels, couldn't let go all the way. She frightened herself out of the prayer, like it was a drug coming on too strong and she was scared of an overdose.

Emer felt something shift inside her; she was so often ashamed of what people did in the name of Christ in her country, but there was a rightness here. She felt closer to divinity in this place, to a Something Else, on this day. She needed more. She had read somewhere once—was it Samuel Beckett again?—"the prayer is the god." And she felt the righteousness of that perception today, the spiritual wisdom. This extension up and out of oneself. This charitable vector. She didn't know what it meant exactly or how it would play out specifically in her future days, but the Sacré-Coeur move centered her, made her feel part of something greater than herself. She repeated it over and over, like a mantra—the prayer is the god, the prayer is the god. The prayers are the gods.

After an indefinite period of this other-oriented bliss, she glanced up and noticed that her father was still inside his confessional. Emer moved up, wondering if maybe she could eavesdrop on the old man. She couldn't make anything out at first, nothing specific, but then an eruption of laughter came from within the box, a startling noise in this place. She rushed up, and just as she opened the door to her father's side, an old priest came spilling out the other, like he'd been stabbed or shot. That was Emer's first thought. Omigod, Dad stabbed the priest! But no, maybe he was giggling, actually holding his sides like an illustration of someone laughing. And now her father came out too, laughing just as hard. The priest dabbed at his weeping eyes with his colorful vestments and walked off shaking his head.

Emer asked her father what the Father was laughing about, and he said, "Laughing? He was crying. I rocked his little world."

"How'd you make him cry?"

"I told him the many ways in which you would have been a better priest than he is."

Her dad was so energized by his confession that he said, "Let's get on the subway."

"Where do you wanna go, Pops?"

"Heaven."

"Not sure it stops there."

"Hell?"

"Let's take the One."

BETWEEN THE DOG AND THE WOLF

O N THE SUBWAY, Emer watched her dad aimlessly enjoy the movement; she tried to talk to him about last night—almost as if she wanted him, in his constant twilight, to corroborate what was real and what was not. She didn't want to ask him outright, that never seemed to work with him; she decided on cavalierly throwing words and phrases in his direction to see what sparked him, like a fairy-tale child tossing bread crumbs.

"Reservoir," she said. "The Central Park reservoir." The old man stared straight ahead. "Should we get some Chinese food tonight? I can order from Dragon King. We can get it delivered." She pronounced it "de-li-vered," like a clue. The old man was silent. She felt like she was losing him to that place he went to, pulled in by an undertow in an ocean of night, again.

"I need to change the past," he said. And then closed his eyes.

"Is that what you're doing?"

"Trying to. But you're talking a lot, Bill."

"How can you change the past?" she asked. "Pops? How? The past is what happened already."

"I need to see the future to figure that out, Bill," he said. "Obviously."

"Obviously," she agreed. And then—

"Goddammit, I wish you'd stop calling me Bill."

She knew her dad had an illness, knew he wasn't being an asshole or forgetful on purpose, but sometimes she simply lost patience. It felt to her sometimes like he did do it purposefully, though she knew intellectually that was untrue. Nice daughter, she thought, to take it personally when he loses his mind or shits his pants.

"Oh? What would you like to be called?" her father asked.

"Emer."

"Emer. Beautiful Irish name."

"Yes."

"Emer the dreamer." Just like that, a moment of past grace in the now, an unexpected lightning flash of salvation.

"That's what you used to call me."

"I did?"

"Yes. And Emer the schemer. And Emer who will never own a Beemer. But mostly Emer the dreamer."

"I shall try in the future."

"Thank you."

"Whatever floats your boat."

He seemed to drift off with closed eyes, asleep maybe. Peaceful, she hoped, and brave in his quest to change the past. She looked around for a Train of Thought to occupy her thoughts, and her eyes met the eyes of a familiar stranger.

He was looking at her. Con was. The one she called Con was staring at her, unblinking, like he knew her. He smiled. She felt herself smiling back, felt her heart beating in her temples. She was excited, turned on, and guilty for some obscure reason, and not because she was sitting next to her father as a stranger flirted with her. Or so she thought. Or so she hoped? She felt something hot at the back of her neck. This wasn't love at first sight. She didn't believe in that. But this was intensity right off the bat. Though it wasn't really first sight, what with the premonitions, dreams, and the other sighting, but it was definitely something at first something.

Noticing that the old man next to her was asleep, and not wishing to broadcast their conversation above the din of the car on the tracks, the familiar stranger mouthed words at Emer silently and she mouthed words back, like a couple of kids trying to have a private phone conversation with their parents nearby, or new parents whisper-shouting, trying not to wake a newborn. They made exaggerated faces to form words, meanings, and reactions, so his initial voice in Emer's mind, and hers in her own, would have been all caps.

"I'VE SEEN YOU BEFORE!" he mouthed.

"YES!"

"WAS HOPING TO SEE YOU AGAIN!"

"WHAT?"

The man pantomimed "hoping" (which looked like praying) and "see" and pointed at her for "you" and made a rainbow in the air with his right index finger for "again."

"WAS HOPING TO SEE YOU AGAIN!"

"SHUT THE FRONT DOOR!"

"WHAT?!"

"YOU WERE? YES! AGAIN! ME TOO!"

Emer found herself in a more outgoing mode of her personality, driven by the mimed volume and charades aspect of the interplay. She felt a certain lightness that was unusual. She liked it, liked this version of herself.

"I'M CON! MY NAME IS CON!"

"I KNOW!"

"YOU KNOW?!"

"I MEAN. NICE TO MEET YOU, CON! I'M EMER!"

"WHAT?"

"I AM CALLED EMER!"

She realized her diction sounded like a racist portrayal of the stilted Native American dialect in old Westerns. I am the one they call Emer.

"EMER!"

"EMU?"

"WHAT?"

"LIKE AN OSTRICH ONLY SMALLER!"

"WHAT?!"

"FLIGHTLESS BIRD! I THINK, MAYBE, NOT SURE!"

"WHAT?!"

"EMU?!"

"EMU?! NO! EMER! ER! ER! ER!"

As Emer was grunting out the "ER"s and flexing her arms like an angry Hulk to put the meaning of the sound over, Con gave up on the game, got up, and walked across to her. He put out his hand. She shook it. It was big and warm. Her own hand disappeared into it.

"Con," he said. He held on to her hand, applying just a little more pressure.

"I am the one they call Emer," she said. Her hand increasing pressure in return. He laughed. He got it.

"Emer," he repeated. "Like *mer*, like the sea, mer-maid. The Emermaid."

"Score," she said. "Yes."

"Far sight better than Emu," he said, still holding on to her hand.

Her father opened his eyes and stared at their hands together. The train—well, not just the train, but the whole damn sweet world—came to a stop. The subway doors opened and Con spoke quickly—

"This is where I get off. Nice to meet you, the one they call Emer. See you around campus." He took her hand to his mouth and kissed it, turned, and exited the train.

Emer drew her first deep breath in a while. Her father grasped the hand that Con had abandoned and said:

"I know that guy, Bill," he said. Bill again. Oh, well.

"Yeah? Really? Where do you know him from?"

Her father nodded, and said, "The future."

THE WOMAN WHO FELL TO EARTH

THE VERY NEXT MORNING, Emer was back on the train. What did it mean that she spent so much of her life underground? Regardless of whether or not she'd ever be crowned, Emer felt in her bones that she was and always would be Miss Subways. And all these other familiar strangers, who every morning walk into this mass moving grave, and get shuttled to another life, modern-day Persephones all—what havoc must this wreak on our primitive subconsciousnesses? To be buried alive every day, to be resurrected for work, buried again, and then sleep. Then, who were we when we woke up reborn? Were we free to re-create ourselves daily—us subway people, reincarnation junkies?

Boy oh boy, Uber was changing things, then. Uber *über alles*. Haha. Was she overthinking things? Uber-thinking things? She was. Was merely thinking actually overthinking? Perhaps. It's just a fucking subway, she told herself, looking around for a Train of Thought to distract her from her personal Notes from the

Underground. Sometimes a subway is just a subway. And finding this:

> The intellect of man is forced to choose
> Perfection of the life, or of the work,
> And if it take the second must refuse
> A heavenly mansion, raging in the dark.
>
> —W. B. YEATS

She really had to meet the city employee whose domain it was to choose these quotes. He or she was quite the card. She marveled that Yeats thought perfection of either life or work was attainable. Wasn't that the stunning male hubris of this sentiment? She looked around, like the sheriff of this compartment, for a possible manspreader to shame with her eyes and a shake of her head, but all the men were well behaved, keeping their laps to themselves. She wondered how many, if any, fellow riders were on their way to perfecting their work this morning, and how many had left perfected families behind to go back to work.

She felt angry all of a sudden. At herself. She wondered if she'd let her job, her sacred job, go a little the past few months and was she shortchanging this year's crop of kids. She often thought she could sail through a year blindfolded with her teaching hands tied behind her back, but surely that would be a sin. Sin. She hated that word, *sin*, it lodged in her soul like a guest that came for a Sunday and stayed for a lifetime. *Sin*—from the Old English *syngian*, related to the Greek *hamartia*, meaning "missing the mark," from archery. The Old Testament, she knew, from her childhood rebellion, sparked by being barred from the priesthood by her ovaries, used six different nouns and three verbs to describe sin. You can tell what's really important to a culture by the number of words it uses for a concept. Sin to the Christians, like snow to the Eskimos. Trying to get it right, capture it, this feeling of sin, shadowing it with imperfect words because one word can't seem to do the trick, can't imprison the feeling linguistically. Sin had never been fully captured, was still loose, an escaped convict or an escaped conviction, in the world and in her brain.

What would her perfect work look like? Hadn't she wanted to leave something behind? A treatise on teaching? A book of some kind, surely, a testament that she'd been here on the planet and seen some things and had some thoughts about things she'd seen. What would the perfect life look like? A husband and children? No children, not after the fucking abortion. Dr. Coughlan, your name will live in infamy, you fucking butcher. But she'd let that go, hadn't she? "Processed" with three separate shrinks over two decades. Why did it bubble up now and then like a murdered thing tossed in the river that washes up on shore?

But she could adopt, couldn't she? Wouldn't that be a beautiful thing? Like Mia Farrow. Adopt a Benetton ad of all races, a model UN of a nuclear family. Didn't even need a husband for that. Just a cagillion dollars. *Cagillion* was a word she would think, but never say, as a teacher of the language and of basic math. She would never say "cagillion" out loud. She had standards. Why was she attacking Mia Farrow? It was easy, but not nice. She took another sip of coffee. Maybe that was the problem.

Looking for a Train of Thought was really just a dodge, she had to admit. If she were being honest with herself, she was hoping to see that man they called Con. And what did that mean— to be honest with oneself? How was that possible? Or how was it not possible? Especially if you were making it all up on a daily basis. Without a husband, without children calling out to her to be a rock of particular form and identity, she was perilously free. To the kids at school, being Ms. Emer—she knew how to do that, all right. That was a set of specifications she could adhere to in her sleep, most of the time anyway. The one who teaches us to read, kindly, real but not too real, Ms. Emer. Just real enough for the first-grade mind. There were ruptures, though, ruptures in time, in cohesive identity. She recalled a few now with a distinct shudder of displeasure—cross words, gossip, instinctive revulsion to certain kids she could never quite get over. But she refused to dwell.

Amid all these trains of thought, there was a baseline of curiosity and want: she was looking for the man on the train, one man, Con—hoping, and also not hoping, that he might be buried alive with her here this morning. She didn't know if this was his daily train, and figured not, as she hadn't seen him before.

At each stop, she looked at the open doorways to see what mystery guest was entering the car. In a city so crowded with people whipping around like electrons in a supercollider, there was so much chance for chance. And then, sure enough, as if she were a witch that could conjure spirits from the air, at Forty-second Street, the very groin of all Manhattan movement, the doors opened, like on the game show *The Price Is Right*, and in walked Con, or rather in ran Con. He hustled to Emer and slipped a piece of paper into her hand, then turned and ran out again before the doors closed. It was kind of comical. And charming.

She unfolded the piece of paper and read his handwriting, which fully covered both sides. Handwriting—how quaint in this keyboard world—dated for this day in April:

The emu (Dromaius novaehollandiae) *is the second-largest living bird by height, after its ratite relative, the ostrich. Emus are soft-feathered, brown, flightless birds with long necks and legs (!). They forage for a variety of plants and insects, but have been known to go for weeks without eating. Breeding takes place in May and June and fighting among females for a mate is common. ☺ The male incubates the eggs, during which process he hardly eats or drinks and loses a significant amount of weight.*

A constellation used in Aboriginal culture in Australia is the "Emu in the Sky." The Emu's head is the very dark Coalsack Nebula, next to the Southern Cross, and the body and legs are other dark clouds trailing out along the Milky Way to Scorpius.

And this myth: An emu with very long wings once made her home in the sky. One day she looked over the edge of the clouds, and down on earth she saw a great gathering of birds. High in the gum tree, the Bell Birds were making sweet music with their silvery chimes, and Kookaburra, perched on the limb of a dead tree, was chuckling pleasantly to himself, while the Native Companions danced gracefully on the grass nearby.

Emu was very interested in dancing, so she flew down from her home beyond the clouds and asked the birds if they would teach her to dance. The cunning old Native Companions replied, "We shall be very pleased to teach you our dances, but you could never learn with such long wings. If you like, we will clip them for you." Emu did not give much thought to the fact that short wings would never carry her home again. So great was her vanity that she allowed her

*wings to be clipped very short. When she had done so, the
Native Companions immediately spread their long wings,
which they had previously concealed by folding them close
against their backs, and flew away, leaving Emu lonely and
wiser than before.*

*She never returned to her home in the sky, because her
wings would not grow again.*

Sincerely, Con

(KLondike5-248-2876)

*P.S. You have the coolest, most beautiful mismatched eyes
I've ever seen. Like Bowie. The woman who fell to earth.*

In addition to the text and phone number, there were some
exquisite drawings in a cross-hatch pen stroke—of the Emu constellation and the long-winged, pre-ruse Emu. Beautiful, delicate
stuff. She was quite charmed by it. She'd never heard of a bird
called a "Native Companion," and rather liked that assignation.
The note was long, and the thoughts it sparked even longer. Emer
missed her stop and had to get out and hump it back uptown
to school in the sudden, unpredicted rain. Her hair and shoes
got soaked. She didn't care. A perfection of something or other
beckoned.

THE WEIRD SISTERS

IN THE LUNCHROOM, Emer sat with Izzy, bullshitting as they ate. Emer kept an eye on three of her girl students who had been giving her a problem all year, and were huddled together at lunch today. Often a class had no dramatic kids, sometimes one, rarely two, three was more or less unprecedented for Emer in her small private school section. But these girls had been conspiring ceaselessly, like a gang of three, and creating unnecessary problems almost daily.

As the year wore on, Emer had gotten more and more fed up. It really affected the feeling in the classroom. Each year's class was like a play cast by fate—there were leading men and women; there were villains; there were clowns. It was pretty much the identical play every year with minor twists and turns differentiating it, so much so that Emer often wondered at how life, even at that age, had a sameness to it, that long-running cosmic dramedy of "the year I learned to read." But this year had been awkwardly peopled by the cosmic casting director, the three "weird sisters" causing the production to be top-heavy with gossip, distractions, and meaningless, stupid incident.

Emer could see from a few tables away that today the weird sisters were concocting a mixture of foodstuffs as if they were paint samples, as kids are wont to do. Into a paper bowl, like witches over a mini-cauldron, they put mustard, ketchup, mayo, salt and pepper, milk, yogurt, cereal, spit. Since time immemorial, such abominable agglomerations have been conjured in grade school lunchrooms, the girls eventually painting with them, while the boys usually ended up daring one another to eat them for some huge, hotly negotiated sum of money, like a dollar fifty.

The gang of three had performed this stupid magic trick a number of times already this year, but seeing this waste of food anew, Emer, unbeknown to herself, hit her limit with these brats. She left Izzy and approached the girls' table with a grim version of Ms. Emer's face these coddled children had not seen before, telling them that waste was a "sin" and they were going to eat what they "made." She wanted them to learn this secular eco-morality and get it good. If God was mostly dead in the curriculum, there was still sin, there was still penance, there was still redemption, even for six- and seven-year-olds. The kids protested feebly, with their already well-honed sense of being affronted in their systemic self-entitlement, but Emer lifted the bowl in front of their faces, holding out a spoon with her other hand, and demanded that they reap what they had sowed. She was about to get biblical on their asses.

Even as she did it, she felt an anger and a righteousness that were outsized to the situation. The episode had quickly escalated to parable, a teaching moment. But she couldn't stop herself. One by one the girls relented and ate. "A big bite," Emer commanded.

The girls did as they were told and immediately started gagging and crying, snot and tears streaming down their faces as two of the three actually barfed up bits of lunch. Still, Emer wrote this up to their need for drama. The girls continued to cry, and spew, and dry heave above the colorful viscous effluvia. Emer felt justified, as she ordered them now, still retching, to clean up the whole mess; but then, and only then, did she dip her finger in the bowl to taste what she had made the girls eat, and realized there was a lot more pepper and phlegm in there than she had imagined. She herself choked back a cough, and felt her eyes water and bile rise.

It was then she knew that she'd fucked up.

THE FATHER, THE SON, AND
THE HOLY GO

AFTER VISITING WITH HER DAD, it was after 10 p.m. by the time Emer got back to her place, and Papa struggled to open the heavy door for her. She wasn't at all sleepy and had forgotten to eat again, so she decided to order in from Dragon King. A couple egg rolls and some hot-and-sour soup should do the trick. While she waited for the takeout, she opened up a file on her computer and started writing down some of the things she had dreamed the past few months. She felt there might be something worthwhile in what she was going through, or at least there might be a through line, and if she got it out there in front of her, maybe she could see patterns and a fuller meaning emerge. Before she got too deeply into it, the buzzer rang, Papa telling her the food was coming up. She saved the file, meaning to label it "Godforsaken," but mistakenly adding an "s" and writing "Godsforsaken" instead. She backstroked to excise the extra letter, but then reconsidered and deemed it a happy accident.

She thought she recognized the Dragon King delivery guy

from the reservoir shenanigans. She wondered how she might broach that subject. As she looked through her purse for a cash tip, she sensed his melancholy leaking into the room. He wasn't just a grown man on a bicycle now, he was a man, no doubt with hopes and dreams and a rich interior life.

She decided to swim against that cold current. Maybe she had prayed for him in her Sacré-Coeur. She looked frankly into his eyes. He was a middle-aged Chinese man with straight, flat graying hair cut in a kind of a traditional pageboy. Unfortunate for a man his age. He wore cheap, shower-ready flip-flops and a button-down short-sleeve shirt with a pack of cigarettes in his breast pocket. And he was crying.

"What's the matter?" she asked. He shook his head—no. She pulled the money away from his hand. "Tell me," she teased as if the tip were dependent on his acceding to communication. He looked at her, as if to question whether she really wanted to perform this serious breach of protocol, her humanity reaching to his humanity across class, language, sex, race, and gluten-free soy sauce. She did. He seemed relieved, actually. He pointed to his cigarettes, asking permission. She said sure and even asked if she could bum one. He gallantly lit hers, then his own.

They smoked together as if they'd just had transgressive sex, rather than a word or two. Emer hadn't smoked since high school. The smoke burned her throat and she coughed, but the nicotine felt good in her blood. She forgot how you get high at first.

When his cigarette was almost down to the end, he spoke. "Need God's help." His accent was heavy, his vocabulary limited and short on verbs and articles, but his intent was focused.

"God's help?" she asked.

He nodded.

"Help how? Like church? You want a priest?"

"Priest no! Interview. You help. You know God?"

"Sure. We've spoken from time to time."

He didn't get the joke; he didn't look like he was in the mood to get any jokes at all.

"Good. Good. You come?" He smiled for the first time; his teeth were a stained and crooked mess.

"Where?"

"You help? Father, Son, Holy Go?"

He reached his hand out again, put the five-dollar tip gently back in her palm, and closed her hand over it. "You help me?"

She was touched by his gesture. "How?"

"I show. You come. I show."

He mimed putting on a coat and made motions with his hands for her to come with him.

"Now?" He smiled like it was the best idea they'd ever had together. She didn't want to go, really. She had school in the morning, but she'd opened this door, and now felt responsible. She reached for her jacket and walked to the elevator with him, smiling and repeating to herself, "Holy Go."

HAN SO-LO

PAPA, LIKE A PRACTICED SITCOM ACTOR, raised his eyebrows at the odd couple as they left the building. The deliveryman stood astride his delivery steed and motioned for Emer to take the seat. "What's your name?" she asked.

"Han."

"Han So-lo?"

No laugh.

"Okay, Han, give me an address, I'll take the subway."

He shook his head. "Chinatown cray."

"I can find, give me address." She felt like a racist, dropping words, dropping the "it," dropping the "the," and resolved to stop that.

"Faster," he said. "I faster. Bike." What the hell—she hopped on the bike seat behind Han, who, remaining standing, began to pedal, heading downtown. It was a long way to Chinatown. She had to put her hands on his waist to keep from pitching off, cutting a slightly more romantic silhouette than she cared to project.

She glanced behind as they were pulling away and saw Papa standing on the sidewalk, shaking his head, giving them the Haitian stink-eye.

The ride downtown was difficult, more difficult for Han for sure than Emer, but oddly beautiful. Han's bike was semi-motorized, so it was more of a bicycle/motorcycle hybrid. If Emer had ever ridden a bike this far along Manhattan, she was never at leisure to look around. She was used to moving underground, or in cars that were moving too fast or crawling so slowly that she could not relax.

They rolled past Times Square, a place Emer hardly ever came to, especially at night, and which now seemed to make *Blade Runner* obsolete, she marveled; the city got sleepier after Madison Square Garden, home of her father's beloved, beleaguered Knicks.

As Han began to sweat, his legs pumping, Emer feared she might be seen by the parents of children she taught in the Village, since many of the St. Margaret's families lived down there. How would she explain her position, riding bitch to Han So-lo? Did she have to explain anything at all? Did it fall within acceptable behavior for Ms. Emer? At stoplights, she looked down so as to be less visible to pedestrians. No one called out her name. Han chain-smoked the whole way down, his nicotine exhalations a kind of vehicular exhaust.

MAY WONG, MISTRESS-DISPELLER

DOWN AROUND MOTT STREET in Chinatown, Han finally slowed and, coasting with one leg on the pedal, skidded the bike to a stop in front of a store. Han hurried into the storefront, saying "please," and motioning for Emer to follow. He led her through the back of the establishment—which seemed to be a cavernous warehouse for those Asian knickknack 99-cent-type stores, like Azuma or Zuma, that used to pop up on the Lower East Side like fungi. It was easy to be dismissive of all the knock-off ceramics and crapola, but Emer always thought it spoke to a more basic human need to fill empty spaces with hoped-for beauty, or something like beauty, more like a plastic simulacrum of the notion of the beautiful, and on a budget. As if clutter could hold the horror at bay.

She waded past what seemed like thousands of porcelain cats, lava lamps, backscratchers, and black light posters, the very source of the dreck Nile, to a hidden back room where a makeshift classroom had been thrown together.

There were ten or fifteen young adult Chinese people sitting at desks in shadowy half-light, while a man in front of a chalkboard—the teacher, she supposed—harangued them in a native tongue. The teacher stopped when he saw Emer. He offered her his chalk, pointed at the blackboard, and said, "Teach."

"Teach what?"

The teacher looked at Han, like—maybe you should've taken care of this already. "Teach them God. Jesus. Judas. Crucifixion. Born again. The whole nine."

"Why?"

"I tell you later. You teach now." Now it was Emer who looked to Han, who in turn smiled back as if to say, Well, this is what we agreed on, isn't it, go ahead. The adults all had notebooks like grade school kids, pens poised and at the ready.

Emer launched into an improvised, condensed version of Christianity. Jesus-lite. She didn't know she had this Reader's Digest Bible tucked away in her brain, but she did. She surprised herself with the details she seized upon. It was the religious version of *Desert Island Discs*—*Who's Next. Nevermind. Thriller* (gotta dance on the island). To the desert island of the one God came—the Virgin Birth, the tripartite God, the Judas Kiss, driving money changers out of the Temple, turning the other cheek (number one without the bullet).

The tripartite God, so difficult to embrace and to digest—the Father, Son, and Holy Ghost—but no doubt a holdover and call back to polytheism. Approach it that way? *Ghost* was a fully laden word to these people; this was a world where ghosts were very active and often malevolent—so she stuck with the Holy Spirit.

She got bogged down in dogma—the fight over transubstantiation and consubstantiation, whether Jesus was the wafer or symbolized by the wafer (had worlds really gone to war over that?), were subjects so arcane that she lost hold of what she was talking about a moment after, like cupping water in her hands. She drew diagrams; she made puns no one got; but no matter what she said, these students gave her absolutely all of their attention. They seemed to write down every word like they were taking transcription at a trial. Emer felt as if she were passing a test she'd been studying decades for. She was a priest today. The Priestess of Chinatown.

After at least an hour of this, and with Emer showing no signs of slowing down, the teacher stood and started clapping and nodding, and walking toward her; all the students followed his lead, they also stood and clapped for a full two minutes. Emer was high, on a roll, and decided to end with a joke, her father's favorite from when she was a little kid—"Thank you, thank you, and one last thing, you probably won't be asked, but—how do we know Jesus was Jewish? Okay, he didn't leave home till he was thirty-three, his mother thought he was the Son of God, and he went into his father's line of work." She saw people starting to write it down—"No, don't write that down. That's not . . . anyway . . . good night, Chinatown, I love you, don't forget to tip your server! Good night!"

The good students abruptly gathered their notebooks and things, and left Emer alone with Han and the teacher. The teacher opened his wallet and offered Emer what looked like a couple hundred bucks. Emer said no, but Han accepted half of it sheepishly.

"Okay, now tell me. What the hell was that?" she asked the teacher.

"Asylum from China."

"Really?"

The teacher looked to Han as if to ask, Is she cool? Han nodded. The teacher handed her a card with a name on it, a lawyer's card. "My name is Dave," he said, continuing, "Asylum from religious persecution. America will save these people, but they need to answer questions about why they were persecuted in their homeland. Religious persecution is best and easiest. Forced abortion, forced sterilization—all go against Christianity. We teach them crash course to be Christian so they can stay in country and live. All they need do is answer a few rubbish questions. Christianity 101. My best teacher quit last month, she got married and moved to the suburbs."

"Knowing this stuff doesn't make you a Christian."

At that, Dave convulsed in laughter. "Tell it to ICE."

"So you're a lawyer, Dave? Dave the lawyer, lawyer Dave."

"Yes," the teacher said proudly.

"You're ripping these people off. What you're doing is illegal."

"I am saving their lives. I have no problem breaking the law for that. I have no problem taking money for that. They have no chance in China. I give them a second chance."

Han, who had been smoking quietly, stepped aside and said, "My daughter." He revealed to Emer a pretty young girl, maybe twenty years old; she had been in the "class." "My daughter live good now," Han said. "She stay New York, she answer Jesuses question right."

"Father, Son, and Holy Ghost," she said, smiling. "Water into wine. Turn the cheek." Her gratitude was so genuine, Emer had to smile and take her soft hand. She began to feel decent about what she'd done tonight, when a heavily made-up young Chinese woman grabbed her arm and pulled it like a leash. "You don't wanna be here with these deadbeats." Emer said hasty goodbyes to Han and lawyer Dave, not going so far as to promise to come back and do it again next week. The woman led Emer back through tchotchke world, then outside to the street.

"You need this," the woman said, handing her a card. "May Wong," it said, "Mistress-Dispeller."

"Mistress-Dispeller?" Emer asked, her head still uneven.

"I get rid of the other woman."

"What other woman?"

"Yes, if your man has been fooling around with another woman, we will approach her with a better offer to move on."

"A better offer?"

"Money, a job, a new city, even another man. Whatever it takes. We make a plan. We use PowerPoint."

"This is a real business, then?"

"Nothing but business."

"But I don't have a husband."

"That is temporary."

"Is it?"

"Maybe. I'm a mistress-dispeller, not fortune-teller." She smiled.

"You've used that one before."

"Never. Just for you."

"So if I did have a husband and he was having an affair, you would find this woman, and say, 'Hey, how about taking this job in San Francisco for a couple years?' Something like that?"

"Yes, something like that. You make it sound easy. It's not. I am a professional. Trained. We are connected. You hire a mistress-dispeller, you don't just hire May Wong, you hire a network you can trust."

"Not very romantic."

"Neither is being alone."

"You've used that before."

"Never. Just for you."

"You work outside of Chinatown?"

"We would like to expand, to franchise. That's why I am talking to you."

"The Starbucks of mistress-dispellers."

"From your mouth to God's ear."

"Why not."

"Yes, why not. It's good business, makes everyone happy. Husband, wife, mistress, kids. All happy happy happy."

"No one gets punished?"

"Not my job."

"No one learns a lesson?"

"A lesson about what?"

"Cheating."

"Not my job."

"You make a good point."

"I make a good living. Champagne dreams. I buy my own tits."

She hoisted her formidably augmented breasts up front and center and made them do a proud little dance. May continued:

"Maybe you get tits, you get man. Men like tits."

"I have heard. Your advice is wide ranging."

"Feel my tit. Feels good. Real." She squeezed them in Emer's direction.

"No, thank you."

"I have same doctor who did Kim Kardashian."

"No, you don't."

"How you know?"

"Well, for one, I think she lives in LA."

"You know her?"

"No, I'm kinda just guessing from her oeuvre."

"Then how you know?"

"You're right. I don't know."

"He do her ass, too."

"No. Stop."

"He put a tit in her ass. Or something like this."

Emer couldn't help visualizing that particular phrase, apart from the medical procedure, as a very ungainly sex act, perhaps. She started laughing hysterically. " 'He put a tit in her ass'? You're killing me."

"Keep the card."

May Wong walked away with her fake tits, red silk dress, and five-inch pumps, navigating and sidestepping the potholes of the Chinatown sidewalk as if by heel sonar. Emer felt faint, like some episode might be coming on, or maybe she was in the middle of one; she felt a ridiculous sublimity in her soul, boomeranging so fast from Christ to Kardashian. She needed to sit, quickly, so she set her ass down in the middle of the street, a mistress-dispeller's card in her hand, and Han So-lo, her ride back home and out of this strange night, nowhere in sight.

LOVE TRAIN

FROM HER VANTAGE POINT on the ground, Emer could see the entrance to the subway, and that familiarity seemed like a good idea. She got herself up, walked to the end of the block, and went underground. She felt better immediately. She would be home soon. The train was not crowded at all. Her mind was fully occupied, sparking in all directions with the night's Chinese fireworks. It was after eleven.

Emer closed her eyes, felt like she might nap on the way home. In spite of herself, by sheer habit, she searched above her head for something to read and found a Train of Thought:

> Forgive me those rough words. How could you know that man
> is held to those whom he has loved by pain they gave, or pain that
> he has given—intricacies of pain.　　　　—W. B. YEATS

Yeats again. The conductor on this line was no existentialist, but an Irish Romantic. She thought of her father and mother, she thought of herself, seemingly unencumbered by such intricacies, and none the better for that. The MTA must be on a Yeats kick, she thought; well, better than Billy fucking Collins, that's for sure. She started to nod off—an amazing thing, that we can sleep in this noise, with this movement, with so many strangers around.

A few stops in, the doors opened and in walked Con. Again. Emer felt a wave of good feeling break over her body. He himself was so stunned to see Emer that the doors closed on his shoulders and he had to hustle inside to avoid being left behind or crushed. He sat down next to her.

"Emu," he said, "I'm not stalking you."

"I'm not complaining."

"You're out late."

"Is that a problem for you?'

"Our first argument."

They laughed.

"You didn't call me," he said.

"Our second argument. This just isn't working."

"Why didn't you call?"

"I don't know."

"You don't know?"

"No, I honestly don't know. I wanted to."

"Okay. Okay. You wanted to is good enough for me."

"But something stopped me."

Con nodded. He seemed to understand what she was saying, even though she really didn't understand what she was saying. That was a neat trick.

"The last few weeks," he said, "I've found myself thinking about you. And I don't know why. Sitting here with you is like déjà vu. I feel like we've done it before. But nothing else is familiar, except you. Déjà you."

"Cheeseball."

"Don't mind if I do."

She smiled. "I know exactly what you mean."

"You do?"

"Kinda."

"Kinda sorta."

"My stop is coming up."

"Don't go."

"Really?"

"Yeah."

He reached for her hand, pointing at the subway map across from them. "Look at that, doesn't it look like that old teaching toy—the 'invisible man,' was it? Where you could see through the clear plastic to all the veins and organs?"

"Yes, we have one of those in my classroom."

"You teach medicine?"

"First grade. Very similar, though. A lot of overlap. Especially about the colon."

Emer wished this were a European train and a discreet professional would walk by at any moment offering cocktails. "I guess you could think," Emer said, "of all the lines of the subway underground like the arteries that pump blood beneath the skin, and we, the riders, are that blood, and maybe the heart has a consciousness, an intention, like a god, that diverts all of us travelers toward or away from one another."

"I like it 'cause it's cheap." He made her laugh while still letting her know her little flight of fancy had registered. "It also looks like the lines on a hand that you could read a fortune with.

Where does this train go till?" he asked, while tracing an imaginary route on her palm with his finger.

"Jamaica."

"Ha! Jamaica."

"Why is that funny?"

"When I was a kid . . ."

"You grew up in Manhattan."

"How did you know?"

"No idea."

"So I did, I did grow up in Manhattan and I loved dinosaurs. Do you see where this is going?"

"Not a clue."

"So if you're a city boy and you love dinosaurs, where do you go?"

"Broadway?"

"No. Funny, but no."

"Museum of Natural History?"

"Of course, yes. And since my mom's Irish, actually from Ireland."

"My dad's Irish."

"Whose story is this?"

"I don't know."

"So my mom, maybe five years removed from a small village outside Dublin, living on Eleventh Street and Avenue A—taking the subway was always an adventure, like a medieval knight's quest or the labors of Hercules. If we didn't end up at Yankee Stadium it was considered a victory."

"That's funny."

"It's true. So one time, dead of winter, we get on what they used to call the BMT, I was about ten, and of course we make a couple of wrong connections—the D, the Q, the R, or some such shit."

"Can I interrupt?" she asked.

"Again?"

"Haha."

"Sure."

"I'm going to kiss you at the end of this story."

This was not the kind of thing Emer had ever in her life said or had thought of saying. It wasn't that it was forward or ballsy, it was just so damn charming. That's what surprised her. And she realized that this man brought something out in her, her own charm. Yes, he had his own charm that he was deploying in telling this no doubt touching and smart New York City boyhood story, but it was her own charm that spooked the hell out of her. Spooky action at a distance—wasn't that some recent Einsteinean thing? *Charm*—wasn't that a term of the new physics? Or some kind of new particle. New to her, anyway. Charm and quark and spin? The cuddly cute nomenclature of the new physics. Maybe we are just like atoms, she wondered, destined by our own unknown internal chemistry to react to the spin and charge and charm of certain other particles. He was smiling now, and charming as fuck.

"You're going to kiss me?"

"Yes."

"Not now, but at the end of the story?"

"Exactly. So take however long you wanna wait. Be as long-winded as you feel the need to be."

"That's how the story ends?"

"I don't know how the story ends, but that's what's gonna happen at the end of the story."

"That was it. That was the whole story. Story's over."

"No, it's not. Come on . . ."

He stared at her and she stared back. Part of the charm of charm was the mock resisting of charm.

"Okay, so in any case, we are on the wrong train, and after Fifty-ninth Street, it seems the train just keeps going, like it's never gonna stop—we go through tunnels, we go through bridges, I swear we go through Middle Earth, ten, fifteen, twenty minutes it seems like, we're like prisoners looking out the windows, help-less, I can see sweat on my mom's upper lip, and finally, after what seemed like hours, we stop at an outdoor, aboveground station, the doors open and reveal this huge sign that says, wait for it—JAMAICA."

Emer laughed. "Jamaica, Queens. Is that the end?"

She leaned in to him. The train car had emptied out, as if a magician had made everyone else disappear.

"Nope. So I don't know from Jamaica, Queens. My Irish mom probably doesn't know either, and I can see she's about to pass out, and I say with like this bad island accent, "Oh boy, Jamaica, did we get on the wrong train, mon!" And my mom just cracks up. She has a hard laugh, like laughing cost extra, and she says, 'Next time we go to the Museum of Natural History, we bring our bathing suits.'"

They kept looking at each other.

Con said, "My subway story. The end."

Emer moved forward and kissed him. First kisses were al-ways so awkward, like a stranger's lips and tongue were speak-ing a different language from yours and you had to settle on some common ground, a shared grammar of tongue and lip. But not this time. It was as if they had kissed before, many times before, spoke the same language, and their mouths had not forgotten.

Con stopped for a moment, pulled back, and said, "I don't want to make you miss your stop."

"I don't give a fuck. And just for the record, I don't talk like that. I never say, 'I don't give a fuck.' And I never kiss familiar strangers on the train."

Con laughed. "I don't give a fuck," he said, adding, "How long do we have? When do you wanna get off?"

"Jamaica," she said, charming as all get out. "Let's ride this all the way to Jamaica."

HAMMER OF THE GODS

THEY DIDN'T GO TO JAMAICA. They went back to Emer's apartment. Emer felt compelled along the streets as they walked home hand in hand, as if she were fulfilling the mandate of some unseen string-puller, and yet at the same time, she had never felt so random and full of her own free will. She was not by nature an exhibitionist, and was embarrassed by the high-school-intensity make-out session she had begun on the F train. She was happy to get home with this man. Papa was still on duty and shot her some serious Haitian shade, which she translated as, Two men in one day? Whatever, she was a grown woman, and he wasn't her papa.

This sense that they were in and out of this world right now, that they were both free agents and pawns, lent the whole night a surreal quality where normal rules didn't apply. There was no talk of birth control. Or disease. They were on each other as soon as the door closed behind them.

As Con's hand found Emer's knee and began its slow, teasing

upward journey to her thigh and beyond, Emer flailed and fumbled for the light switch behind her, so they could get up to god-knows-what in the darkness. Con found her hand on the switch, and with his hand over hers, flicked it back on. She looked at him. He was smiling. "I'm in my forties," she said, and flipped the light back off.

His other hand was already caressing her sex. She felt so wet, embarrassingly so, and wondered why she should ever be ashamed of passion, of the material proof of said passion, and what type of world was it where you'd want to hide that? Her mind started fleeing the scene. His lips knocked the thoughts right out of her again. She saw an image of an eraser on a blackboard wiping a slate clean. His lips were like that sci-fi tool in the movie *Men in Black* that make you forget everything. If his lips could do that, she wondered, what would the other parts of his body do? He kissed her again and she stopped wondering. His fingers dallied on her upper, inner thigh, which was slick with her welcome. "Sorry," she said.

He turned the light back on.

"For what?"

"Nothing."

"You're sorry for being turned on?"

"I guess."

He took her hand and squeezed it over the conspicuous bulge in his pants.

"I guess I'm sorry, too." He smiled.

She got lightheaded with desire and anticipation. "Oh boy, howdy, yeah, you're really sorry."

"Not sure I've ever been this sorry."

"You are one sorry guy."

He switched the light off this time.

"Thank you," she said. "I'm in my forties."

"I've heard. Me, too. You're forty-what?"

"Thirty-eight."

"Very early forties."

"Can we just leave it at that?"

"You can be thirty-eight as long as you want." His mouth found hers again. She felt herself opening up in the darkness into a kind of synesthesia; she wasn't sure where her lips ended and his began, what was his body, his pleasure, and what was hers. It felt like a most benevolent form of insanity, a waking dream.

As he removed her dress from her shoulders, he shook the material down her body rather than over her head, and he had to kneel, and, as her dress fell in a bunch around her feet, he stayed down there.

She felt alone until his lips made soft contact with her belly, his hands reaching around her ass and pulling her underwear down and off to join her dress, like mounting evidence, like a prophecy, at her feet.

She wondered if she'd been working out enough lately, then told herself to shut up and enjoy. His tongue flicked at her belly button, and it felt nice, though she worried that she might have lint there; but before she could make a joke, he had continued his journey south to the last stop on this line. He was kneeling before her, like she was some type of goddess and the prayer on his tongue was making her feel divine. It had been so long, so fucking long. She could almost cry.

"Oh, God," she said, "oh, God." Not yet. She couldn't give in yet. She turned the light back on. He stopped praying for a moment and looked up at her. In his eyes, she could see he was fully

DAVID DUCHOVNY

aware that he was in a funny position down there between her legs, and she appreciated that.

"I'm sorry," she said again.

"I know," he mumbled, "we covered that."

"I just wanted to see what you'd look like with a beard." And this cracked them both up.

As he was laughing, he rose up and took off his shirt. She was relieved to see he wasn't in the best shape. He wasn't fat, but he was clearly no narcissistic gym rat either.

"You looking at my two-pack Shakur?" he asked.

"Hubba hubba," she said.

"Hubba hubba?"

"I have no idea where that came from. I think my mother used to say it when Captain Kirk would come on the old *Star Trek*."

"That," he sputtered, in imitation of the famously herky-jerky, stop-and-go delivery of William Shatner, "is the. Sexiest. Thing I've. Eh-ver . . . heard." He kissed her again so deeply and well, she felt like her head was opening up. The ceiling blew off the apartment and you could see the stars. He removed his pants and underpants in one motion.

"That's a neat trick," she said.

"I practice at home."

"Make yourself comfortable."

"Don't mind if I do."

She felt like they were a comedy team, but she didn't know who the writer was. And it was as if they were trading roles—for a riff, he'd be the straight man and she the fool, and then they'd switch. It was heady and destabilizing in the best way. He reached to turn off the light for her, and this time, trading places, she stopped him. His cock was fully erect and beautiful to her, insistent, like it was pointing out something of interest in the sky. She took hold of it like she was shaking a stranger's hand. Nice to meet you, good sir.

And she flashed back on a college class she had had on Milton, of all things, and the temptation of Eve in *Paradise Lost*. Well, not really all that odd, as she dwelled upon it. And she remembered that the seduction of Eve by the snake had begun with his tongue, with words, and that there was a continuum of intercourse, from verbal to sexual. It was intercourse that made Eve fall, that made Eve human. It was all intercourse. And Emer was on her way to human again tonight.

"I'm tired of talking just now," she said. "Take me to bed."

He was man enough to do as he was told.

That was the end of the speaking portion of tonight's program. From that point on, the intercourse was physical and wordless, though punctuated by many a moan. They made love like a long-time married couple who are still in love. Like an old improvisation. It was urgent, but practiced. What had been true of their first kiss was true of all the ways they touched each other, as if each had been schooled in the art of the other. How could this be? Emer stopped asking questions; the answers, if inchoate, were obvious, and she would happily leave them unworded tonight.

After they had finished, she was still hungry for him, but needed sleep. She was afraid of sleeping with him, afraid that her body might emit noises and gases while she was unconscious and make her disgusting to him. She wanted to issue some sort of blanket biological denial. He said, "I have trouble sleeping."

"I don't. And I have crazy dreams."

"Do you want me to stay?"

"Do you want to stay?"

"Of course."

Both were afraid of seeming to insult the other, their intimacy so quick and intense that it felt almost embarrassing and unwarranted, and therefore suspect. Emer was aware that she either wanted him to stay forever or leave immediately, and she was never going to utter either of those thoughts.

"Can you do me a favor, then?" he asked.

"Maybe."

"Can you just sing me to sleep?"

"Sing you to sleep?"

"It helps."

"I don't really know any songs."

"You don't know any songs? That's not possible. Nobody doesn't know any songs."

"I know 'Kashmir' on the uke."

"Zeppelin 'Kashmir'? I had you pegged for a Depeche Mode gal."

"My dad loved Zeppelin."

"On the ukulele? That's the stuff of nightmares. Anything else?"

She got up to fetch her instrument. He recoiled in mock horror. She played a little of Zeppelin's "Immigrant Song":

"Ah-ah, ah! Ah-ah, ah! We come from the land of the ice and snow / From the midnight sun, where the hot springs flow . . ."

"Wow, that's . . ."

"Amazing?"

"Sure, but also . . ."

"Awesome?"

"Sure, that's a word."

"You hate it."

"I don't hate it, no, you're like every guy's dream, a Zeppelin-lovin', uke-playin' chick—I'm just scared a mite by it."

"Wait. I got it." She reset her fingers on the uke and began to sing him the "Vowel Song." "This is what I sing to my kids to teach them how to read. My very own composition. Ah Eh Ee Oh Eu . . ." She strummed along on the uke. Con's eyes grew heavy.

"That's beautiful," he said. "Don't stop. That's a hit. That's perfect. Top Forty."

"Ah Eh Ee Oh Eu . . . Ah Eh Ee Oh Eu . . . Now we say our vowels, now we say our vowels."

And just like that, the man in her bed, the familiar stranger with whom she had just made love, was asleep.

THE IMMIGRANT'S SONG

EMER AWOKE BEFORE DAWN to find Con up on his elbow staring at her.

"That's kind of creepy," she said.

"Right?"

"Do you have to be somewhere?"

"Not really. You?"

"Yeah, I have to be at school in a couple hours."

"That's all I need."

"Haha."

He reached up to stroke her hair, and found the ridge of the scar on her scalp. Emer pulled away, self-conscious. No one had ever touched her there before.

"How's the writing going?" she asked.

Con stopped moving. "Writing?"

"Yeah."

"Why do you assume I'm a writer?"

A very good question. Why did she assume he was a writer? From her dreams, from her remembrance of things that may or may not have passed. None of it admissible in court and perhaps not admissible in casual conversation, even.

"Your Jamaica subway story was writerly."

"Writerly?"

"Not very writerly of me to use that word, is it?"

Con smiled, but she had disturbed him.

"I'm an actor," he said. She burst out laughing. But he wasn't kidding.

"You're not kidding."

"No."

"Well . . . that's amazing."

"Is it?"

"Sure. I mean, maybe that's why I think maybe you look familiar or you seem familiar to me."

"I'm not famous. When I say 'actor,' what I'm really saying is 'unemployed.'"

"Stop bragging, maybe I've seen you."

"I've done a bunch of commercials and some weeks here and there on soaps, and I've done four *Law and Orders*, and recurred on *The Good Wife* as the brother of a sister of a cousin."

"I watched that show!"

"Did you?"

"Saw it once or twice. I think they shot in my building one time."

"You don't remember the famous brother of a sister of Julianna Margulies's cousin role?"

"Sorry. Maybe?"

He laughed and looked away, sadly, she thought.

"I don't care," she said. "And besides, I think I've always wanted to be taken advantage of by a gigolo."

"I'm flattered?"

"I shall call you 'Sergio.' Sergio the gigolo." She was staying light as air, but she felt them descending into a more real world despite her efforts, like a plane through clouds about to land. An actor?

"It's funny you say that about writing, though," he said. "'Cause that's what I would've said I wanted to be when I was a kid. That's what I wanted to do as a man. It's actually how I got into acting— to see writing from a different angle, I guess. But then . . ." He seemed to almost say something else, or he seemed to be exhaling a very articulate and telling silence, like he was looking deep down into himself and wasn't sure he liked what he saw.

"What is it?" Emer asked. Even though she hadn't been in lover's company in a while, she was surprised to still find herself so immediately in tune with a man's easy slide into self-loathing, and the coincident feminine impulse to pull him away from that navel-gazing, self-abnegating male darkness.

He took his time, as men do, used to having the floor. He began speaking at the tail end of a long exhale. "Anyway. I guess I got lazy."

The "anyway" was the lie, Emer knew. The "anyway" covered all the things he didn't feel he could tell her yet but would have to if they somehow continued to get to know each other. The "anyway" was the drawing of a curtain.

"I got lazy or I was born lazy and just didn't have the balls to sit alone in a room typing. I guess I wanted to have more fun, and now here I am, kind of a nonwriting nonactor, nonentity."

"You have really got to stop bragging. It's unseemly," Emer said.

He smiled, but remained blue. "I'm in my forties and just getting started. I also do a lot of voiceover work."

"You have a nice voice."

"You think?"

Emer got up to run her mouth under the bathroom faucet. This man seemed too smart to be an actor. What a waste. It was hard to be a man, with all those demands for worldly success and the vanquishing of dragons. She didn't care. And yet she did. She didn't have a ton of experience with men, but she knew well enough that a man of a certain age who had not slain a dragon was a dangerous, sad thing. It seemed Emer couldn't slake her thirst, taking huge gulps of the cold water, like trying to swallow something back, drown something, or water a deep-seated, neglected, arid need.

She felt as if she had split in two, and that Con was part of herself, call it the male half of her brain, call it the male imago— the part that felt it could play fast and loose with power and appropriation, the part that felt capable of anything, potent enough to go out into the world and remake, play with its forms like a child with Play-Doh. She remembered some old Emerson quote about not writing, not respecting your "genius" or something, and then reading someone else who has written your story, and feeling the prickly shame and despair of that recognition. Someone else had done what you were supposed to do. She wanted him to leave. Because she, too, had wanted to be a writer as a child. His not writing made her want to write. She wanted him to leave so she could begin.

But she wanted him to stay. She wanted to tell him she knew

exactly what he was talking about and that she was living it, too. But then she checked herself; she really knew nothing about this man.

She stopped drinking the cool water and came back to the bed.

"Sex makes you thirsty, huh?" he said.

"Yes," she lied, and then thought, My first lie to this man. And she recalled an article in the paper about how little lies make bigger lies possible, that a type of acclimation, or a wearing of a groove is how she envisioned it, happens in the amygdala, the infamous, so-called reptile brain—when a little lie is told, literally paving the way for more, and bigger lies, from dirt paths to asphalt roads to superhighways, just a slippery slope of mendacity.

"I've got to head to work soon," she said, which was not technically a lie, but might as well have been. She kinda wanted to be alone. Con stood up and put his left leg in his underwear. She glanced at his flaccid prick in the near dark, illuminated only by the slanting bathroom light, hanging somewhat forlornly to the left, not proudly pointing at the sky like the night before; she quickly looked away, as if staring at a limp cock was somehow rude, like lingering too long looking at a car accident, too much softness and vulnerability. It had been so long since she'd seen one up close and personal, it was like looking at an exotic animal in the zoo. She thought she'd like to make it hard again.

Con looked up and said, "There's something. Something you're not saying."

He zipped up his jeans—zipper, no buttons. She knew that probably meant something, it meant something about style and whether he was hip or not hip, whether he was trying to appear younger than his years or not, but she couldn't remember, just as she could never remember which pocket with the bandanna meant you were a top or a bottom in the gay community, or what color the Bloods and the Crips were. All these signs and signifiers she knew and forgot and mixed up put her in ignorance and sometimes even danger. And every few years the signals changed, like those gods, like these gods, she thought, but no, the gods remain.

"There's a lot I'm not saying. I'm sure there's a lot you're not saying too."

"Yes."

"But I really do have to get ready. I never do this." She sounded so prosaic to herself. She already missed the poetry of the night before.

"I don't care if you do or don't."

"Yeah?"

"Is that your way of asking if I do this all the time?"

Emer had to take a moment with that. Was it? Maybe, but she didn't think so. Con continued, "I don't care. Even if you're doing stuff like this all the time, doesn't matter to me, I don't judge."

"So you wouldn't judge me if I was a big, fat subway slut?"

He smiled and went into the bathroom and finished dressing. She heard him raise the creaking toilet seat and urinate forcefully, and she thought, How strange, I doubt that toilet seat has been raised in years. Over the sound of his urine hitting the water, he called out. "You're not fat," he said.

A MOSQUITO, MY LIBIDO

AFTER CON LEFT, THE SUN ROSE. Emer tidied up. She took the sheets off the bed and cleaned the bathroom, and felt for a moment like she was cleaning up a crime scene. There was a solitary cracked sunflower seed by the window in the living room. Emer kept finding signs that Corvus occasionally visited. Never when she was home, however. She tended to leave the windows open and some seeds and grapes out, and often there was food missing. So either Emer was sleep-eating or fostering a nasty rat population in her building. Or, better, Corvus was making furtive visits to his home nest.

She ended up taking out some of the old notebooks she had recovered after her mother's death. She began jotting down notes in the "Godsforsaken" file again. All this writer talk, and all these strange experiences, these dreams and visions, had her wanting to make sense of things. Clearly this was a through line in her life, a notion of divinity or the supernatural, and she wanted at the very least to document it for herself, if not come up with a coherent view of God and gods. Sounds like a minor project, yes, but wasn't that every adult's almost responsibility—to square oneself with the divine? She doodled around in the "Godsforsaken" file until it was time to go to work.

In the subway on the way to school, she wandered through a few cars till she found a Train of Thought that made her self manifest to herself this beautiful blue morn. She found this:

What if some day or night a demon were to steal after you into your loneliest loneliness and say to you: "This life as you now live it and as you have lived it, you will have to live once more and innumerable times more" . . . Would you not throw yourself down and gnash your teeth and curse the demon who spoke thus? Or have you once experienced a tremendous moment when you would have answered him: "You are a god and never have I heard anything more divine." —FRIEDRICH NIETZSCHE

The night before had been just such a "tremendous moment." Would she run into a god or demon today with whom she might make this deal to relive yesterday forever? And though she looked around for Con, she wondered if she really wanted to see him again already. Her life was not making out with strangers on trains. It felt unreal. She needed to talk to Izzy about it. That would make it real. To tell another soul, to put it out there in the world, that would shade it, give it weight. And once it felt real, Emer would know better how she truly felt about it.

For the moment, though, she chose to close her eyes and forget about it. But, even in that enforced act of forgetting, of sweeping it aside, she felt a surge of excitement; the notion that her life, so predictable, could also embrace something so out of the ordinary. She realized she was wet. But it wasn't sexual, or not merely sexual. It was her primordial soul oozing to life, and this was the only way her body knew how to chime in.

Saying good morning to her students felt oddly fraught. She felt raw, like an actor who couldn't remember her lines. It was as if Emer thought the kids, with their pure receptors, could smell it on her, a change, an excursion, something naughty. She imagined they were looking at her askance, imagined their heads tilted slightly to the side in skepticism. But no, that couldn't be. I'm projecting that, she thought.

Her favorite child, Alice Freundlich, though she never played favorites, appeared beside her at her desk during a reading exercise and asked, "Are you okay, Ms. Emer?" Emer entertained a moment of imagining giving young Alice Freundlich a blow-by-blow account of the previous night's events, but, because she wanted to keep her job, did not.

"Thank you, Alice," she said. "I guess I didn't sleep so well."

"My mommy never sleeps unless it's in the valley."

"What's that?"

"She always says, 'I need the valley-yum.'"

Emer nodded at the child. "Go back to your desk, honey, I'm fine."

"Okay. Here."

As she left, Alice handed Emer a shiny red apple. That clichéd symbol to curry favor with a teacher. Emer laughed at the innocence of it.

But wait, was the child being symbolically cagey? Was this a descendant apple of Adam and Eve? From the tree of knowledge? Was the child implying that Emer had lost her innocence, been charmed by the snake? This child, who didn't know what

Valium was—or did she? Had that little back-and-forth been a test? How should a child handle the overwrought symbolism of this apple?

Emer took a big bite. It was one of those awful, mealy Red Delicious that looked like a jewel and tasted like waterlogged cardboard injected with stale fruit essence. Not much more of an apple than just a red, semi-edible thing. Forget about being a symbol for good and evil, it was barely a symbol for what an apple used to be. It was as hard as a stone, and she felt her teeth shift as she bit into it. She realized she hadn't eaten since lunch the day before. She soldiered through to the core, symbolism and taste be damned.

When the lunch bell rang, Emer excused herself and went running to Izzy's office. Emer said as she was opening the door, "I ran into that guy again."

"Ran into him?"

"Bullet points?"

"Fuck bullet points."

"I ran into him on the subway last night and we talked and then we made out. A little bit."

"Talk about burying the lede."

"I made out with an almost total stranger on the F."

"Big deal."

"It's a huge deal."

"For you, yes. But it's also not. It's what people do. I'm giving you what the pros call 'perspective.'"

"I don't think people do this."

"No, just animals. Really? Was it strange? Kinky?"

"I don't think so."

"Tell me about it."

Emer opened her mouth, but nothing came out. Finally she said, "I don't know how to talk about it."

"Here: show me on Raggedy Ann and Andy."

Izzy handed Emer two stuffed dolls that she kept in her office in case a child was having difficulty talking and needed a proxy. They were especially effective when asking about any physical confrontation of where a child was touched by another child or an adult.

"You're such an asshole."

"Yes, but I'm your asshole."

"Ew."

"Use the dolls. And your words."

Emer touched the lips of the dolls together.

"Very good."

Izzy took the dolls and turned them into a 69 position.

"Did this also happen?"

"We were on the train!"

"So?"

"People do that?"

"Maybe. I don't know. I hope so."

"Well, we took the train to the end of the line. We stood between the cars so we wouldn't be seen."

She didn't know why she was lying to Izzy, as there was no reason—Izzy truly would not judge her. Maybe that little lie road had been cleared earlier in the morning with Con, and now she was making it a bigger, two-lane lie. Regardless, the gist of what she was telling Izzy was true, but for some reason, she didn't want to tell her that she had taken Con to her bed in her apartment. Like this was somehow worse or sluttier? Worse and sluttier than fucking a guy standing up on a train? Emer marveled at herself, her shifting standards bubbling up from the unconscious.

"Like this?" Izzy stood the dolls to face each other. Emer took the Raggedy Ann, Izzy played the male. Raggedy Andy said, "You . . . are a doll. And that was amazing. You tore my stitching out. You put the 'raggedy' back in Andy."

"He doesn't talk like that."

"How does he talk, then?"

"I can't. This is stupid."

"You be him and I'll be you."

"No, I can't."

"Okay, okay, back to bullet points—did he put his man-thing in your lady-thing?"

"Yes."

"Okay, not what I'm into, but"—Izzy sang the chorus of Handel's *Messiah*—"Hallelujah Hallelujah Hallelujah Halay-uh-loo-yahhhh . . ."

"I think so."

"You think? Oh dear, that's not good."

"I mean I think we did. No, we did, we did. Jesus, Izzy, I did."

"How was it?"

"Great?"

"You're asking me?"

"For standing up on a train it was amazing, and it's been so long."

"Well, with stuff like this, I think it's like figure skating, or diving. You have to factor in the degree of difficulty before you can multiply and get a true score."

There was a knock on the door. Izzy looked to the window

and saw no one and assumed it was a child she could send away for now until she got the rest of Emer's download. "Yes?" she called out in an adult-to-child voice.

"It's Sidney," came the annoyed reply. "Is Emer in there?"

Izzy opened the door for Sidney. His face was cloudy. He clocked that the two grown women were holding dolls. "Izzy, my dear, can we have this room of yours for some privacy? I need to have a word with Emer." Izzy looked to Emer. Had he been eavesdropping at the door?

"Sure. I'll just need the room back in half an hour."

"It won't take that long."

Izzy left. Sidney shut the door behind her, and locked it.

"Bit of a kerfuffle," he said.

"What is?"

"You don't know?"

"Sid, don't do that, please."

"Right. Did you force three girls to eat something a few weeks ago?" Emer's prophetic heart was right. Her act of righteous anger had been a pebble tossed in a pond, the waves moving out from the center, landing now.

"*Force*? I don't know that I'd use that word."

"Recommend?"

"Well, maybe more than 'recommend.'"

"Fucking hell, Emer, I'd be okay if you shoved their bloody little brat faces in it, but I'm in damage control, as per usual."

"What's going on?"

"They want me to fire you."

"Who does?"

"The parents."

"And?"

"And I told them that that was out of the question. That you were a beloved teacher, a master teacher, and that this incident, when I would have the chance to delve deeper, could be chalked up to a bad day and a bad decision, but was in no way indicative of your character or of your pedagogic modus operandi."

"Thank you. Thank you, Sidney."

"But they want their pound of flesh, and I have to give it to them, or more precisely, you have to give it to them."

"From what body part will this pound of flesh come?"

"Your pride, I reckon. I'm going to set up three separate meetings with the three sets of parents, and at those meetings you will apologize and seem to grovel, you will say 'mea culpa' thrice times, and you will sing the praises of their brilliant kids and you will be your absolute best, most smiling self."

"Or?"

Sidney had the oddest look on his face, at once ancient and youthful, scolding and playful, like a man beholding Hell for the first time and thinking—at least it's not cold. "Come on, Emer, I'm your ally here. You know damn well, or. Or you'll be fired. It's a brushfire right now, but if it catches, you will be tossed on the conflagration like a witch, and believe me, I've seen cities aflame with less of a spark than this, so please, tread carefully."

"I hear you."

"Will you allow me to set these meetings for you?"

"Yes, Sidney."

"All right, then. They will happen within the next week. These parents have the patience of honey badgers."

"Is there anything else?"

"Is there?"

"What?"

"Anything else?"

"Not from my end."

"Excellent. Well, I'm sure we'll have a new crisis soon enough, won't we, Emer?"

That strange look came over his face again. Emer mustered a weak laugh and agreed, though she wasn't quite sure what she was agreeing with or what she was laughing at.

EMILY D

EMER'S EVENINGS HAD BEEN PRETTY SET before Corvus had thrown everything out of whack. She did yoga twice a week, and she did a spinning class at Soul Cycle one night a week and on Sunday morning. On other nights, she might run on the treadmill or do the Versaclimber at Equinox. In good weather, she might run the loop around the reservoir. But she favored the gym. The gym functioned like a church in some other life. She had superficial acquaintances there, people who knew her by name, seemed pleased to see her, and kept her from feeling too invisible in this city.

She didn't know why she worked out so much. She didn't think it was to attract a man, or a more generalized vanity; she had vague notions of health about it, not letting her old lady bones decalcify, and an oblique belief in both the meditative power of yoga and the rah-rah ethos of spinning. The mélange of approaches worked for her and kept her from feeling or appearing too obsessed with any one physical activity. She flitted, hummingbird-like, from one life-changing health fad to the next—from vegan to paleo, from no fat to lots of fat, from statins from heaven to statins from hell. The science behind all these trends seemed iffy, temporary, and possibly manipulated by Big Pharma, swinging like a pendulum. She therefore tended to stick longer with what tasted good. Right now she was into megadosing vitamin B_{12}, which was supposed to protect the aging brain (spooked by her dad's genes running wild and replicating ceaselessly within her), and bulletproof coffee—a high-fat ritual out of California or Hawaii that consisted of adding butter, coconut oil, and cream to her morning joe. It ended up tasting something like liquid buttered toast. She gave her father a sip of hers once and he literally spat it out on his chest like she had tried to poison him, screwing up his face and saying, like it was a last straw in the culture wars, "For the love of Mike, Bill! Let coffee be coffee."

After Corvus's departure, she quickly resumed her untroubling OCD leanings and her "healthy addictions," which she also filed under the broader phylum "obsessive activities that don't hurt anyone"—such as cleaning, the Sunday crossword puzzle, and making sure her vibrator and emergency flashlight always had batteries. In her closet, at any given time, there were at least twenty AAs and Ds standing at the ready like a tiny reserve army, and she didn't even use the damn things that much.

Though in the last week or so, since the train ride with Con, she might've been throwing herself into her extracurriculars more intensely than usual. She still hadn't called him. Not because she was playing it cool or anything, she just didn't know what to say, did not know how she would fit the event into her life and square it with her character, did not know that she could continue.

It reminded her of a being she had seen in one of her old

notebooks, called a Gancanagh—an Irish folkloric entity whose kiss was addictive, or rather a toxin he secreted through the skin was addictive. He kind of slimed you. With opium resin. When the Gancanagh departs, his lovelorn and detoxing victims waste away to nothing for want of his companionship. Some even fight to the death for his love, which, of course, they can't really possess. She wondered if Con was somewhere feeling the same way about her kiss, her addictive toxins.

This Tuesday, she would miss her yoga because Sidney had set up the mea culpa teacher-parent meetings. The incident had quickly become a low-key cause célèbre at the school, so Sid wanted it handled and tucked away asap before it snowballed into legend.

Emer was, in fact, in danger of losing her job. It was "out of character" for her to have acted thus. Was it? Her job depended on that interpretation of events. She was prepared to sit contritely and swallow her medicine the way she had made the girls swallow theirs. One set of parents "got it," and thought it was fine the way Emer had responded, and didn't need to take the meeting. Actually that was a mom, whose first husband, a firefighter, had died in 9/11. The woman had remarried and had more children, and her daughter, Maya O'Connor, was the one weird sister who actually had the most intense physical reaction to eating the mess. So that left only two meetings tonight, with the parents of Ashia Waters and Shoshanna Schwartz-Silberman, back to back.

Sometimes, looking for a Train of Thought, she told herself, This one will be an omen. Straight from the subway gods, meant for me and me only about right now. She was feeling a little nervous tonight, a little in search of succor, yet she was hopeful when she spied this:

Long Years apart—can make no
Breach a second cannot fill—
The absence of the Witch does not
Invalidate the spell—

The embers of a Thousand Years
Uncovered by the Hand
That fondled them when they were Fire
Will stir and understand—

—EMILY DICKINSON

Dickinson was like that Witch to Emer, that uncanny and disorienting. She was able to perch in a twilight world between sense and nonsense, full of dread and hard truth, yet still retain an essence of the mundane, a whiff of her uneventful life, spent as a conscientious objector, hiding in plain sight in Massachusetts, to an establishment not yet ready to read her. Do not venture into her desk drawer unless you have balls of steel. She accessed the simple, natural horror, speed, and beauty of an actual lightning strike. Dickinson had no voice in her own time, as a woman, so she stuffed her silent screams, more than eight hundred of them, in a drawer and waited for eternity to hear. And eternity did hear. As did Emer.

The spinster of Amherst was both a cautionary tale and a role model; she, too, had believed in God, for a time. Dickinson once said, "I never enjoyed such perfect peace and happiness as the short time in which I felt I had found my savior." Short time. Eventually, her sense of eternity grew too large to be constricted by the one-named God.

A short time. Was that what was happening with Emer? Perhaps that's all the time we get with God. Why do we ask of him, as we ask impossibly of a romantic lover, to last forever? But it's the memory of that oneness with the holy that persists, even from childhood, and forms the template for all subsequent romance. Come to Jesus. There was Con and his kiss creeping in again. She deflected thoughts of him, consigning them to the distracting rumble of the tracks.

So Dickinson was the true underground woman, an authentic Miss Subways, and Emer aspired to her own grace and truth as a woman in and out of her own time. "Meet Emily, a native of Amherst, Mass. Our May Miss Subways spins a horror at death and nothingness into jewels of insight on the loom of her soul. She also enjoys baking, wearing white after Labor Day, and oblivion."

Thank you, MTA. The subway had again been her oracle. She took a deep breath. She would bow down when need be and rise up when need be. She would scribble in "Godsforsaken," and file it away in the unpublished drawer of her desktop screen. Con had been a goad to her, and a rod—she would take the reins and write her own story, of her own gods, planted in her head, as she envisioned it, by her very own tumor or ghost of a tumor. She would see him again, and make love to him again. Or she wouldn't. The tumor was growing again, or it wasn't. She would publish her thoughts on gods, or she wouldn't, and it would be left to future generations to find nourishment in her corpse like mental carrion, or not. Oh, that's pleasant, she thought, but also knew from the Witch that "after great pain a formal feeling comes." This is the feeling of form beginning, the word moving across a chaos of waters and making waves. It was all gonna be okay.

THE SCHWARTZ-SILBERMAN EFFECT

EMER GOT TO HER CLASSROOM a good half hour early to set up two chairs by her desk. She wanted to maintain the space between her and the parents and preserve her position of authority. There were no big person seats in her room besides her own. The parents would have to sit in the kids' little chair/desk combos. No matter how tall these adults were, Emer would be taller.

Of course, she had met the parents before. At the beginning of the school year, and at a regularly scheduled parent-teacher conference mid-year. But it was the mothers of these two kids, not the fathers, whom Emer remembered. The mothers had been strong, had taken the lead in conversations about their children, while the fathers had hung back. Ashia Waters was an African American kid whose mother, Emer recalled, had a vague connection to show business, and Shoshanna Schwartz-Silberman's mother was a lawyer who worked in the DA's office.

First up were the Schwartz-Silbermans. As soon as the couple walked into her classroom, Emer knew it was going to be a rough ride. Shoshanna's mom, Debbie, tossed her an ironic smile and refused to shake Emer's hand while the father, Ron, looked almost apologetic about his wife's unbridled anger, yet also relieved, as if he was happy to share the brunt of it with someone else for the evening. Emer smiled and said, "Thank you for coming in tonight. I'm sure you're both very busy and the last thing you wanted to do was—"

Debbie cut her off. "The last thing I wanted to do was see about the welfare of my child?"

"Of course not," Emer said. "I'm sorry if you heard that. I didn't mean to imply . . . I just am sure that you are very busy . . ."

"This is like something out of the Middle Ages."

Emer decided to nod her way through. She didn't want to apologize too early or too much, she wanted to let Debbie tire herself out, if possible.

"This is no different from spanking or hitting a child," Debbie went on. "I don't know why we are even sitting here tonight, I don't know why you weren't summarily fired. It's out of respect for Sidney that we are even here at all."

"I understand your concern."

"My concern? You assaulted my child in the safe space of a classroom."

"*Assault* is a powerful word."

"Yes, assault. Sho is traumatized. She's a gifted kid with a strong imagination, so she's willful, and because you can't handle that, you try to break her?"

"Nobody was trying to break anything or anyone, Mrs. Schwartz-Silberman. I can assure you. Shoshanna is highly intelligent, with all the energy that comes along with that. I value high-spiritedness in my kids, believe me, and I try to give it free rein as much as I can until it starts to interfere with the cohesiveness of the classroom."

"This was at lunch."

"That's right, it was at lunch."

"Lunch has to be cohesive?"

"This had been going on for a while. Sho, Ash, and Maya can get pretty powerful when they join up. They'd been at it for much of that day, and, in fact, much of the year. That's not to excuse what I did—mine was a failure in judgment and patience, and I sincerely regret it, and apologize from the bottom of my heart, and can assure you and promise you that neither it nor anything like it will ever ever happen again."

Finally, the passive father, sensing an opportunity to divert his wife's attack on the teacher into an attack on the other kids, and by extension the parents of those other kids, chimed in, hoping to make it more fun for everyone.

"Yeah, we've been hearing that Maya is the ringleader, the instigator."

"Please, not now, Ron."

But Ron was rolling—"Well, poor kid, her dad died in nine-eleven—that house must be like a morgue."

His wife shut him down. "Not her dad, not Maya's dead, Ron, I mean not Maya's dad—fuck me—Maya's mom's previous husband."

Ron persisted limply, "I still think it's a valid read on the situation."

Emer all but asked permission to speak. "If I may, I'm trying not to assign more blame or anything to any one of the three girls."

Debbie's eyes flashed again. "I agree. I don't think one of the girls gets blamed more than the other, thank you very much, Ron, I don't think the girls get any blame at all. The blame is yours, the adult here, the teacher."

"She apologized, Debbie."

"If you're gonna sit there and take her side, why don't you just go the fuck home and watch Maddow, Ron."

"Fuck you, Debbie."

"And you," Debbie said, zeroing back in on Emer, "don't be calculating in your head that because Shoshanna's parents speak like this to each other, she is now 'acting out' at school."

Emer had just been thinking exactly that and replied, "I was thinking nothing of the sort."

Ron, injured now and humiliated, stood. "She apologized, Debbie, more than once, she said it would never happen again. I don't know what else we can achieve here. Thank you, Ms. Emer, we appreciate your time. Let's go."

"You can go," his wife said. "Go."

He went.

Once again Debbie Schwartz-Silberman turned her full ire on Emer, like the prosecutor she was. Emer began to pity Shoshanna. She began to know the girl. This meeting was actually helpful to her, as a teacher, she thought. She mustered an incipient sense of gratitude for the whole episode.

"I just can't imagine," Debbie said, gathering up as much courtroom mock sympathy as she could, "how you treat your own kids."

That stunned Emer. That level of attack. She steeled herself not to cry, she wouldn't give this woman the satisfaction. Debbie Schwartz-Silberman saw the tears behind the steel, and while that wasn't enough—nothing would ever be enough, no amount of contrition or prostration or penance—it would do for now, this little bloodletting, and save Emer's job.

"I don't have any children," Emer said, wanting to but not looking away.

Debbie nodded angrily. "Maybe that's just as well." With that, she left to join her husband, who'd been audibly shuffling his feet and sighing impotently just outside the door. When Emer was safely alone, she gave herself over to a few tears, trying not to hear the Schwartz-Silbermans going at each other as they retreated down the hallway.

Sidney popped his head in. He was not a part of these meetings, or even listening, but he was "around if I'm needed." He shot her a big fake smile and did a little dance shuffle.

"Two down, one to go. You okay?"

She nodded.

"I am here and not here, as the need arises." He disappeared again.

Emer grabbed for the Kleenex, omnipresent and within reach anywhere in a first-grade homeroom, blew her nose, and looked up at the big clock that she used to teach the kids time. She had five minutes to get her shit together before the next inquisition.

THE WATERS

ASHIA WATERS'S MOTHER, who went by "Mama," was from Africa, though Emer couldn't remember which country. She spoke in that singsong accent that Emer couldn't help hear as cheerful. When Mama Waters walked into the classroom, unlike Debbie Schwartz-Silberman, she did not launch into an immediate attack. She shook Emer's hand, and even kissed her cheek hello, and laughed as she struggled to sit in the child's desk seat.

"Shall we wait for your husband to get here to begin?"

"No."

"How would you like to begin, then?"

"In the beginning . . ."

Emer laughed. "I was raised a good Catholic, so that's fine by me."

Mama Waters did not laugh. She just nodded and repeated, "Catholic."

Emer decided that she couldn't read Mama's affect clearly, that there was a bedrock cultural difference between her smiles and frowns and Emer's smiles and frowns. This is what it must be like to be a little autistic, she thought, to be unable to read faces, to not pick up on the social cues. She forged ahead.

"Then I'll just start, if you don't mind. Ash is a great kid, smart and full of energy, as I'm sure you know." If Mama Waters did know, she wasn't letting on. Her quiet unsettled Emer further—was it anger or politeness? Emer began to miss the direct fight and hostility of Shoshanna's Upper East Side parents.

Truth was, little Ashia Waters was the ringleader of the weird sisters. The one who usually came up with the games the three would play and who had definitely started the witch's brew that day in the lunchroom. The kid was a lot to handle—a trickster and inveterate liar, but charismatic and funny when she wanted to be. Emer thought she had the right amount of ego and self-regard to become a surgeon, or in another future scenario, an actress playing a surgeon. Ashia was her favorite of the three, even though she caused the most trouble. The other two girls were like sheep. But Emer had decided, in conferring with Izzy, that the three would be treated as one in these meetings—they would all be equally culpable, all equally harmed, and all equally apologized to.

"So, I am deeply apologetic about the way I handled the situation. It was out of character for me, and your daughter deserved better and will get better in the future. Has she said anything about it to you?"

"Yes. On the day she did. But not since."

"Was she traumatized?"

"This is a stupid word. This *trauma*. No, she was laughing about it." Emer flinched at the word *stupid*. It was verboten in the school of the twenty-first century. It was the *fuck* or *cunt* of a bygone era. About the worst thing you could call someone was "stupid." Emer chalked it up to Mama having grown up elsewhere, elsewhere being outside Manhattan or Brooklyn.

"That's good." But was it? Emer immediately regretted saying that.

"Was the whole stupid thing Ashia's idea?" Stupid again.

"No, no," Emer lied, "not that I know of."

"Listen, Ms. Emer, when I was a child, Muslim in Nigeria, I was caned for being late to school, welts on my rear end. I was slapped for chewing gum, blood from my lip—and I realize we have different customs, we make changes, we adapt to our home, our circumstance. For instance, my family name is Wati, not Waters, but I got tired of spelling my name over and over and people fawning over my exoticism . . ."

Emer squelched an urge to fawn over her exoticism and ask more after her name and origins.

"I guess what I am wondering here tonight is," Mrs. Wati/Waters continued, "what took you so long and how can you claim to educate my child unless you lay hands on her when she is bad?"

Wow. That was a different perspective—"spare the rod, spoil the child"—Emer had not anticipated. She had a vague feeling she was in deep waters or that she was being entrapped. She decided to timidly pull back.

"That's just not my style, Mrs. Waters. Or the policy of the school."

"You can call me 'Mama.'"

"All right, Mama." She felt odd using that honorific, especially with a black woman; it sounded to her that she'd entered into a blues song refrain—*well, all right, mama.* "Maybe we should wait for Mr. Waters?"

"It's not her father. Her father is in Africa. I'm no longer with her father. It's my boyfriend here."

"Does he live with you?"

"Why do you ask me that?"

"Oh my god, I don't know. Forgive me. It's none of my business." Emer felt like an idiot for asking that question, and she began to feel the chasm between her and Mama widening by the moment. She needed a third party there to adjudicate, or translate.

"Shall we wait for him?" Emer asked almost pleadingly. And just then she heard the footsteps coming down the hallway, and a knock on the door—Sidney come to save the day.

"It's open," Emer called out.

And in through the door walked Con.

At first, Emer simply thought he was mistaken, or brazen, coming to see her at school like this, when the timing couldn't be worse—setting aside for the moment that it would've been borderline stalking to figure out where she worked. And yet she was also excited that he'd gone the extra mile to seek her out. And she was, she realized, happy to see him. All of those thoughts passed in the millisecond that their eyes met, and then Con said, "Sorry I'm late," and went to join Mama at one of the desks.

If Con was in shock, he was very adept at hiding it. Emer was unable to process what she needed in order to navigate this moment—everything, her career, her reputation as a teacher, a woman, her very character—all of that was in play. All the questions she had for Con—Did he know? What was he thinking? Was he fucking insane or just a fool or an asshole?—would have to wait for another day, if ever. Was this what had somehow blocked her from calling him again? Had she met him before? Emer just needed to get through the next minute or so without throwing up, which she was in real danger of doing. The best she could come up with was to introduce herself—"Hello, Mr. Waters—have we met? Maybe we've met at a previous thing?"

Thing? What did she mean by "thing"? You mean a thing like a maybe-we-fucked thing? That type of thing? She glanced quickly at Mama to see if she had picked up on the "thing." She thought about calling out for Sidney or excusing herself to go to the bathroom. Con said, "No. I haven't been to one of these meetings before. I missed the, what was it, first two?"

"Three," Mama corrected.

"I wasn't sure," Emer said. "I thought maybe. There are so many and . . ." Emer simply did not know how to finish her thought.

"All of us look alike?" Mama asked. And then, adding off Emer's stunned look, "All of us parents." Con laughed. Mama laughed. Emer laughed. Emer inhaled for the first time in a while.

"What do I call you?" Con asked. In her funk, Emer had absolutely no idea what that meant, and she saw Mama was puzzled at her confusion. Then it came to her; he was asking her name.

"Emer," she said, "but the kids call me Ms. Emer."

For the rest of the meeting, Emer tried to keep from hyperventilating, and continued to address Mama, though when she realized freezing Con out might look conspicuous, she looked at Con, only to go back to looking at Mama when she thought looking at Con was becoming fraught. She felt she had the attention span of a fly being swatted at in a bedroom. There was no exit and no safe place to land. She sought out an open window.

She couldn't think. Time was moving too fast and yet not moving at all. The meeting was eternal. She looked at the clock and couldn't read it. She was afraid to get caught looking at the clock, or her watch, or her phone on the desk. Surely, they'd been sitting like this for hours, days even. Where the fuck was Sidney? When she could think of nothing else to say, she would merely repeat a variation of "I'm sorry and it will never happen again."

Finally, mercifully, Mama rose, and said, "Thank you for your time, Ms. Emer. You have no need to apologize further, if at all."

"Thank you," Emer replied, extending her hand to Mama, who pulled her into a cheek kiss again, which made Emer feel even worse.

Mama turned to Con. "Do you have anything else on your mind?"

Everything was freighted with too much meaning. Emer felt herself losing a grasp on what words meant at all. What did *else* really mean anyway? What did *mind* mean? How was it different from *soul* or *heart* or *conscience*? Emer felt her knees buckle. She just wanted to go home and sleep for a day.

"No. I'm good," Con said. What did *good* mean? He continued, "Seemed like a tempest in a teapot to me anyway."

Emer extended her hand to Con, feeling, so close to the end, that she momentarily knew what this was all supposed to look like. He seemed surprised by the gesture, but then smoothly took it, as he had on the subway the first day they talked. She felt the buzz in his touch.

"Nice to meet you," she lied.

"Nice to meet you, too, Ms. Emer," he lied back.

SPOOKY ACTION AT A DISTANCE

EMER WAS EXHAUSTED by that ordeal, bone tired, but she felt the need to see her dad before heading home. Something about his unspoken love for her, a father's love that abides and transcends the actions of a child at any age. She didn't need the assurance of it, or a demonstration of it, she just needed to sit with it, be in the presence of it. When she got there, her father was asleep. Ging-ging was watching *Dancing with the Stars*.

Emer sat down beside her and watched a couple of C-listers do a rhumba. Ging said, "I like the dance." And Emer could agree, there was something reassuring in the blanket mediocrity and gung-ho spirit of that world. Emer felt it pull her in and down, with something darker and more nefarious waiting just on the other side of the dance.

"We have long walk today. He loves to play the Pokémon Go," Ging said.

Emer looked over at the old man, his body rising and falling, doing its own, simpler dance before death. "That's nice, Ging.

Good for him. Tell him I came by, and I'll be back soon. Tell him I love him."

"He know," said Ging.

"But tell him anyway."

"Okay, miss."

"Tell him I screwed up and he's not gonna love me anymore."

"I won't tell him that, miss."

"Why not?"

"Not possible," Ging-ging said, and turned back to the shadows dancing on the screen. Emer decided to stay and watch a little more *Dancing with the Stars*. Ging-ging came to sit beside her and held her hand.

WOMBAT

THE NEXT MORNING, Sid was waiting outside the school for Emer, a big, unreadable smile on his face. "How was the faddish inquisition?"

Emer sipped her Pain Quotidien coffee and said, "Good, I think. Coulda been worse, coulda been a lot worse."

"That's what I'm hearing."

"Good. Thank you, Sid."

"I think we can put this matter to bed. Swing by my office after three and we can compare notes, cross *i*'s and dot *t*'s."

Sometimes she really liked Sid and got a kick out of him. He had a steady hand. One of the first things he'd said to her as a young teacher was "When in doubt, do nothing. It's never as good or as bad as it first appears." He was a big one for aphorisms. On the average, three out of ten of his maxims were worth remembering.

During the day, she was very keen to pick up signals, any signals at all, from the weird sisters. She had to guard against being

DAVID DUCHOVNY

oversolicitous, though she did treat the kids to a ukulele version of Taylor Swift's "Shake It Off" as she sniffed around for any lingering hostility, blame, or hurt, especially around the mercurial Ashia Waters. How could she treat this child evenly now that she had slept with her father? Well, not her father, but the actor who played the role of her father.

Jesus fucking Christ, what have I done? Did the child know? They know everything, don't they? No, they don't. That's a myth of a perfect child whose "receptors haven't been corrupted" or some such New Age bullshit that raises the child to a god. A child is not a god. How long till the end of the year and the god moved up a grade? A month? That was doable, a month was doable. And then that horrible mistake would be dead and buried in the past forever.

No, Ashia knew nothing and, today, she was having a lot of fun with the word *wombat*. Ashia had decided that the answer to everything today was going to be "wombat." Two times three equals? Wombat. Benjamin Franklin discovered? Wombats. Rock, paper, scissors, wombat. Far from being annoyed at this last-stand rebellion, Emer was pleased that Ashia still had her spunk. And soon, of course, the other two girls were answering "wombat" to everything. Well, shit, Emer had to admit, it's a funny word.

The wildfire spread, and by the end of the day, the whole class had caught wombat fever. The answer to everything, the name of everyone, the key to all mythologies, was "wombat." As the ultimate olive branch, right before the end of the day, Emer surreptitiously googled "wombats," and announced, "Last quiz of the day—what is the short-legged, muscular quadrupedal marsupial that is native to Australia?" To her delight, the class was stumped. It was too obvious. "Here's another clue. You gotta get it before the bell rings. They poop square!" An explosion of laughter and playful disgust for the miracle of square poop. Emer drew her eyes right to Ashia Waters. "Ash, any idea what animal I am describing?" Ashia shook her head no, the first time she had been silent all day. Little fucker. "Come on, the bell's about to ring."

Ashia gave over, unsmiling, defeated, subsumed, not unhappy—"Wombat." She sighed and then proclaimed by way of letting Emer know she was no one's bitch, shouting, "Ewww—they have square buttholes!" That brought the house down. Emer had engineered a moment of unity. She joined with her nemesis to make a small, transcendent moment.

Emer gathered up her things and went down to Sid's office. It was a beautiful spring day, and she hoped the meeting would be short and she could head back uptown, take a walk in the park and think. Maybe give Izzy a call.

Sid was seated behind his desk when she walked in. He rose and remained the same height. "Well, all quiet on the western front," he said, gesturing for Emer to have a seat. "Had a nice chat with Mama Waters and the dreaded Schwartz-Silbermans. Do you know this is the third Schwartz-Silberman we have passed through these hallowed halls, like so many undigested meals? We should have a limit on kids here in this country. Like China. He must fuck her to shut her up, don't you think?"

"Jesus, Sidney."

"What?"

"I love you."

"Anyway. I think we dodged another bullshit bullet here."

"Thank God."

"If you must. But it was more me than Him."

"Thank you, Sidney."

Sidney shut the door to his office. "How was today?"

"Fine. Good. Like nothing ever happened."

"Well, nothing did."

"Not exactly. I screwed up, Sid. I shouldn't have."

"Maybe, maybe not."

"I know better."

"We all know better, Emer, but we're human, most of us any-way, and we fuck up, we lose our temper, we do things. How are we to know what our character is unless we step outside it and look its way now and then?"

"That's quite nice."

"Might even be true. Would you like some examples of me being 'out of character'? Mostly from the '70s, mind you."

"No, thank you."

"Good answer. Let's color inside the lines, shall we? I'll save it for the memoirs. Tentatively titled *More Cocks Than Frocks*."

"How are you not in jail?"

Sidney was often profane, but never quite like this. It was like he was trying to clear out psychic space in the room. Emer sensed in it a condition of safety. He continued, "Well, no harm, no foul. I think it's over. I can't be sure. These issues can be like zombies, lying dormant and dead, and then one day, George Romero is back in town."

"*Night of the Living Dead?*"

"Good catch." Sidney went to the door to adjourn, but Emer, emboldened by Sidney's "confession," felt like this was the place to confess something of her own.

"There is one more thing," she said.

"Oh?" Sidney said, and went back behind his desk.

"And it's awful."

"Something with your father?"

"No, no, no . . . something unexpected, inconceivable . . . I can't believe I'm in this position."

"Is it my business, Emer? You don't have to tell me if you don't want to."

"It is your business, yes, unfortunately, it is."

"Best to come out with it, then."

"You don't know me away from school, but I'm boring. I haven't had a steady boyfriend in years. My life is here at the school, really, and my father, that's it."

"Okay."

"I've been noticing a man on the train to work the last couple months and I have this very strong attraction/connection to him."

"Do you mind if I pour myself a drink?"

"Of course not."

"Would you like one?"

"Maybe in a minute. Just let me get through this."

"Go ahead." He went to pour himself a tumbler of Bushmills.

"So the other night, late, I'd been in Chinatown."

"What were you doing in Chinatown?"

"Doesn't matter. Well, there he was. And we talked, and we kissed, and more."

"Sounds like a nice story."

"It's not."

"No?"

"Can I have that drink now?" she asked. Sidney handed her his glass. "So last night, in the middle of the meeting, the second meeting . . ."

"With the Waterses."

"Yes, the dad was late and in walks the dad."

She let it sit there. At first, Sidney was waiting for the rest of the sentence with a rather bland aspect of anticipation. Then, all of a sudden, he got it and his mouth opened slowly.

"No."

"Yes."

"No."

"It was him."

"Fuck me running."

"Yeah."

"Emer!"

"It won't happen again."

"You didn't know?"

"No!"

"You never met?"

"I'm almost sure of it."

"Almost sure?"

"If I did, I didn't remember. I'm sure of that."

"Fuck."

"Yeah."

"Did he know?"

"I don't know. I don't think so."

"Does she know?"

"I don't think so. No."

"Fuck fuck fuck. No one knows?"

"No, not that I know of."

"Fuck fuck fuck."

Sidney rubbed his mouth with his hand, as if trying to mold the next words, like a sculptor with a formless piece of clay. He shook his head. He raised his eyebrows a few times as if to begin speaking, but couldn't. He said finally, "This. Is a situation."

"Yes. What should I do?"

"What should you do?"

"Please, help me."

"You can't see him again."

"No? I mean, no!"

"No! This is like living under a volcano now, we don't know when or if it will erupt. Or a bomb, a volcano or a bomb."

"What's the difference?"

"A volcano is the hand of God. A bomb was built and set by man."

"You think this was a setup?"

"I have no idea."

"For what reason?"

"No idea. Maybe reasons that we don't yet know."

"I'm so sorry."

"I understand you are, Emer, and the way you tell me this story, if you are, as you portray yourself, an innocent in this, which I believe, then it is just a divine coincidence. And I believe you. I believe you and I thank you for coming to me."

"Thank you."

"Would you like my advice?"

"Please."

He took a few moments to choose his course and his words. "I think we let this sleeping dog lie. I'm sure this guy is in no hurry to admit an adulterous affair to his wife."

"Not his wife, apparently."

"Whatever. Semantics. An adulterous affair with his kid's teacher."

"She's not his biological daughter."

"Emer."

"Sorry."

"Maybe you get away with it."

"Me?"

"If the shit does ever hit the fan, Emer, I will have to cut you loose. I will deny this conversation ever took place. I will lie and I will call you a liar to your face. You will not recognize me, and people will believe me, and not you."

"I understand."

"Does anyone else know? Izzy?"

"Izzy knows. Of course. She knows I had a thing with a guy, but she doesn't know who the guy is."

"Well, I would counsel that you don't tell Izzy anything else, not what you've learned about this schmuck. And Izzy cannot know that I know. Anything. Are we clear on that? I'll let go of both of you before I step down."

"I understand."

"Do not call this man. Do not arrange to meet him, even if it's to tell him it's over."

"What if he tries to contact me?"

"You're a big girl. No contact. Take cabs. Uber. Cold turkey. Absolutely no fucking contact. This is not gonna be my legacy. I didn't put almost half a century of blood, sweat, and tears into this school for some stupid one-night stand to be my legacy."

That hurt. Was that what it was—a one-night stand? She didn't like to think of it that way, didn't like to think of herself that way, but thought it best not to quibble at the moment. They sat in silence.

Emer began to cry. Big, fat, hot tears. Sidney offered her his hanky. Emer felt so appreciative of that, and for the lost art of the hanky, that it only made her cry harder. It began as a cry for this situation, but soon became a cry for everything. Everything that was, and everything that wasn't. Sidney realized this and did not try to console her. This cry was too inclusive to be given short shrift. He sat back down in his chair and waited until the storm passed of its own course. After a few minutes, Emer's breathing began to return to normal.

"Okay, now?" Sid asked.

Emer took a deep breath and bit her bottom lip like one of her own students. "As okay as it's gonna get for now."

"Yeah? I'd like a plan B."

"What? What's plan B?" she asked through tears.

"Plan B is what makes plan A work."

"So what is it?'

Sidney pondered, his eyes drifted heavenward. "Don't have a plan B. Plan B is to keep trying plan A and hope that the next month or so is as uneventful as a postmodern novel."

"That's not very comforting."

"That's my point. Alrighty then—shoulder to the boulder?" Sidney said by way of bucking her up after fucking her up.

"Shoulder to the boulder," she echoed, and nodded, but didn't move. "But now what, exactly?"

"Now," Sidney sighed, "we wait."

"For what?" Emer asked, handing Sid back his wet hanky.

"Nothing. Hopefully."

DONKEYS SEE WHAT HAPPENS

FOR SOME REASON, the catastrophic image Sidney had planted in Emer's mind, of a volcano or an explosive, took root and blossomed. Each day thereafter at school, Emer felt hyper-aware, like a bomb-sniffing airport dog, attuned to smells and sounds humans could not hear—the ticking of the clock, the rumblings of the nearby subway, the rush of a class of little feet up the stairwell were all harbingers of a natural or man-made disaster about to come down on her head. Sidney had requested they speak no more of the matter unless there was a "conflagra-tion." A few days later, Emer had texted Sidney to ask how he was doing, and he texted back that she shouldn't text him, that he was too old, "like Hillary," to know how to put electronic things in the trash.

Emer shared his helpless paranoia before the "cloud," and thought that was good thinking, so she typed back, "Okay, let's see what happens," and sent it, only later realizing that autocorrect had chosen the more colorful if less comprehensible "Donkeys see what happens." Sidney had not responded. Apparently he was okay with letting donkeys see what happens, and that had been that for their texting.

She had also been barred by Sidney from confiding to anyone else what had happened, especially Izzy, her closest friend on the planet. This isolated her further in her own world of paranoid perception and heightened awareness to clues and conspiracies, either real or imagined. She felt the processes of her brain tilt away from left to right, from the rational to the intuitional, from logic to superstition—gathering patterns and subtexts, and storing them, the way a person badly lost during an afternoon hike in unfamiliar woods might, as the sun went down and the temperature dropped, begin to conserve water. Just in case. She saw double-dealing and plots everywhere.

Of course, Izzy noticed that Emer was "off," and inquired after her. But Emer was able to keep her emotional distance and generally avoid her at school, dodging most of her phone calls and texts. When Izzy confronted her one day, and Emer was on the verge of telling her best friend the truth, Izzy threw her the bogus lifeline of suggesting that maybe she had been seeing the mystery man. Emer gratefully latched on to that, admitting that the relationship had continued, but that he was married, and that was the cause both of Emer's secrecy and of her apparent recent increase in self-loathing and inauthenticity.

Sweet Izzy pooh-poohed the idea of adultery as something Emer should take responsibility for, telling her that was between the man and his wife, and that she was a free agent. She scolded her mildly about harming a "sister," but was more happy that Emer was finally into a guy after so many years. Emer felt relieved, but also burdened by the fact that she would now have to falsify updates about this relationship for Izzy. This increased her sense of isolation and bifurcation. She figured that eventually, in a month or so, she would tell Izzy that they had broken it off, and that would be that. She felt like an actress in a play who had forgotten her lines and was now improvising "in character," hoping the audience would not catch on before she could get back on book again.

A few weeks of Uber, Lyft, and taxis went by, and Emer was beginning to resent the amount of money spent, so she ventured back onto the subway one late spring morning. She did miss the commute, the crowded privacy, the loud quiet, the Train of Thoughts.

And sure enough, a week of subway riding to and from school eased her up a little. Like things were gonna be okay, the bomb wouldn't go off, the volcano wouldn't erupt; this was not Pompeii; Con would not reappear. Once, she saw a man on the train who fit Con's silhouette, and she was surprised by her reaction. After the initial rush of fearful adrenaline, Emer felt a wave of hope, a flirty, giddy anticipation, which made her realize she really did want something more from this man. Maybe an explanation? So she kept riding the subway, telling herself it was over, hoping, and barely admitting this to herself, that it might not be.

During these weeks, she spent a lot of time with her dad, who, true to Ging's report, was deeply into Pokémon Go. When Emer wondered aloud if this was dangerous to her father, Ging-ging pointed out that "at least it gets him out of the house. No Pokémon in this building." She went with him and Ging on one of these hunting excursions, her father in a wheelchair, holding the phone in his hand like it was a Geiger counter.

As a young man, and after he retired, Jim had loved to fly-fish, and even disappeared upstate now and then to rent a cabin in the Catskills with some buddies. Emer saw this game as an evolution of fly-fishing or even the big-game fishing of Hemingway and the machismo of the previous century—these strange new gods and creatures, with their specific natures and tendencies and dangers, were very similar to the strange world below the surface of the waters. So she signed off on all things Pokémon Go, resolved to study its ways so she could converse knowledgeably and engage with the old man, gave Ging the rest of the day off, and wheeled her father into Central Park for some big-game hunting.

Once in the park, the old man said, "Alice," so Emer rolled him to the statue. He asked her to wheel him around and around the figures, as if looking for something, a crack or an opening. He pointed to the ground, where Emer saw a business card of some kind. She picked it up. It said, "Go Ask Alice Enterprises / 23 Central Park Westeast." There was no such address on the city grid, and this was indeed a nonsensical, Alice in Wonderland type of address. Emer figured it must be part of a game or social movement of which she was unaware, and was about to toss it, when her dad said, "Keep it." Then he said, "Reservoir."

Emer wheeled him north along the Bridle Path, and parked him within sight of the fountain and its geyser. He tried to get out of his chair, to move toward it, but he didn't have the strength. He was like a believer at Lourdes, Emer thought, remembering his *Cocoon*-like rejuvenation of that night, or her dream, she didn't really know which. Was he asking for help or showing her his vision? "Think there's any fish in there, Pops?" she asked. Jim nodded—like, oh hell yeah. Emer laughed at his happy certainty. "Sharks?" Jim shook his head no, just as certain. "You're not afraid of sharks, are ya, Pops?"

"No."

"No, not my pops. My pops isn't scared of nothing."

He shook his head in somber agreement, and then dead-panned, "Your mother." And they both laughed and cried a little.

"You wanna go for a swim, Pops?" she asked him. He looked up at her, tears in his eyes, and nodded yes. She pondered what she could do—hoist her father over the fence where he would then drown, and she would spend the rest of her life misunderstood as a patricide and pariah? He was staring through the fence at the shimmering, liquid oval as if it were literally the reservoir of his lost hopes and vitality. She wondered if it hurt to be so close to the cure for loss. It must.

She wheeled him around to face away from the water and pointed him back home. "Another day," she said.

He craned his neck back to meet her eyes as she pushed him. "Promise?" he asked like a child.

"Promise," she promised, not even knowing what her promises meant anymore.

LOVE IS THE DRUG

A COUPLE OF TIMES THAT SPRING, Emer spotted Con picking up Mama's daughter after school. They made eye contact and Emer, as subtly as she could, even though it felt cartoonishly big, shook her head and mouthed the word *no*. Con just as subtly and resignedly nodded yes, as if to himself, looking down, and that was that. Emer felt emboldened by these ghostly exchanges, and the next time she saw Con in the main hallway of the school, waiting to pick up Ashia, she took Ashia's hand and walked her over to the man. She would now take it to the next level, she was going to move past what was, erase it, and normalize this nasty situation. She felt tall enough to ride this roller coaster. As Emer and the little girl approached, Con held his hands out at his sides in confusion, looking like he was about to be arrested for a crime he wasn't sure he'd committed.

"Introduce me to your father, Ash."

"He's not my father. My father's in Africa. This is Con."

"Nice to meet you, Con."

"You've met him, though."

Already this had gone sideways. Why had she asked to be introduced to a man she'd already met? And fucked. Con took her hand again and shook it. He was good at that.

"At parent-teacher meetings. Yes, you're right about that. Nice to see you again, Ms. Emer."

His touch was still powerful to her, like that addictive entity, the Gancanagh. What the hell was that? She felt like she'd been given a morphine drip. She tasted sugar at the back of her throat, dreams knocking at the back door of her consciousness. What was this man? What was this man to her? She pulled her hand back too quickly, too violently.

"You guys are weird," Ashia said rightly. "Let's go. I'm hungry." And she made to leave the building.

"Good to see you," Con lamely said, and took a step to the side, as if to retreat, yet remaining open to being asked to stay. Emer had no words. She was both high and hungover around this man; he was the drink and the morning after. She was looking at her hand like it was the site of some sort of penetration, where the needle had just been.

He said, "Can we talk, please, somewhere else. I want to explain."

"No."

"Okay."

And then for some reason, she said, "You give up easy."

Before Con could respond to Emer's sudden and inadvertent charm, Sidney appeared from behind a much taller adult, like a sideways jack-in-the-box. Emer actually jumped.

"Sidney!"

"Hello. Hello."

"Do you know Ashia Waters's father, Con? It's not Waters, is it?" She was using too many words.

"No, it's Powers. Con Powers."

"You know our headmaster, Sidney Crotty."

"Yes, of course, of course," Sidney said, but did not extend his hand for some reason. They stood in triangular silence for a moment, until Con said, "I'd better get going," and took another step back. He gave a harmless little neutered wave/salute, and then, as no one stopped him this time, off he went.

After watching him disappear, Sidney, speaking out of the corner of his mouth like an untalented ventriloquist, hissed, "What the fuck was that?"

"Nothing. Nothing. There's nothing."

"Nothing will come from that nothing, my dear. Speak again."

"What?"

"The bard. Parse it out later. You are opening the proverbial can of worms. For fuck's sake, Emer, don't be stupid."

A third grader overheard the tail end of the conversation and announced, "Mr. Crotty just said 'stupid'!" Sidney gave Emer one last hellish look and then grabbed the little boy up in mock anger, quickly defusing his use of the most controversial word of the twenty-first century. As Sidney roughhoused with the little boy, she turned away and closed her eyes for a second, and said silently to herself, This must be what fate is.

SOUL TRAIN

SOME QUIET DAYS WENT BY, but now Emer half expected, half dreaded that she'd see Con on the subway. She knew she'd foolishly picked at the scab, rubbed the lamp, opened the box. She kept a seat open for him by doing her own miniature version of manspreading—womanspreading. She was in the vanguard of this as yet unacknowledged phenomenon. So she wasn't all that surprised when Con appeared at Fiftieth Street and stood above her. She pulled her legs together and he sat down next to her. She laid down the law: "You have three stops, speak."

"Hold on, let me set up my Teleprompter so I stay on message."

"Funny. Wasting time, but funny." She felt herself in some kind of character, like the hard-ass best friend. She liked herself in this role.

"Okay. We'd never met. Never. I didn't know who you were."

"I believe that. Doesn't make this any better."

"It kinda does."

"It makes our mistake morally defensible, which is more than I can say for this moment right now."

"I'm not married to Mama. We used to date. We haven't been together like that in about three years."

"Bullshit."

"It's not bullshit."

The train stopped at Sixty-sixth Street and got quieter as people shuffled off.

"But you live with her?"

"Yes, I live with her. But as separate . . . entities. She sleeps in one room, I sleep in another."

She wanted to believe him. But it would be easier if he were full of shit. She didn't know yet.

"Why have you stayed together?"

"It's a long story."

"Too bad for you, only a couple stops left."

"It's too complicated for right now."

"Try me."

"She's very wealthy, money from her family, the family is very old-fashioned African. But they like me well enough. They like me with her. She's afraid the money will go if I go."

"And you spend this money, too?"

"Yes, I suppose I do."

"Charming."

"Emer, I have asked to leave. I have made all the arguments, but she won't allow it."

"Won't 'allow' it?"

"She's from a very powerful family. I swear it makes sense. That's what it feels like."

"Whatever. You're saying you two have an 'arrangement.'"

"Something like that."

"'Something like that' meaning there's one arrangement for you and another for her?"

"No. We're in a 'you do you' mode."

"Is that the mode you like?"

"It's the mode I find myself in."

"So you're passive, a victim of cushy circumstance?"

"I like to think of it not as passive, I like to think of it as complicated."

"Is there a difference between 'liking to think' something and just 'thinking' it?"

"I like to think so." He smiled, pleased with himself.

Seventy-ninth Street came and went. They sat in silence as the doors opened and closed on Eighty-sixth Street, which meant that Emer was not going to visit her father this afternoon. Each little step she took, each moment she dallied, she knew which way she was headed, but she told herself, at any minute she could stop, there was always the opportunity to pull the emergency brake. She'd done nothing wrong. They'd done nothing wrong. He was a nice guy. She was a nice girl. She reached for his hand. "Jesus," she said.

"What?"

"When I touch you. It's like. It's like a drug."

"You sound like my Irish grandmother."

"Gross."

"No, not like that, she used to tell me that I was handsome, you know grandmas, she said I was one of the Gancanagh."

"I actually know what that is."

"Yeah? What is it?"

"Kiss me."

He kissed her. She felt the drug enter her through their shared saliva. The next stop was hers.

"Why me?" she asked him sincerely. "Of all the women in New York, of all the women on the subway, you pick a thirty-eight-year-old first-grade teacher. It's bad TV writing."

"Well, I was on *General Hospital*. Three-episode arc."

"Don't ever say that again."

"Maybe you don't see yourself the way I see you."

"Yeah?"

"Maybe you're my Gancanagh."

"Gancanaghs for each other?"

"Sure. That just sounds like what people call chemistry. Chemistry squared. Simply."

"It doesn't work that way. You can't have a female Gancanagh."

"Why not? Like a succubus or a Lilith? I've heard of those. Can't we make up our own rules?"

"No," she said. "There are so many reasons why this is a terrible idea, and they only start with the aboveground shit of what you'd call polite society. My life—I have seen these visions and I have made deals, and I am in danger."

"We've all made bad deals. Life is hard."

"You don't get it. On some fundamental level of morality, of God's will or the will of the gods, I am not allowed to see you. Specifically."

"I feel like you're being dramatic. Ever so slightly." He smiled.

"Feel my head." She took his hand and traced the scar where her tumor had been removed. "I had a tumor."

"I'm sorry."

"No, ssh. Don't. Long time ago, I had a tumor and it gave me visions, and I'm okay now, but I'm still witchy, I still have these visions from this ghost tumor, ghost visions. And I'm not crazy."

"I don't think you are."

"You're not just saying that? Maybe you wanna get off this train right now before I take it all the way to Crazytown."

"No, I don't think so."

"So my visions—whether they're visions or reality or dreams—don't matter to you?"

"Might matter."

"Might matter, right you are, okay. But these visions offer up a world and a world that has rules, and these rules say you can't just make up your own rules. That's when society breaks down, all hell breaks loose, and chaos reigns."

"Cats and dogs living together?"

"What?"

"Bill Murray? *Tootsie*? I'm desperate."

She felt like she should tell him the secret. He deserved it, or she deserved to say it out loud and tell him.

"I think you're a poet and you're just beginning to know it," he said.

"Thank you."

"Maybe we can collaborate."

Emer had had enough of this banter, and yet she felt she hadn't even begun to partake of this familiar stranger's sweetness. She straightened her shoulders. "Yeah, why don't you come home and collaborate with me," she said, "now."

She could still pull the emergency brake at any time. Sure she could.

MEET THE GANCANAGHS

THE ODD THING ABOUT HAVING A DOORMAN in your building was that they became surrogate parents in a way, without the power. All censure and no agency. Mostly mute witnesses to your life, without the authority to intervene. Like a Greek chorus without lines. You could only guess at their judgment and opinion, as Emer could guess Papa was judging the shit out of her as she walked Con past him on their way to their afternoon delight. Trying to show she had nothing to be ashamed of, rather than scurry by with her head down, she stopped to bump fists with Papa as usual. He dutifully and mirthlessly gave Emer some dap, but then again, that was his job.

On the elevator up to her apartment, Con kissed her. Even though Emer knew there was a video camera in the elevator car, one that broadcast to the front desk, and god knows where else. Mid-kiss, she opened her eyes and looked at the camera; she was thumbing her nose at all authority, real and imagined, at all those who would take away what she, for once, knew she wanted. Bug off, eyes of the prying world.

They stopped and kissed in the hallway before they got to Emer's door. Fuck you, any neighbors that might possibly empty the trash right now. None did. They kissed when she inserted the key in her door, but before she turned it. Fuck you, uh, everybody else. Once inside, Con spun her back to the front door and pressed up against her. She could feel how hard he was again. She wanted him inside her as fast as possible, because she didn't want to get caught up in whether this was wrong or right. She didn't want to think at all, she just wanted to do, to be. There would be time later for dwelling. She stopped the kiss, put her finger up to his lips to quiet them, grabbed his hand, and led him into her bedroom.

THE SALMON OF KNOWLEDGE

EMER AWOKE ALONE. She raised herself on an elbow and listened for Con in her apartment. Nothing. He probably had to get home to Mama. That was reality. Already reality, so soon nipping at the heels of reverie. It occurred to her that this was like one of those old movie cutaways in the age before they could show you everything on screen. The couple kisses, a door shuts, a train goes through a tunnel, fade to black, the sun rises, the girl wakes up, the man is gone, her virtue compromised forever. The best bits happened offscreen, but they were fresh on the screen of Emer's mind.

She went to the fridge and got herself some après-sex ice cream. Oh yeah, she was all about "all decadence, all the time" now. There was a piece of salmon in there so she downed a little protein before her treat, ever the responsible girl. She opened her computer to "Godsforsaken," and started writing about what had happened. Or so she meant to. Her fingers took on a life of their own, and she found herself watching them type from some place above her head, just letting it fly in free association, the trippy words appearing on the screen like an articulated lava lamp. Deep into the wee hours, when the cawing of a crow shook her out of a trance.

She whipped around to see Corvus on her windowsill, something in his mouth. The black bird dropped whatever it was and flew away. Emer approached the window, and in the moonlight, she could make out a baby mouse (rat?!) or squirrel, bloodied, tiny, badly injured, squirming, hopelessly broken—its head twisted, neck partly snapped. Emer picked the poor creature up in her hand, its speck of a heart fluttering against the sappy bones of its almost transparent breast. It was a baby squirrel, she saw now. A beautiful creation in miniature.

It wouldn't live. It was in pain. She knew this was a thank-you note from Corvus, but it was gross and sad, and she also couldn't help thinking of it as a dark omen. She thought back through her studies to the significance of squirrels and crows, but her full-chested empathy for the dying "crater" (as her dad would've called it, Gaelic for "creature") blocked associative recall and memory.

She thought of cupping it in her hands, running to the bathroom, and flushing it down the toilet, but then hesitated to add drowning to its miserable short stay on this planet. Maybe just toss it out the window? But what if it didn't die from the fall and only suffered more? Emer apologized to the baby—its features were both remarkably blunt and fine up close. What the hand, what the eye. Pinkish, the eyes barely open, the eyes that would soon close forever. She kissed its tiny bloodied snout, laid the broken body on the floor, put a sneaker on her right foot, and crushed its skull under the instep, brain blood swiping on wood like ominous calligraphy as she cried "sorry, sorry, sorry" through gritted teeth.

She picked up the carcass, satisfied it was dead, and only then flushed it down the toilet. She mopped away the remnant stain. She went back to her kitchen nook, sat down, and started sobbing hysterically.

She didn't know how long she'd been crying when there was a knock on the door. It was 2:45 in the morning. Instinctively, she called out "Con?" as she went to open the door, only, as once before in a dream or another life, to find a tiny doorman there.

CONNED AGAIN

I T LOOKED TO EMER as if Sidney was wearing a doorman cos-
tume for Halloween, which was months away. She laughed.
"What are you doing here, Sidney?" Sidney was not pleased.
And then she remembered her evening with Con and hoped to
God Sidney didn't know anything about that.

"Not Sidney," said Sidney.

"Not Sidney what?"

"Can you invite me in?"

"Come on in."

"Them's the rules," he said. She followed him into the living
room, scanning nervously that there were no signs that Con had
ever been there.

"What's with the getup?"

"This was not the deal."

"What are you talking about?"

He turned to look at her, hard. She felt deeply unsettled by
his gaze.

"Stop calling me 'Sidney,'" he said. "I am Sidhe."

"I don't understand."

"You understand fine. You're just too nervous to comprehend at the moment."

"No, I really don't understand."

"Remember the terms of the deal, and remember who I am."

"Sidney, this isn't funny anymore."

"I am Sidhe."

He raised his voice; for a small man he had a lot of menacing power. Emer flashed on an image of a superball of concentrated rubber that could bounce dangerously, impossibly high. Like this little man. She was terrified.

"The terms of the deal," she repeated to herself, puzzling, gnawing at the phrase. Whatever much was unclear in her mind, hazy shapes from memories and dreams flashing by clamoring for emphasis and attention, what was clear was that Sidney somehow knew that she had seen Con.

And why not? It's a city of millions. How did they think they might sit and talk on a crowded subway? All it takes is one piece of bad luck—one relative, or parent, or friend of a friend of a friend who recognizes her or him—and in three minutes, with the help of smartphones, in Afghanistan, Australia, Bumfuck, Idaho, and even Staten Island, all the tweeters and instagrammers know about the fallen schoolteacher and the parent.

But, she also thought—maybe I should play it cool until I know for sure that he knows. She was terrible at playing it cool, but figured she had nothing to lose and it might buy her some time. She flicked her hair back casually.

"Why are you wearing a doorman's uniform?"

"Because I am a doorman. Of sorts."

"Of sorts?" Repeating phrases, treading water—maybe he doesn't know.

"Yes, I prevent certain things on one side from crossing through to the other side and vice versa."

"Sounds like a doorman." She laughed a crappy little fake laugh.

"Jesus Christ!" he exploded. "He was here. I can smell him, your chemicals together. Your Gancanagh. You were not to have any contact with him, that was the deal." Busted. Better just come clean.

"Sidney—I don't know what to say. I saw Con on the subway and we talked and he came over. He doesn't love her—whatever she is to him—it's a loveless thing."

"Spare me the human details. You think I give an ancient fuck about your *Cosmopolitan* magazine analysis of his 'relationship'?" He said *relationship* like an exterminator might say *vermin*.

"I don't know why you're yelling."

"You're shitting me!"

"You can fire me, or I can quit. I'd prefer to quit. Actually I'd prefer to stay, but if you feel you have to fire me to protect yourself, go ahead. This is not unprecedented. It happens. Shit happens. People fall in love in difficult circumstances. Most songs are about it."

She hadn't prepared that particular line of argument, but was pleased to watch it take shape as it spun out of her mouth. Except for "most songs are about it"—that was rather lame, and of course, Sidney seized upon the weak link.

"Most songs are about it? Jesus, I'm thirsty."

"I'll get you a glass of water."

He laughed scornfully. "Not that type of thirst."

"Oh. Whiskey?" Images from a dream came back to her, and she heard herself saying, "Irish whiskey?" Sidney put his finger to his nose in assent.

As she poured his drink, she took a healthy swig herself. Sidney inhaled his and offered up his glass again. She filled it. "Good money after bad," he said, and downed the second. It was all coming back to her, but the all was incomplete and confusing. She felt like she was herself and not herself just as this was Sid who said he was not Sid.

"Okay," he said, "now I can breathe. And think. Now, lass, you were given a card recently?"

"A card?"

"Yes, like a business card."

"No. I don't know. I don't think so."

"May I check your purse?"

"Sure. I have nothing to hide."

"Please don't say things like that—so boring."

Emer pushed her purse across the tabletop. Sidney rummaged through it. He helped himself to a piece of gum. He examined a lipstick, seeming to disapprove of the color, and then produced a business card as promised. The one that she had picked up off the ground in Central Park by the Alice sculpture on a walk with her dad. She had completely forgotten about it. The one with the impossible address.

"Here it is," he said.

"How did you know?"

"Let's agree on a moratorium on questions like 'How did you

know?' Let's just say the answer is—because I am Bean Sidhe, that's how. Okay?"

"I guess."

"Stop guessing and start knowing," Sidhe said. "Come. Walk with me."

23 CENTRAL PARK WESTEAST

NOT SO FAST, Giantess," Sid said, hustling down the hallway of her building, trying to keep up with Emer's long strides. Nearing the entrance, Sid called out, "There he is, Papa Legba!" Papa lit up to see Sid. It was the first time that Emer could remember ever having seen the man smile. "The once and forever Haitian king." Sid bowed. "Irish prince," Papa replied, and bowed back, doorman to doorman. What the hell is this nonsense? wondered Emer.

As they walked toward the park, Sid pulled out his phone. "Let me bring you up to speed," he said. "Sometime ago, we made a pact, you and I, the terms of which—this king, this Gancanagh, Cuchulain, would live, but he could not know you and that you would stay away from him. The signs have been all around you, and yet you miss them or consign them to a dream. This is not a dream, Huge Woman, or if it is, it's the dream you are waking into now."

They entered the park, heading southeast. Sid kept on,

"Everything. The bird, your father, the old-people orgy at the reservoir—now that was somewhat untidy, I'm sorry—the dreams—how dense are you gonna be?"

Had he been following her all this time? Had he hacked her computer?

"How steadfast is your belief in what you think of as real going to be before you can see it for what it is—merely a version, and a lesser version at that." He offered her his phone. "Press play. Take a look at that. Maybe you'll remember more."

Emer pressed PLAY and watched as Con and Mama Waters walked holding hands and appearing to kiss through what looked to be a SoHo street in the rain.

"When was this?"

"Wrong question."

"I'd like to know."

"Today."

She couldn't believe Con had been lying to her today. Didn't want to. "Impossible. I was with him today."

"Aha!"

"Dammit."

"He loves her. He lied to you."

"I don't believe that. When are these pictures from?"

"Yesterday."

"No. I call bullshit."

"Tomorrow."

"What?"

"Yesterday, today, tomorrow, right now. All of the above. I told you it was the wrong question. Keep watching."

Emer watched on the screen as the scene played out like a

movie, it was even scored like a film, the jaunty piano, old-timey rom-com music segueing into a darker synth-horror mode as the lovers walked down the street and a car suddenly sideswiped them, hitting Con and throwing him in a slo-mo stuntman-flailing arc fifteen feet in the air.

"Jesus! What is that? What just happened?"

"That is what will happen if you continue to see him and break your deal."

"You're sick, Sid."

"I am fair, but you are trying me!"

They stood beside Alice. Sid took out the business card. "So what you just showed me," Emer asked, "could happen?"

"Did happen." She tried to take it in and square it like a math proof, but it was beyond her. "Has happened. Will happen."

"You make no sense."

"It happened and it unhappened, and it will happen and un-happen again. It's happening and unhappening right now. Until you put an end to it. Till you stop the eternal return."

"How? How would I do that?" There were actually crickets in the park, which stopped their chirping en masse just now as if signaled to hush by some cosmic conductor. How wonderful and sad, stranded as they were in a little patch of green surrounded by an asphalt moat.

"Educate yourself. Reeducate yourself. Know the gods that came before your mind."

"Why can't you just tell me instead of speaking in riddles?"

"I am telling you, Gargantuana, you're just not listening with your dream ears. Wouldn't it be too easy for me to just give you the answer? And it would sound ridiculous. A child's fantasy of adult life. Fucking humans, you race of time-bound fools, want it all spelled out for you. No wonder you like the big boss, union-busting Jehovah."

Sid's rant, and the crickets that took up again, merged to wash over Emer like the roar of the ocean. She was less in the act of piecing things together rationally; it was more like she had a sense of one reality transposing itself over another, as if one part of her brain was being folded into the other, or a world of dreams was being layered over a so-called real world to form a hybrid whole. And as you might, when your left brain folds over your right, Emer felt a little dizzy.

"I'm not sure you're taking me seriously," he said.

"I am. I'm trying to."

"Are you? Just because I'm funny doesn't mean I'm not lethal."

He extended his arm like a falconer awaiting a falcon. Emer felt a powerful shudder behind her head, and her hair flew to the side. A large black bird landed gracefully on Sid's shoulder.

"Oh my god! Corvus?"

The bird walked down Sid's shoulder to his hand, perching there like a pet parrot. Sid offered Corvus to her, saying, "The proverbial bird in the hand. For we are in the land of proverbs now."

Corvus delicately hobbled from Sid's hand to hers. She felt an immediate and profound reconnection to this being, and through him, to all living things. She felt her chest tighten. Corvus extended his cold hard beak to her lips.

"I missed you," she said to the bird. Sid gave them a moment, and then extended his hand to receive the bird again. Corvus, like a trained act, high-stepped from Emer's hand, back to Sid's.

"It was a beautiful thing you did. Saving this crater."

Emer was now tearing up.

"But it was against nature, against the overall deal. He was weak and was meant to die."

The bird looked to Sid and cocked its head curiously to the side, as if to say, "Really, bro?" Sid nodded. Corvus puffed his chest out and rose to his full height, turning his head toward Emer, and then continued to keep turning it, till he had made a full Linda Blair 360 revolution and snapped his own neck. The sound made Emer gag. The bird fell off Sid's hand to the ground, motionless as a black stone, dead.

"Corvus!" Emer knelt on the ground and picked up the bird. But his spirit was gone.

"What did you do? What did you do?"

But Sid had moved on. He was on all fours under the sculpture, checking the business card in his little hand.

"Okay, okay—I believe you," Emer cried. "I respect you. Whatever you want. Just stop killing things." She walked over to Sid on buckling knees.

"Here we are," he said, with some effort, pulling at something on the ground, a handle.

The covering gave. A bright light rose up from beneath the ground, impossibly, casting a vertical shaft upward, like when the city commemorates 9/11 downtown. Emer got down on the ground, too. She tried to peer into the light, but it burned her eyes, and when she looked away, she saw dozens of ghost moons transfixed upon the night sky. "Come under here with me," Sid said.

"What is under there?"

"The furnace of making."

"The furnace of making what?"

"Exactly."

"Another riddle."

"Another stipulation. You must translate what you see and share it with the world from the hand of a human, from the mind of a time-bound, earthbound Deathling."

"I'm not a processor like that; I'm not a systems maker. I'm just a teacher."

"You'll be a publicist of sorts. A visionary. Or dead."

"What if I say no?"

"You're already in the game, Deathling. You have no choice but to play on."

"I want out."

"Your wants are what got us here."

"I'm afraid."

"You damn well should be. You're scrapping with gods and monsters now."

"You're not Sidney, are you?"

"Yes and no. No and yes—told you I'm a doorman, sometimes I'm on this side, sometimes on that side. I tire of your vacillating jibber-jabber. You may enter."

Sid pushed her forward and down, into the light. She saw shadows, what Plato must have seen in his cave a couple of thousand years ago, in Technicolor, what John Lennon saw when his mother died, what Leonardo saw when he met Lisa Gherardini.

Shapes came in and out of focus as if the world turning on its daily axis were itself the turning of a lens in her eye, her soul camera. Emer fell down slowly face-first through heavy liquid space, and felt her fingers moving, as if to gain purchase on a passing ledge, or to write upon the air.

THE WORLD NYPL

EMER AWOKE WITH HER HEAD on her computer keyboard. It was day outside, and by the angle of light, past morning. She didn't know how long she'd been writing, or how long she'd been asleep, but the keys had made small square indentations on her hot, glistening forehead. She felt feverish. She glanced at the bottom of the computer screen and saw that the word count of this file, labeled "Godsforsaken," was over 55,000. Impossible, she thought, must be gibberish, but saved it anyway.

Tomorrow was graduation day, so Emer didn't have to go into school today, which was just as well. She needed to talk to Con, to see him before she would run into him again at the ceremony. She called his number for the first time since she had called and hung up. They arranged to meet at the main public library at Forty-second Street. She wasn't sure why that location, but it seemed inherently neutral, public yet private, quiet, quaint, and safe.

She grew up using the New York Public Library and even

came to adore the unfortunate-sounding acronym—NYPL—as being apropos, as we all were suckled on the teat of this knowledge. And she just loved that main building, with its stone lion sentries and the books—the magnitude. It was a palace built for books when books were royalty, like a still-standing ruin of a religion long dead, the religion of the written word. Somehow she felt as safe in there as she would in a church. "Sanctuary," like Charles Laughton, the Hunchback of Notre Dame, lisped, "sanctuary."

Emer entered the main hall and went to find an out-of-print book she remembered from her childhood revolt against the God who would not let her love him like she wanted. It was called *The Old World Book of Faeries and Demons* and it couldn't be removed from the library. She perused it in a corner, and saw much that made her pause in wonder and sudden recognition—it was all in there, the Bean Sidhe, the Gancanagh, Papa Legba, the Dragon King, and Anansi the trickster, the spider goddess, and much more. She took pictures of page after page with her phone.

Con showed up a few minutes late. They kissed hello. She felt the tip of his tongue on her lip, drawn to his taste and his scent. Gancanagh. He pulled at the old hardcover to get a better look. "What's this crazy shit?"

"It's crazy shit, yes, that's what it is. I have to tell you some things, and it's probably gonna sound crazy metaphorical, but I want you to know I am not crazy, or metaphorical. I am being sane and literal."

"I have no idea what you're talking about, but okay, go ahead."

She told him all she could remember of the first dream—of Sidney and Sidhe, of Anansi, the video of his death, of the deal and whether or not the deal was adhered to, of Nietzsche and the eternal return, of her personal intersection with the immigrant history of this country writ small here in New York City, of deliverymen and mistress-dispellers, of parallel universes and the new physics corroborating the essential oneness of matter—stuff she knew nothing about really, but intuited from fractured firsthand experience. Con sat and listened, stone-faced, it seemed to her. Emer's sincerity precluded any jokes. Finally, she fell quiet, having exhausted herself after what must have been twenty minutes.

Con, with the practiced timing of the actor he was, waited the requisite number of beats before saying, "So . . . are we gonna have sex again or what?" Emer didn't react.

Con breathed out audibly. "You're serious?"

"Yeah."

"Well, I'm confused."

"It's confusing."

"No, not all this," he said, waving dismissively at the giant compendium of folktales and folk deities.

"About what, then?"

"About this . . . I don't have the words for it . . . fantasy?"

"It's not a fantasy."

"Then it's, fuck, I don't know. I mean, if you don't want to see me anymore, I get it, but this is so weird."

"You think I don't want to see you?"

"Emer, you just told me a ridiculous story about fairies and spiders, basically the gist of it being that my life is in danger if I continue to see you."

"I'm not making it up."

"Oh, because it's in this comic book here, you're not making it up." He angrily pushed the big book away.

Emer paused and tried to stand for a moment in Con's shoes.

His reaction made sense, probably a lot more sense than anything she had been saying. She felt desolate, alone again, naturally.

"How else can we explain our feelings?" she asked. "The intensity, the feeling that this is not the first time with us?"

"I don't know, but there are a thousand explanations I'd go to before this."

"Like what?"

"Like love, like fate, like we fit, like you got chocolate on my peanut butter. I don't know. I'm not a poet. But this is not literal. Love is big and we are small. Love is bigger than us and in order for us to embrace it we make stories up. Don't start believing the stories we make up to explain things that have no explanation. There's such a thing as mystery."

Emer saw she'd been a fool to share her madness. She should have just told her father; he had a mind that could accept this beautiful nonsense. As right as Con was for her, she was not right for him. She could see that now. And yet she did not give up. Almost from outside herself, she heard herself keep at him.

"But maybe . . ."

"What?"

"Have you heard of ghost planets?"

"Ghost planets now? Jesus, you jump around."

"What is the moral reason to do anything? Is it my pleasure? Or is it simply some imprecise calculus of figuring out the greatest good for the greatest number? Or is there a hard and fast thing called the right thing?"

"Goddammit, you lost me. I always get in over my head at the library."

But Emer was gathering steam again. "I think of morality as

like the Earth, this lonely planet in cold space. And we are influenced by the things we see and know we know—the planets in our orbit that exert ethical gravity over us, et cetera."

Con countered, attempting to bring the discussion back down to earth. "Can you try to be a little more monosyllabic—I'm an actor." Emer smiled sadly at his habitual self-effacement, his chronic short-selling of himself, as he continued, "It sounds to me like you're upset at some, like, religious notion of being a quote unquote adulterer."

"No. Not exactly. But I am worried about the unknowns and the unseen."

"Ghost planets in the mind?" he ventured, sounding like a game show contestant unsure of his answer.

"Exactly. What if we use God—or gods, or past lives, or future lives, or heaven and hell—as spiritual dark matter, all things that cannot be seen or proven, all moral ghost planets that we allow or conjure up to inform, influence, our morality? And we choose to act as if these things are not now real at our spiritual peril?"

"Let me try to follow—so in this way, we jerry-rig moral lives in this life, this life the only one we can see and touch at the moment and know for sure?" he asked, as if he had lost belief in what he was saying mid-sentence.

"Something like that."

He paused. She could see that he was breathing hard.

"If you just don't want to see me anymore, then say it. Have the balls to say it."

"If I knew what I wanted to say, don't you think I'd come out and just say it?"

"I don't know at this point."

"No, but I do know, I just can't find the words. But I have the sense that neither of us is what we could be."

"Meaning?"

"Meaning—you're an actor."

"Hey now."

"No, what if you haven't challenged yourself in this life because you've been made comfortable, your mind has been lulled to sleep? What if you're really a king in disguise who has forgotten his true nature?"

"That's kinda Disney," he said dismissively.

"I was thinking more Lotus Eaters."

"Hey, it's the fucking ghost planet of high school literature."

"Yes, you're angry! But yes. And you recall that knowledge from some other place, but maybe you are a sleeping Ulysses, or maybe I am too, and maybe the only way we wake up is to reject this love, is to choose perfection of the work. You have been relying on looks and charm, and relying on the kindness of women—first Mama, and now you want to rely on me."

Emer could see that Con was stung.

"So you're doing this for me? Your not seeing me anymore is for my own good, a silly fucking actor? So you leave and I leave Mama and then and only then maybe I can pee standing up and be a man without the help and love of women?"

"Maybe. I don't really know; it's all so hazy to me."

There was a palpable shift. Con stood back up, brushing something invisible off his chest. "Look, Emer, we got lucky."

"What do you mean?"

"We had some fun that we probably shouldn't have, and we got away with it, we didn't get caught."

"We did get caught."

"We didn't get caught, and now maybe you're right. We should just walk away from it and bury the bodies as deeply as we can and hope for the best."

"That's what you want?"

"It's what you want, for Christ's sake!"

He said that too loudly for the library. People turned and glared.

"Don't tell me what I want," Emer said, "and don't put words in my mouth. I believe I'm trying to help both of us."

"I guess I don't want your help. I guess I'll put on my big-boy pants. Let's forget this ever happened."

"Not possible."

"We'll see."

He left without kissing her goodbye.

IF YOU SEE SOMETHING,
SAY SOMETHING

EMER SAT FOR A WHILE, unable to move. Alone. But she was less alone among these books. She could stay in the library forever, happily enough entombed. She decided, strangely for her, to steal the old book—fuck it, you know, where had playing by the rules got her? She was mad and wanted to lodge her protest, if only with the ether; she would take this book. Her heart was beating fast at the prospect of literary theft.

She looked for her backpack to smuggle the pages out. The backpack was gone. It had been right at her feet. She looked around the room; she retraced her steps since entering the building. Nothing. It had her wallet, driver's license and ID, MetroCard, everything. Even her phone. This was a situation. She slipped the ancient book under her shirt and tucked it in. She looked pregnant.

On the verge of panic, she exited the NYPL without triggering any alarms or arousing suspicion, and prepared herself for the lonely walk back home, when she caught sight of a familiar-looking bag sitting atop the trash of a nearby can. She hustled over to it—it was the fabled, the dreaded unattended backpack in midtown Manhattan. It looked very much, no, exactly like hers—but what if someone had put a bomb in it? Or anthrax? Or plutonium? Or whatever the new terrorist sarin du jour was? It could've been out of her sight for over an hour. How long did it take to plant a bomb? How heavy was a bomb? What color was plutonium? What did anthrax look like? She had no clue. We think we have been prepared for modern times, but we have not. She spent most of her time in a school, she was a baby out in the big, bad, real world.

She picked it up. It was heavy, she thought, heavier than when she packed it this morning, it seemed. She unzipped the top slowly to look inside. She got scared. It was definitely her bag. Her wallet and cash, phone, everything still inside. She looked around to see if anyone was watching, transferred the book from her belly to the bag, then slung it over her shoulders, and began jogging uptown to blow off some adrenaline and disappointment, and hoping not to blow up.

Once she got home, she placed the wayward bag on the bed and gingerly went through it more thoroughly, trying to understand the extra weight. It was one of those backpacks for serious hikers, had been a present from Izzy from her Dykes That Hike club a few years ago, with a thousand zippers and what seemed like dozens of different hidden compartments and pockets. She went through them all and couldn't find anything except maybe a strange bulkiness to one of the panels.

She got a knife from the kitchen and cut into the bag, into its lining. A Polaroid picture became visible, and then another. About three stacks of forty old-fashioned Polaroids each packed neatly like bricks of cash or drugs, hidden in the lining of her backpack. Strange enough, but what was even stranger was the relationship documented in the Polaroids. One stack was all of Emer and Con, but not one moment that Emer could remember. Seemingly taken on long-ago vacations, even some taken in Emer's apartment, for which she had absolutely no recollection. Wonderful moments all. It was like a greatest-hits compilation from a band that never existed.

One entire stack seemed to have been taken at a fair where you pop your head through a cardboard diorama and some carny, for a couple bucks, takes your picture as Wild Bill Hickok and Annie Oakley, or Antony and Cleopatra. She flipped through these funny ones—Con as Muhammad Ali and Emer as Joe Frazier, Abbott and Costello, Bonnie and Clyde, Dracula and a victim, Johnny Carson and Ed McMahon, Beavis and Butt-Head—Con and Emer as just about every duo, tragic, comic, and farcical, in history.

The third stack was even more puzzling. It seemed to consist of photos taken from the future. Emer and Con were progressively older in these. This sequence ended with a sweet shot of an old man and woman with their backs to the camera walking away into the sunset on a deserted tropical beach. Into their own sunset as well. Emer couldn't help noticing that her ass had held up pretty well in old age. She laughed at the thought, then froze, overwhelmed finally. Something or someone was really trying to teach her, or touch her. Or fuck with her.

All of a sudden, she felt strangely energized, and ravenous. She didn't feel safe going outside again, so she ordered in from Dragon King.

THE WIFE-DISPELLER

HAN GOT THERE FAST. Emer understood from Han, she thought, that his daughter was doing well, and had passed muster as a fake Christian; she'd been given asylum for now, and was even seeking employment at a local church. Emer didn't know if he was kidding about that last part. Han would not accept payment for the food or a tip, and before he left, cigarette drooping from his lip like a Belmondo with dumplings, asked, "You okay, Teacher?"

"No, Han, I'm not okay."

"Very good."

"Nope."

"Very, very good."

"Glad we talked, Han. Hey, listen, if I need you and your boys tomorrow to, you know, just kind of ride with me, protection, can I call on you?"

"I owe you," he said, and off he went.

Emer poured herself a glass of red wine and ate a little. The doorman, Novak, buzzed up. "May Wang here to see you."

"Wong?"

"What you said."

"Send her up, thanks." Emer couldn't remember if she had exchanged addresses with May. She unlocked her door, and, a minute later, May Wong, Mistress-Dispeller, flowed in dramatically like she was being trailed by an invisible retinue of chattering attendants.

"I have excellent deal for you," she announced, precluding any discussion of how she came to be here by launching immediately into the why.

"What deal?"

"It's a good deal. You know what I do."

"Yes. So?"

"Baby doll, what are you? You're a mistress."

"Oh, fuck. I'm a mistress. I'm not, no, I'm not, but okay, okay."

"A someone come to me and ask me to get rid of you this week."

"Mama Waters."

"Someone, I say. I'm like a priest or psychologist. I don't name names."

"A woman?"

"A woman. Or a man. What's the difference?"

"Black woman? Mama Waters?"

"Mama who-who now? I am like the grave. But if my grave had a headstone, maybe it says Mama something on it." She laughed at her own wit and looked around. "Nice place. Small. Clean."

Emer gulped at her wine; it wasn't strong enough. Of course Mama knows, she thought. And that bitch, she thought. Emer felt a jealousy rise in her she hadn't felt in years, and the will to compete poking out like the sun from clouds.

"And just how did she propose to get rid of me?"

"You're saying 'she,' not me. I found a job for you in Los

Angeles, teach at private school, Crossroad—famous people's kid school—Tom Hank, Henry Winkle, the Fonz—heyyyyy—rent-control apartment in Santa Monica, Tesla—he/she/it/they have a lot of money."

"All that for me? For me to leave Con alone?"

"Yes. You take? We shake."

"I'm tempted. Getting pretty tired of New York."

"I'll go with you. Leonardo DiCaprio is my jam."

"Tesla, huh?"

"Or Porsche. That's what I would choose, Carrera, and Brentwood over Santa Monica, I think—if you wanna play baseball, you can get all that and a bag of chips."

"Would you like a glass of wine?"

She poured May a glass and she poured herself another. The wine made May's cheeks red and relaxed Emer's wild mind, slowed things down a bit for her. How small is the world we live in, she marveled. New York City is still a town, still small in some fundamental way, still human-sized. No matter how big we get, we remain human-sized, she thought, it's our nature. And then again, how many mistress-dispellers must there be in New York City? Five? Twenty-five? One? Another couple sips helped her move from paranoid to comforted by the seeming coincidence in long red nails sitting in front of her.

"May, I'm wondering if you've ever flipped the script."

"What do you mean?"

"I'm wondering if you ever work it the other way around."

"What way round is that?"

"You know, like get rid of a wife, get rid of a wife for a mistress."

"I get rid of man-mistress when man has a mistress who is a man."

"I'm sure. But that's not what I mean."

"But, no, never get rid of wife."

"Wife-dispeller."

"Wife-dispeller, no."

"I don't know. I'm just thinking out loud. You never know, maybe she's not in love anymore, looking for an easy way out."

May Wong shrugged. Emer shrugged in response, and said, "Sometimes people do things just 'cause they think they have to."

"That's American psychology. I say—you make a choice, then the choice makes you, and not vice versa."

"I don't get it."

"Kill her."

"What?"

"Have wife killed."

"You can have her killed?"

"Everybody dies sometimes."

"No!"

"I didn't say I'd do it, but I know people. It's not my preferred way of business, but it's business. You have money?"

"Not really."

"No money."

"Schoolteacher salary."

"Then I'm no wife-dispeller." And she laughed again.

Emer had to laugh with her; the woman had an undeniable force, so Emer felt the need to go on record. "Let's be clear, okay, I do not want to kill anyone, okay?"

"Whatever."

Emer stared at May, but could not figure out the moral code at work here. "Or hurt anyone," she added.

"Yeah, yeah. Boring." May sighed, then continued spitballing. "But what if this wife had another man?"

"What do you mean? The wife is cheating too?" Emer, having narrowly called off a hit on an innocent woman, was now seeking crystal clarity at every foggy turn.

"No," May answered, "but maybe you could find her another man, and she'd be better than she is with this man who cheats."

"Huh."

"That's not really my job, though. You need a professional yenta for that. It's a Jewish area. I stay out, maybe take a finder's fee."

Emer liked this less bloody idea. "But there's something there; it's another way out. Listen to this . . ."

Emer read from her huge, stolen faerie book: "The female Sidh, as well as faeries the world over, such as the Anansi of Africa, or the Salaceto of Brazil and Yitzang of Mongolia, seek the love of mortals. If the mortal refuses, she must be his slave. If the mortal consents, he is hers and can only escape by finding another mortal to take his place."

"That's some kooky shit there. If mortal refuses, then god must be a slave."

"But it's saying—there can be substitutions."

"Gotta serve somebody. For Chinese, three is a lucky number, for marriage-dispeller, two and four are lucky numbers. That's a numerology I like."

"One is the loneliest number."

"Three Dogs Night." Surprised, Emer laughed out loud. "Hey," May said, "don't underestimate me 'cause a my accent, bitch." Then adding, "This wine is nice. So, we have a deal? Should I book your travel to California? I'm also a travel agent. First class."

"Not just yet. Have another glass with me."

THE CALCULUS OF LOVE

GRADUATION DAY at St. Margaret's was a traditionally joyous occasion, though it had been relabeled "Moving Up Day" for terminologically neutral reasons Emer could not recall. Emer had not slept. She had drunk wine and plotted with May Wong all night and then drank coffee all morning—a winning combo breathwise. She looked and smelled like damp laundry. She didn't want to shower, but she forced herself.

She jumped on the subway with her hair still wet and saw that the final voting for the Miss Subways reboot was at the end of the week. She wondered what the polls were saying. She remembered a conversation that her parents had had, more of an argument really, during a presidential election when she was a kid. Maybe it was Bush/Dukakis? And she heard her mom keep repeating, "But the polls are saying something else." And her dad saying, "Fuck the polls, you can't trust the polls!" Young Emer had worried that her parents were weirdly and specifically racist against just Poland and the Poles.

Instructed by May and true to his word, Han and a handful of other Dragon King deliverymen on bikes had accompanied Emer from her subway stop to the school. They hung discreetly on the outskirts of the building smoking cigarettes, looking ridiculous and bad-ass at once. Emer went inside.

As Emer was tidying up her homeroom for the summer break—all the detritus of a year, the nubs of pencils and discarded work sheets—Izzy came to see her. Emer filled her friend in on the pertinent details while omitting almost everything, telling her that she would not see Con anymore (in the cover story, his name was Ken), and adding fictional touches to make the story seem seamless. Emer was surprised at how easily wholesale lying was coming to her, so much so that she preferred to think of it as a "gift for storytelling."

Izzy said the general rule for the length of time to get over a breakup is half the time you were together. Izzy said that Con and Emer were together possibly two days, a few weeks if you take into account the amount of time she spent fantasizing about being together, so she's fairly certain, by her nontrademarked, nonprofessional, nonmathematically rigorous "calculus of love," that Emer would get over Con in anywhere from five minutes to ten days max.

Izzy was optimistic about the whole episode. She was just happy Emer "broke the schneid" and had got back up on the horse and all that shit people say when you get laid after a dry spell. She wanted Emer to think of Con as training wheels for the real man, or bicycle, who's about to come a-callin'.

Hearing Izzy's trivialization of Con made Emer feel more lonely and alone. She just had to get through the rest of this day, and then she was free for the summer. In three months, she lied to Izzy, this thing will become clear, she thought, away from school, away from Sidney, away from New York City, even. Maybe she would quit. Maybe she'd travel Europe before she got too old, write a book. Her dad would miss her, but she thought he'd probably want her to go; the younger version of her dad would've wanted her to go, anyway. She wasn't sure which version of her dad she should be intuiting.

When Izzy left, Emer sat behind her desk, looking out at the empty chairs. She said one last goodbye to her homeroom. She was sentimental like that, attributing feelings to things, and she didn't want the homeroom to feel abandoned. She promised she'd be back. Once she felt the room was properly consoled— didn't take long, rooms were pretty used to being left—she leaned back and could place all the faces from this year in their assigned seats. And she could do the same for last year and the year before, up to maybe five years ago—interlaying the faces of the children with the faces of the children that came before, like trick photography, the faces morphing, like in that old Michael Jackson video, "Black or White," was it? Where what was amazing was not how different the faces were, as you might expect, but how similar, even through drastic changes in skin tone and features. It didn't seem like there was much that needed to be changed to get from face to face. We all look alike, are alike.

This sameness, over the years and from day to day, weighed upon Emer in this moment, and it did not feel liberating, it felt incarcerating. Black or white, today or fifteen years ago, now or then—the difference was a trick, an optical illusion, the sameness was the truth. Time seemed to move, but only laterally.

She closed her eyes and heard the ticking of the clock; the spell was broken by the sound of Sidney's singing coming down the hallway toward her: "In the words of the immortal Barry Manilow—'looks like we made it.'"

When Emer looked at Sidney now, she saw Sidhe, and when she thought of Sidhe, she saw Sidney; it was frustrating and unsettling. "So far, so good," she replied.

"You haven't seen him?"

"No," she lied.

"He hasn't tried to contact you?" Sidney sat down.

"No, it's over."

"You know, Emer, I am of two minds." That's exactly what she had been thinking, yes. Was she a puppeteer and the world on her string? Or was she a puppet convinced by the string in her hand that she was not?

"Yes, I know." She vaguely agreed so as not to show her hand.

"I am both what I do and who I am. I am the head of this school, but I am also a man. I am your boss, but I am also your friend, at least I hope I am."

"Thank you, Sidney, I think I understand."

"I prefer when you call me Sid, it's been almost twenty years." He laughed. "May I confide in you, Emer, as you have in me?"

"You don't have to."

"But I feel that I own this terrible secret of yours and it gives me a power over you I do not want and I do not enjoy, and if I were to repay you in kind with a secret of my own, we might recover more even footing."

"That makes sense, actually."

"I am also dealing with love." Holy shit, this was not what she bargained for. "Also a love that dare not speak its name. And I have been thinking about love, all different kinds of love, the love we have for a lover, the love we have for Christ, and speaking to you as a friend now, I wonder, I guess I'm wondering aloud, isn't it all part of the same love? Isn't all love good? Isn't love what binds us all together? Not in who we love, but in the mere brute fact that we love?"

"Yes, Sid, I think that's true."

"I've spent my life, lifetimes it seems, denying who I am. Is that what God wants?"

"I don't think so, Sid."

"Lifetimes, my dear. Do you know what I'm telling you now, as a friend, as a man?"

"Not really, but enough."

"We are all doubles of ourselves. We all inhabit our prosaic space and our magical space, like a strobe light. At rare times, the spaces line up and we are one thing. Like now. You know now who and what I am?"

Emer allowed that declarative question to settle like a pebble falling through water. She faced up to Sidney, held his gaze and held her ground. "You are Sid."

"Then speak to me as Sid."

"I'm afraid."

"Figure your way through."

"I feel like my deal sucks."

"You want to renegotiate?"

"Why was I picked?"

"Picked?"

"I did nothing to bring this on."

"Of course you did. And anyway, inaction is a type of action, so I daresay you are damned if you do or don't. Causality is a road from nowhere to somewhere else called nowhere. Do you know about our school's namesake, Saint Margaret of Antioch?"

"No."

"She took a vow of celibacy, but was forced to marry a pagan. The vow didn't sit well with him, so he had her imprisoned. Satan visited her in jail in the guise of a dragon and swallowed her. She used the handy cross around her neck to cut her way out of the belly of the beast. That was Saint Margaret. Damn, I miss those days."

"Was that advice?"

"I'm not sure myself. We are limited by our masters. You cannot be a priest, I cannot be a lover. Listen, Emer, if you want to renegotiate something, you need to offer something else in return, for new terms."

"That's what I'm talking about."

"What have we got?"

"Maybe I just quit. Maybe I choose perfection of the life over perfection of the work."

"I don't know that quitting is an option."

"I'm not sure perfection is either."

"I can't believe I'm weighing in on this like I said I wouldn't, but maybe you have more power than you think you do, and maybe the other woman doesn't have the power she claims to have. Maybe she's all talk."

"And maybe you are too."

Sidney smiled and got up. "Well, that is another gamble you have to be prepared to take, I suppose."

They stared at each other. She wanted to scream. She wanted somebody to level with her, or at least tell her what level she was dealing with. Finally, she spoke.

"Isn't there anything I can give you just to leave me alone?"

Sidney seemed saddened by that request, almost hurt. "There

could be, though I think I've been clear with you. Schools have rules. Obedience to the rules is how we pay our debt to the future. Speaking of which, congratulations on another year in the books—tits and teeth, Emer—all is as it is. One of the lies we tell these children is that reason will get them through life."

He broke out in a laugh so violent, dismissive, sad, and downright weird that Emer recoiled slightly. It took him almost a minute to compose himself. "Okay, let's graduate these brats and show them nothing of the hell that awaits them. Tits and teeth."

Emer straightened her back. "Tits and teeth," she hissed back at her boss through gritted teeth. "For sure, but Sidney, I want you to meet someone first, someone who understands dual nature and doesn't give a rat's ass about any of it."

Emer called down the quiet hallway, "May?"

Stiletto strikes echoed off linoleum like a queenly fanfare, and May Wong materialized in the doorway.

"I want you two to talk," Emer said.

PEACE TRAIN

TITS AND TEETH" was another Sidney-ism. Emer thought he might've stolen it from the dancing world, where choreographers would tell their charges not to show the strain and sweat but only the pride—the leading chest and white smile. It was a variant on "stiff upper lip," but Emer much preferred it. How the little priest had intersected with the world of dance, she would speculate on some other day.

As Emer stood and sat and stood and sat in her row with her nineteenth graduating class, singing the obligatory hymns and listening to speeches these children would never understand or remember, she cried big fat tears. It was an occasion like that, so she felt she could cry for everything under cover of graduation day; tears in drag, in a way. The children sitting next to her felt a little concern for their blubbering teacher, but even this Emer felt to be a "teaching moment"—to show the kids it was okay to cry, okay to give in to deep joyous sadness in public.

Whenever she felt safe enough, she would glance to the back

of the church to see where Con and Mama were with Ashia. She didn't see him, but they both most certainly were present for their daughter's last day of school; she could feel eyes on her back, like she might be ambushed. She saw Sidney and May talking. She saw Shoshanna Schwartz-Silberman and her parents. She even kissed Debbie Schwartz-Silberman's cheek. All was water under the bridge. She saw a happy Maya O'Connor and her mother. Her phone dinged. She wouldn't look. Little Ashia hugged her from behind and gave her a big kiss, and it was then she saw Ashia's parents hanging back politely. Everyone was being well heeled, thus far.

Summer was almost here. Ah, summer. One thing about teaching was you never gave up that blessed relief come summermertime—it still meant freedom from work and all those things that it means to little children. Some days, Emer liked that she retained this childish glee at coming June, some days she felt ashamed that she had never grown out of it.

As the procession came to a close, Emer stood at the head of a receiving line for her kids—to kiss them and shake their hands. This was the final goodbye. Her posture was perfect and she had the easy magnanimity of a head of state receiving guests, five seconds at a time, at some ceremonial function. Like a prince, she never looked down the line to see who was coming up, only straight ahead at who was directly in front of her. She had seen Bill Clinton in person once act like this—focused on a point two feet directly in front of his nose as the people entered his space, into his focus and out, yet his sovereign focus never changed. He made you feel like there was no past or future, only this present with him, and then it was over.

Emer did her best Bill Clinton. Moving on. Most of the rest of the parents and kids waltzed in and out of her focus as her thoughts wandered to the subway and getting out of there. And it went off without incident. They were all civilized twenty-first-century people. Apparently.

UNDERGROUND WOMAN

THERE WAS STILL A CROWD to get through outside the school, kids of all ages and their parents, and though Emer wanted to avoid everyone, she was stopped and pigeonholed by a few upperclassmen, former students who wanted to show off how mature they'd become. Though it was mildly unsettling when the fifteen-year-old boys wanted to flirt harmlessly with their passably hot former grade school teacher, calling her by her first name or using "Ms. Emer" with sly imprecise irony, Emer knew they simply yearned for acknowledgment as the men they'd become, or were becoming. Emer understood it was her duty to mirror their masculinity back to them without confusing them with any actual intent, crossing any lines, or blurring any boundaries. She knew how to do it, how to act slightly abashed yet impressed at their literally sophomoric innuendo, though her awareness of lines and crossing them was in a bit of disrepair at the moment.

She backed away and nodded and smiled and inched her way to the perimeter of the crowd. She stepped off into the street, turned, and pointed herself to the subway. Three blocks to freedom. As the delivery convoy fell in around her, she felt nearly invincible.

She also felt like she was being followed, by whom she wasn't sure. It could be Con, it could be Mama, it could be Sid. Six months ago, no one would follow her to the train, now maybe three people were. Things were looking up. She noticed Han, with a worried aspect, at the entrance to the station. "Can't go underground," he said. "Get ticket. Moto." He pointed to the motor on his bike. Foiled by the rules again. Emer waved goodbye to the two-wheeler armada and descended. It was her graduation day too, and she'd have to go it alone.

She swiped her MetroCard and waited for the train. An a capella quartet sang the Clash's "Should I Stay or Should I Go" as the waiting people wearing headphones ignored them. Emer knew now that riff would take up residence in her mind for the next hour, or week—"If I go there will be trouble / If I stay it could be double." She scooped her hand along the bottom of her knapsack and came up with a handful of change and some gum. She put the change into the hat by the singers and the gum in her mouth. The train came and the doors opened.

As she was stepping aboard, she glanced right and left, and caught a glimpse a few cars down of what might've been Mama. Emer got on the car, walked to the window where the cars were connected, and peered through. It was. It was Mama, a couple cars back, walking toward her. Emer turned and headed up the other way. She walked through two cars. When the train stopped at the next station, she poked her head out and looked left. Two cars down, Mama had her head out of the car, looking around. Emer felt Mama couldn't really pull anything in public like this. Could she? Emer knew she didn't have to run, but she was running anyway. She kept moving up the cars.

At the next stop, she repeated her lookout. She looked down and left—there was Mama again and this time their eyes met. Emer stepped out onto the platform, Mama followed suit about twenty yards away. As the doors were closing, Emer lunged back in. She'd seen that move done in movies. It didn't work in movies and it didn't work today. She saw Mama successfully reenter the car, heading her way.

Emer walked all the way to the front of the train, moving slowly from the lit platform into darkness. She was trapped. She reached up and put her hand on the emergency brake. She'd never done that before. In New York you'd have to be pretty fucking sure some apocalyptic shit was going down before you pulled that thing—like a damn velociraptor on the loose would be the bare minimum reason. She wasn't even sure it was connected. But she pulled it, hard, and it worked. That it worked exactly as it was supposed to surprised her and made her laugh.

Even though the train was not nearly at full speed, some people were thrown off balance by the sudden stoppage, and Emer took advantage of the confusion to head to the doors in between the cars. She got out and jumped down on the tracks. She was aware she might be completely overreacting. It was like she was hearing another voice in her head, and that was the voice she decided to listen to; it would tell her what to do.

MYSTERY TRAIN

SHE'D NEVER BEEN DOWN on the actual subway tracks before. It was dark and hot, and the filth seemed sedimented but somehow loose. Even the detritus had detritus. She had to squeeze her way along the wall for the length of the lead subway car before she could see open track.

The tunnel felt more, when you were in it, like a cave than something man-made. It felt as wild as untouched nature somehow. The tunnels were built in 1904, and well over a century of hidden, festering shit down here threatened to overload Emer's already feverish imagination. There was some light thrown by the grimy bulbs along the way. Emer was scared of being crushed, but she felt she'd be able to see the headlights of a train coming down the darkened track and get out of the way in time. She didn't know what the next station was. She hadn't thought that far ahead, she hadn't thought ahead at all. She kept walking on toward a light that was reaching her weakly around a curve in the tracks a few hundred yards away.

She tried not to look down at her feet or get consumed by the fear of skittering noises and darting shadows—rats, no doubt. Somehow rats were the most mundane explanation for the noises and movements; the alternatives were even more ghastly and terrifying. There were plenty of signs of life down here, too many, actually. She never thought she'd be comforted by the thought of giant rats at her feet, but she was. Almost.

She followed the curve toward the light, and saw ahead that it was the Eighteenth Street ghost station. But before she made it to the platform, awkward, angled movement—like big animals, not rats, awaking from sleep—caught her eye and stole her breath. She turned to see a figure, a man it must be, or a bear, walking slowly toward her. As her eyes became more adjusted to the darkness in the tunnel, more shapes became apparent to her—people—men, women, and even little tents. This was some sort of encampment. This must be one of those homeless communities she'd read about that somehow survive winters, summers, and persecution in the tunnels. The ghost station would make the best place for the forgotten ghosts among us to make a home.

The hulking man approached. There was no emergency brake to pull now. He flashed a bright light in Emer's face, blinding her—he had a cell phone with a flashlight app, of course he did, of course a homeless man had a smartphone. He grabbed her, hoisting her over his shoulder as easily as a backpack; he was preternaturally strong, and moved with the impossible, jittery speed of a horror-movie predator. He carried her deeper into the tunnel and away from the light of the tracks.

He put his hand, the size of a skillet, over her mouth, nose, and eyes. Now she felt real, focused, pointed fear, enveloped in his moving embrace; he smelled of piss and shit and a long-unwashed *Homo sapiens* musk. Her bile rose.

"Please don't hurt me," she said.

Finally, he put her down. She didn't know where she was, but she could see it was inside this camp of sorts. There were twenty or thirty people living in the abandoned tunnel, as well as some dogs—but no, as Emer calmed herself a bit, to her amazement, what looked to be dogs were . . . alligators? Whitish yellow alligators, mythical albino alligators, maybe five or six of them in a makeshift pen. She'd heard all the apocryphal stories since childhood, of the pet baby alligator craze in the '50s that had people flushing the growing beasts down their toilets when they had gotten less cute, and the amphibians had survived in the sewers, so the stories went.

She'd thought so much was myth before the last few months. Her mind immediately started to square this impossibility to a new worldview. It made sense that the alligators would become a race of albinos, never having seen the light of day—thank goodness. Then she caught herself making sense within the nonsense. Amazing how life adapts, it all makes scientific sense, blah blah blah, but the white lizards were terrifying to look at. They were smaller and less muscular than their aboveground swamp counterparts, but eerie, uncanny, and the color of dead fish.

The area was lit by candle and cell phone. There were drawings on the walls like the cave paintings at Altamira crossed with Keith Haring graffiti. Many images were crude and silly and pop culture oriented, a hodge-podge pantheon—a lot of Michael Jackson, Prince, some *Game of Thrones*, Kurt Cobain, but there were also some Egyptian-looking ones that had bodies of people and the heads of these albino alligators. Like the white alligator was their totem.

"I know you," her abductor said.

"I don't think so."

"They call me Golem," he said, covering himself in the dark cloth of the mythical Jewish Frankensteinian avenger entity. "We've existed throughout most of European history. Jews made our particular race down here in the subways in the late '30s and '40s, but don't have much use for us anymore, it seems. But we wait, we wait. You never know when our time may come again."

She tried to define his features in the near dark, and they did seem to be melting, morphing in the flickering light—half formed, blocky, left in haste by a maker; as if indeed conjured from the clay of disenfranchised, human despair.

"I know you," Golem said again vehemently.

Emer pulled back, relieved to create distance from the veritable force field of his funk. "Well—you live here in the subways, I take the subways, I look out the windows, maybe you've seen me on the trains?"

"Yes, yes, that's it!"

Emer was relieved that it was so easy.

Golem took an instinctive, reverent step back, lowered his gaze, and dropped to one knee. "You're Miss Subways!"

Emer wasn't sure she should accept or reject this homage. "No, no, I'm not, that's not right. The voting isn't even over."

When Golem looked up again, there were tears in his eyes, streaking darkly down the soot on his face, smearing the clay cheeks. He pulled a loop of string from his pocket, and something dangling caught the light.

"How long I've been searching for you. I've caught glimpses of you, in my mind, I thought. Ages searching. To give you this." He spread open the string with filthy, giant, gentle hands and placed the necklace over her head. Emer could now see clearly what it was—the silver token, the trophy given to every Miss Subways winner. "So no harm may come to you."

He called out to the rest of the encampment—"Hey, everyone, over here! Miss Subways!" He turned back to Emer and whispered, "I was created for the likes of you. Many of us were created for you. We are the offspring of the disempowered and the weak. We are their fears animated, made quasi-flesh, given all the strength of their hopes and desire for revenge. You know what golems are."

"I've heard and I've read. But it's an Eastern European myth. I mean, I'm sorry if that's insulting. To call you a myth. I'm just so confused."

Golem reached down to the subway rail beneath him, saying, "Is this a myth?" and with one hand, twisted the third rail at a right angle to itself.

"You make a powerful case," Emer said.

"And you," Golem continued, "you are Miss Subways. Stop denying your power."

One by one, the homeless came toward her, shuffling and groaning in spastic motion, as if a movie were playing with random frames spliced out.

"It's time to engage with your adoring public," the man said. "Meet the ninety-nine percent."

She had no idea what they were going to do to her now. A few of the men and women began to emulate Golem and kneel at her feet, murmuring about Miss Subways this and Miss Subways that.

"They won't hurt you," Golem said. "You are their token woman, their queen, their genius loci. As long as you remain underground, we will give our lives, such as they are, to protect you."

"I'm no one's queen."

"Everyone is someone's queen."

"Are you keeping me here?"

"That medallion ain't chopped liver," he said, touching the token around her neck, making it swing into the light. "You are Miss Subways, you ride anywhere for free."

TOKEN WOMAN

DEATHLING!"

From the darkness, the shout came echoing down the tunnel, and again, "Deathling!" The homeless, the unemployed golem, turned to face the approach, casting their candles and cell phones that way, creating a spotlight for the entrance of a villain. Emer recognized the voice of Mama Waters, but the golem were suddenly perturbed, whispering among themselves a name, in tones respectful and afraid—Anansi. Emer knew the name from dreams and half-remembered reading, but now something clicked, as when one goes from learning a language to fluency one day.

The golem backed off a bit. Emer felt a chill on her skin as their warming bodies withdrew. Golem cast a disapproving eye upon his brothers and stood tall with his Miss Subways. He steadied her with his bloodless, cold clay hand. Emer faced her accuser, Mama, no, Anansi. Anansi spoke first. Her long dreadlocks had turned into hissing red, yellow, green, and black snakes, all traces of Mama's politeness erased by the haughty grandeur of a goddess.

"There you are, Deathling. You can't hide from me, even amongst your tough Jews here."

"I'm not hiding."

"I see your talisman. You are hiding underground. You're trying to steal my man."

"But I didn't know."

"This is not a court of law. You will soon find that out."

"Do you even want him?"

"It does not fall to you to ask questions of the gods, Deathling. You have injured my pride. In your racial, cultural ignorance, you may not know me well, but you know your Greek myths, your Western ways, think back on those instructive stories and how the gods punished the humans who stole their men or their women—turning them into trees and deer, drowning them in their watery reflections."

"But I didn't know."

"That is precisely the human crime."

Emer looked at Golem, whose blunt clay face remained impassive. He shrugged. Emer somehow found courage in that.

"But what of your crime?" Emer shouted. "You stole Con from me with the promise of talent and fame, but you gave him nothing."

"I keep him very well."

"You keep him, yes, you keep him silent, unrealized, like a half-made man."

"You know nothing of our deal or of the way I make deals. My deals change with the wind."

Emer felt like a child arguing with an adult who held all the cards. "Can't we reason together? Come to a new arrangement?"

"You ask a goddess to negotiate?"

"Why not? We are women. Rational women."

"I will roast your eyes on spits and drink your blood."

"Okay, well, that's . . . that's an opening position."

"Shut the fuck up."

"That's not fair."

"Fair? Who ever promised you fair, Deathling? You are in the realm of gods now. You will feel fair ripped from your weak whining heart soon."

The raised voices were riling up the albino alligators; they snapped at the air with their terrible teeth, the palpable confusion compelling them to nip at one another, seeking an outlet. But they seemed to calm when Emer got near them, and even wag their tails like dinosaur dogs. She saw a flicker of doubt in Anansi's eyes, and it emboldened her. She put her hand on what appeared to be a gate, a threat. Emer pressed—"And what of your real remaining powers in this new world and here, underground?"

"My powers?"

"You are far from Africa. It's been hundreds of years. You have lost your flock. Maybe you've lost touch. Maybe you're obsolete."

"Keep at it, Deathling. You will soon feel what is left of my power."

Emer felt a child's righteousness rise up within her, a wave of unearned certainty that she had no choice but to ride. She surmised from her knowledge of aboveground deities losing potency in the underworld, and took a flier—"Your magic and your deals and your wagers, your pride and your beauty, have no place down here where I am queen."

Emer opened the gate. The ghostly alligators spilled out one over the other and surrounded her like spastic plastic bodyguards. Anansi's dread snakes recoiled, and the goddess took a nervous step backward.

"I am Miss Subways," Emer announced, "and I have powers of my own."

The rest of the golem stood up a bit straighter.

"You don't know who or what you're fucking with." Anansi sounded hollow.

Emer pushed forward. "How can you know what love is? You can't die. All you have is pride, that's not love. In order to love, you have to know what death is."

"You lecture me. You make no sense."

"I make sense to the living. You've come down here to teach me a lesson, but it's you who will learn from me."

The homeless, rallied by Emer's speech, goaded by their queen, their very own Miss Subways, had now fully recovered their nerve. They joined the alligators in a shrinking circle around Anansi.

"Look at your timebound minions, deformed losers and reptiles!"

"You sound scared."

"The deathless cannot know fear."

"Maybe that's the problem right there. How can you love without fear?"

Emer knew that as she could not die, Anansi's deathlessness was the key to her misunderstanding. For a moment, Anansi's head tilted and her eyes refocused, like a dog hearing a new word, a new command she could not quite fathom. Just a moment, though, and then the familiar superiority returned to her gaze.

"That's fine," said Anansi, recoiling as an alligator snapped at her foot. "But what happens when you resurface, Miss Subways? Are you sure your newfound influence extends to the up-top world?"

Emer hadn't thought this through. She knew about "fight or flight." She knew she was running toward something more than she was running from something. She hoped that fine distinction would save her, but of course, she wasn't sure. With Anansi stalled, ringed by snapping alligators and powerful golems, her Medusa snakes turning on and biting at one another, Emer backed away and ran down the dark tunnel. She was fleeing to the next station, and from there to where, she didn't know.

REVENGE OF THE DEATHLINGS

WHEN EMER, WALKING UPTOWN she figured, got to the next live station, she climbed up on the platform, and stood and waited in the light for the train. She did not want to go aboveground; she was in her element. She felt deputized by Golem, and at least part goddess-like. She could hear Anansi screaming like a banshee down the tunnel from where she had come. But then suddenly all went unnaturally silent from that direction.

A train moving downtown pulled in at the platform across the tracks from Emer, and then moved on. When it had cleared, two men and a woman were standing on the platform. Con and Sidney, or this must be Sidhe, as he had the doorman's livery on again. Sidhe stood a step behind Con, in the classic old-movie pose of one man surreptitiously holding a gun to the small of another man's back. But Sidhe didn't need a gun; he had the power of the ages in his tiny hands. May Wong stood with the two men.

"We make deals," May Wong crowed, grimacing while trying to remove a wad of gum from a stiletto.

"Emer!" Con, his voice tight, rattled out.

Before Emer could say anything, she saw Con look back uptown on the tracks. Emer followed his eyes, but could only make out a large shadow moving inhumanly toward them, as if floating, or scuttling without ambulatory gait, low to the ground. With a surprising speed that seemed to ignore gravity, the shadow scampered up the platform and into the light—a man-sized spider.

Emer felt the revulsion rise up in her throat as the giant spider, followed by a repulsive retinue of New York's finest plump and nasty gray rats, slid to within a few feet of Con and Sidhe. When the spider came to a stop, though it wasn't quite a full stop, as appendages and hairy antennae-seeming protrusions kept pulsating and wiggling, Emer could see blood dripping from its saber-like, mammalian-thick fangs, bits of albino alligator flesh stuck between, spraying out. The rats, like the remora fish that tag along beneath sharks, fought over scraps of bloody flesh and clay.

Emer looked north and south, uptown and downtown, but there were no signs of more trains coming or going. There would be none for a while, she figured. By pulling the emergency brake, she had brought the system to a temporary standstill. Tens of thousands of New Yorkers, above, below, and on all sides of her were, at this very moment, though they had no idea who she was, cursing her quite creatively.

The giant spider advanced slowly on Con, oozing some sort of sticky web-making matter from her belly as she dragged along. Anansi's voice was altered through her new physiognomy, sounding still human enough to be understood, but also mealymouthed and underwater, as though her vocal cords were located in her wet and bloody guts.

"Connie," she said, "you can't leave me. You know what happens if you do."

"Yes, I know the threats."

"You call this a threat, Deathling!?"

The spider rose up vertically on two of her eight spiked legs, her hourglass figure now looming over Con, her serrated back teeth exposed and gnashing. Veering suddenly toward May Wong, the spider unleashed a torrent from her abdomen that covered the mistress-dispeller from head to toe in a web cocoon, wrapping her with articulate legs like a butcher wraps a cut of meat in brown paper. She stuck a fang in the white bundle; blood oozed. Emer heard a muffled, moaned terrified curse escape from within the web.

Con found the nerve to insert himself between May and the spider. As the rats began to nibble at the squirming, screaming cocoon that had been May moments before, Emer watched the spider turn back to Con and release from that red mark on her abdomen another stream of what looked to Emer to be cotton candy. Even from across the tracks, Emer could smell the rancid earthiness of this ejaculate. The spider slung a few strands jauntily about Con's midsection.

Sidhe had backed away and remained apart, seemingly unperturbed. He looked admiringly at Anansi the spider in much the same way one god might admire the special powers of another, like Zeus contemplating Neptune's special way with water.

Emer called out to Con from across the tracks. "If you reject her love, she has to obey you."

Con took that in, clearly frightened into near paralysis, and called back to Emer, "Are you sure?"

"Not at all!"

"What?"

"Try it!"

Con turned to Anansi and pleaded, "Mama, please stop."

"No!" Emer shouted. "Reject her love, goddammit! Man up!" The spider kept wrapping sticky strands around Con's legs. It seemed to Emer that Anansi was all spider now. The webbing reached Con's knees; he turned back to the mammoth spider busy entombing him to eat later.

"I reject you!" he managed, choking in fear. The spider paused for a moment, then went back to wrapping him.

"Louder!" Emer yelled. "Say it again! Reject her love! Be a king!"

Con spoke up this time. "I reject your love!"

The spider stopped in mid-stranding, its awful belly opening-closing anxiously, like the nostril of a winded beast. For Emer, Con had found an ancient reserve of power, and he doubled down. "Remove this web!" he commanded. "Now!"

Dutifully, like a dog, the spider began unwrapping the web from Con, inhaling the sticky substance in reverse.

Con had to hide his disbelief and pleasure. Emboldened, he turned back to address Emer across the tracks. "What you did for me, the sacrifices you made. I understand now. Sid told me everything. Told me what you did before, in other times."

The spider seemed to find something new to be angry about, turning her attention from Con and advancing upon Sidhe, flashing fangs, spraying bloody alligator flesh. "You! You Irish meddler. You've been messing with me from the start, for centuries. I may not kill Cuchulain, but I will relish a small meal, a fucking appetizer, like you." She sprayed Sidhe with her web material, but he nimbly avoided most of it, light on his toes like a river dancer.

"Whoa, whoa, hey now—the Deathlings have a point. You have not been true to your word, the deal you offered him."

"No one here has been true! Dwarf! If she has contact with him, are you not supposed to collect her life? Are your powers so diminished?"

"I may not be the demon I was, but mark me, Spider, I will still give you fifteen seconds of hell."

"So you say," Anansi continued, extending one of her eight legs to point at Emer across the tracks. "But if she were dead, Cuchulain would love me again."

"Ah, that is so, Spider. That is so. Emer . . ." Sidhe called over to Emer. "That is so. But you and I . . ." He turned back to Anansi. "We are defined by where we came from and our ancient loves and hatreds, yes, but are we not also defined by our adaptability, by our uncanny knack for survival?"

Sidhe reached out and grabbed a handful of the web that clung to him, then he put it in his mouth like the cotton candy it resembled. If spiders could blush, perhaps Anansi did, or so it seemed to Emer, from where she stood.

"You Irish, little Irish thing, think you can consort with me?"

"Why not?" answered Sidhe, his mouth half full of web. "I know it sounds disgusting to you, and perhaps we'd make a laughable couple walking down the street, but I have to say, lass, you are a beautiful thing yourself, and maybe it's time, after all these years in the New World, to lay down our arms—in your case, all eight of them—and embrace. I am for you what you are for me—your way out, and your way in."

The spider grew still, six of those eight legs motionless, and looked across at Emer, then she looked at Con. Sidhe continued, "I believe we are talking about pride now, not love. Believe me, I know of injured pride. I've had to swallow mine and take Jesuit orders for the past hundred years! Me, a proud natural son of pagan Ireland—a fecking priest!" Sidhe's pain and humiliation were real, and the spider saw it.

"Isn't it just that you need someone to worship you? What matter if it's this handsome Gancanagh, a king, or a demon like myself? Is it not more epic to have conquered a miraculous thing like me?"

Sidhe managed, high on his own deal-making sprezzatura, to shoot a wink at Emer. Anansi nodded.

"Would you like to approach me?" the spider asked/threatened Sidhe.

"Oh, very much so. I think."

Emer didn't like this, she feared for more bloodshed. She warned, "Careful, Sid."

Still, Sidhe walked to the spider. He reached her red navel.

"You're repulsive," the spider told the demon.

"I'm repulsive?" He laughed. "Have you looked in a mirror recently? Ah well, even through that hairy skin, I can see you. You're beautiful."

The little man kissed the spider's hideous, fanged mouth. Sidhe pulled back and looked out at Emer, stage whispering, "Not great. I'm not gonna lie, that wasn't great, but not terrible either. As first kisses go, I've had worse. Once in County Galway, after a long night drinking . . . well, that's a story for another time." He rose up on his tiptoes and kissed the drooling maw again.

Instantly, miraculously, Anansi was transformed into her stunning self again, with her perfect skin and piercing yellow-green parrot eyes.

"I am beautiful, thigh-high."

"You've been beautiful for centuries."

"Centuries?"

"From the first time I laid eyes on you, the real you under that Harryhausen disguise, when you came to this country four hundred years ago."

"Came? You mean kidnapped. Enslaved. Not by love, but by greed."

Sidhe kept talking, like the snake charmer, like the spider charmer, he was. Though Anansi was a beautiful woman once again, he still came only to her waist. Sid kept at her, though, drowning her in waves of words, like waves that wear down rock. "We've both been abandoned by people. We're both lonely. I'm crossing that ancient street, my dear, my spider—this Irish demon knows you as woman, goddess, spider, trickster, all your names— all that you are, and he loves you as you really are, as you always were."

Sidhe, on tiptoe, reached up and put his hand gently, but firmly, behind Anansi's neck, pulling her face down to meet his, and kissed her a third time. This time with her full acquiescence. In the middle of this long embrace, he was lengthened out as if in a fun house mirror, but still handsome, transformed to her height.

Sidhe smiled and took a step back so they both could take in his full measure, saying, "Love makes a man grow." Anansi tilted her head to the side coyly, her green eyes fluttering—

"This whole wager with the Deathlings was for me? To get to me?"

"Would you like me to say yes?"

"Yes, Changeling. That pleases me."

"Then, yes. All for you. It has all been for you. We must

be changelings, goddess. Adapt or die. And love is the agent of change; love is a changeling. You must admit—Sid and Anansi has a ring to it. We will have beautiful, powerful children with unknown powers," Sid boasted.

Anansi smiled. "Don't get too far ahead of yourself there, big guy."

Emer believed everything now, like a child. She smiled, like a child. She was free. And Con was free.

During the confrontation between Sidhe and Anansi, Emer had pretty much forgotten about Con. He had moved away down the platform from the supernatural couple, and now he yelled back, "We also need another start, Emer."

"What do you mean?" Emer had a bad feeling again.

"Too much history, there's such a thing as too much history. We've fucked it all up. I fucked it up. It's me. We need a clean slate. I can never repay your bravery and sacrifice. I'll always be in arrears with you, like I was with Anansi. That will doom us. That won't work. I want to be with you, but not like this, not as the man I am. You were right about me, Emer, I've been lazy and asleep."

Emer felt the ground rumble, and that rumble building. The subway must be up and running again. A 1 train was coming.

"You've proved your love for me, but I've never proved anything for you."

"That's not true!" Emer protested. "You just did!"

The train moved closer. Emer craned to look down the opposite tracks and saw the headlights pointing their way.

"A deal's a deal," Con said.

"Wait," Emer called to Sidhe. "You're still telling me I can't see him?"

Sidney echoed Con, "A deal's a deal, and a man's greatest treasure is his word, but maybe we can work something out. Anansi, my dear, do you think you might unwrap the Chinese woman? She is quite the deal maker."

Anansi looked at the bleeding cocoon as if for the first time. "Oh Lord, I'm sorry. I go into a funk when I change."

"No need for apologies, my arachnid," Sidhe said.

Anansi and Sidhe began to unwrap the still-breathing May Wong. When her mouth was clear, May threw some legit shade at Anansi. "You a bitch, bitch."

"You hear that, Con?" Emer called out hopefully. "Maybe we can work something out. All of us."

"No," Con said darkly. "No more deals. No more shortcuts, no more half measures, no more lies."

Sidhe moaned, "Oh Jesus Christ, a romantic," and then took out his phone to film the action.

"Emer!" Con called out, and locked his eyes on her. Emer locked back. He announced: "I am coming for you."

As the train barreled forward, Emer watched Con take another step toward her, as calmly as a man walking in the park. His feet were now on the pebbled bright yellow that forms a type of warning track on the edge of the platform.

"Con!" Emer screamed. "No!"

"See you soon," Con promised as he took one more step toward the tracks and the oncoming train, his eyes never leaving Emer, and for a moment hung in the air like a man flying, like a man free.

Then he disappeared with a sickening thump.

And the world went black.

PART
3

Well the danger on the rocks is surely past
Still I remain tied to the mast
Could it be that I have found my home at last
Home at last

— STEELY DAN, "Home At Last"

"GODSFORSAKEN"

EMER CLOSED HER EYES and did her best to shut out the nervous noises. She allowed stray sounds to swirl into an undefined oceanic swell, an ear trick that was the aural equivalent of letting her eyes unfocus. The blackness and blankness calmed her. The dark—nothing—nothing is nothing to be feared, her father always said. This was the nothing before the something. The nothing before and after the something. The nothing was there before there was something and would be waiting when the something was done. From nothing to nothing we come and go. She breathed it in.

She found nothing comforting. So comforting that she opened her eyes.

Good evening. My name is Emer Gunnels and I want to read to you tonight from a new work of mine called Godsforsaken. *I don't want to be prejudicial, but as a historian turned novelist, I do want to give you a context, share my frame of mind as I sat down to write this book. It was during that horrible election year, and there was all this talk of men being afraid of women, and the changing of the guard, and real vitriol about immigration and terrorism and building that stupid wall. I was thinking deeply about the immigration of people and the immigration of those people's god or gods from whatever countries they were coming from—Mexico, Syria, Niger—wherever. And how our xenophobic response to them was twofold—both as physical beings who would use up our precious resources and as spiritual/religious beings who would undermine our monotheistic Judeo-Christian resource—and it got me thinking about all the waves of spiritual immigration that we have undergone as an immigrant nation and whether our response now would be a contraction out of some neurotic need for purity and order, or an expansion and embrace.*

My mom loved dogs. But she loved mutts most of all. She said they were inherently grateful, and that gratitude was the "queen of all feeling." But most of all, Mom said that mixed breeds had "mongrel vigor"—you know, the crazy expansion of the canine gene pool. And I started to think, in the time of the first incarnation of the Orange Julius, shouldn't ideas and gods and spiritual health adhere to the same law of mongrel vigor? You know, let the best woman win. Let the best ideas fight, fuck, and win. Let the fittest gods survive, and by fittest, I don't mean most powerful, I mean the ones that help us live best and attain our full and contradictory human potential. This struggle is a moral good. As John Milton put it centuries ago in Areopagitica: *"I cannot praise a fugitive and cloistered virtue, unexercised and unbreathed, that never sallies out and sees her adversary." Ideas should be engaged in the same Darwinian struggle as all the rest of life. Everybody in the pool!*

But this sounds like a lecture, and what I set out to do was create a thing of pleasure for y'all—a story. Part history, part shaggy-

dog story or fisherman's tale—Fishtory, if you will. Beyond any moralizing, you see, I wanted to write a nouveau New York docu-noir, that went from black and white to Technicolor when you blinked your eyes.

Emer inhaled deeply, opened the book in front of her. She began to read from her sovereign work.

HOME AT LAST

SHE WAS AT THE AFTER-PARTY for her reading, a glass of wine in her hand, and Izzy by her side. "It's your best work yet," Izzy said, already half in her cups. "Before, you were good, but I felt, 'cause I know you, you were writing like twenty percent dumber than you are, but now you're writing like fifteen percent smarter than you are, somehow, which is a full fifty percent smarter than me so I don't know what the fuck I'm talking about—'cause some old Russian Jew lady poured me a bunch of Manischewitz from a Gucci flask, I shit you not, I'm wasted big-time, like Passover wasted, like Yael Horowitz's bat mitzvah wasted, oooh, there's someone I want you to meet that wanted to meet you. Did that make sense? Let me find him again." Izzy peeled off mid-monologue in search of her prey.

Emer went to check on her dad, who was propped alertly in a wheelchair with Ging-ging in the center of the room. Emer approached, asking, "How'd you like it, Pops?"

Jim Gunnels teased his daughter. "I loved it, Bill, but Ging thought it was a piece of shit."

"Not true," protested Ging, laughing wearily yet happily, accustomed to the old man's hard wit.

"Well," her father said, "I'm looking forward to you reading me the whole thing, Bill. And I don't know why people think it's a novel, sounds like a goddamm straight-up history of New York City to me."

She kissed him on the top of the head, and as she straightened up she noticed a couple in the far corner smiling at her. A tall, dreadlocked black woman and her very handsome, very Irish-looking consort. Standing at his father's side was a mixed-race young man that must be their son. A passing gent patted the boy on the head. She watched as the boy's eyes turned red and his loose, pocketed 'fro seemed to become a nest of snakes. The boy's father leaned down and whispered calmingly in his ear. The boy's eyes returned to green, the snakes returned to hair. The father looked at Emer, shrugged, and mouthed, "The sequel."

Izzy interrupted this, towing a man in with her hand. The man seemed both embarrassed and charmed by Izzy's boisterousness. He was handsome in an Ivy League way, sporting a slightly unraveled, tweedy flair that smart college girls would cotton to. When he offered his hand to Emer, she felt a current run from him up her arm that was so startling, she had the urge to check if he had one of those dime-store novelty buzzers secreted in his palm. She recovered and spoke first. "Hello, I'm Emer Gunnels."

"I know who you are. I just spent the last ninety minutes trapped in the web of your imagination. Oh, that's a terrible line."

"I'll take it."

Izzy prompted him: "Do you have a name?"

"Oh shit, my manners, my name is Cuchulain Constance Powers."

"Jesus, that's a mouthful."

"That's what she said," Izzy offered up, going for that old chestnut, and continuing, off Emer's look, "Too soon? Too soon."

The man continued, "I'm a professor of comparative religion, actually, not true, associate . . . professor of comparative religion at the New School, well, again, wait, at the New School . . . Annex."

Emer smiled. "You're an honest man, Cuchulain Constance Powers."

"Some people call me CC, or Ken, or Cahouligan, but Con is fine. You know, I feel like we've met before. Jesus, another line. I'm just gonna walk away while I still have some dignity."

Izzy held his arm. "You can't get away now. We've got you."

He smiled. "Well, every year, I teach *Read Lightly, Goddess* to my sophomores."

Emer smiled back. "That should keep it in print, thank you."

"And you actually came to lecture my class once about five, six years ago. So we have met. Briefly."

"I'm sorry, I don't remember."

"I'm quite forgettable, that's like the most memorable thing about me."

Izzy was basically drooling on the side. "See that? He's got the funny, chicks dig the self-effacing thing. The funny and the smarty-pants combo platter. Good-looking man, too, I wouldn't toss him out of bed for eating crackers. Go ahead and tell her she's a genius. Emer—present your tush so he can blow smoke up it."

"Izzy."

"It's the wine! In vino veritas, queen."

Con looked gently at Izzy, and then turned back to Emer, noting that she was not apologetic for her rambunctious friend, and liking that.

"I'd be happy to blow smoke. I think you have cojones, great big cojones."

Emer nodded. "Okay. Thank you? Go on."

"I think you're gonna get attacked left and right by the PC police over stereotyping and fast-and-loose appropriation of cultures, but I also think you don't care; I think those are just red flags for the bullshit bulls; I think you're playing a longer game."

"I won't disagree. I mean, my great big cojones won't disagree," said Emer.

"Neither will I," said Izzy, " 'cause I have no idea what y'all are talking about."

Con took a step closer to Emer. She noted for the first time that he was tall; she found herself looking up to meet his eyes. It was a pleasant sensation.

"Can I ask you a question?" he asked.

Emer nodded.

"Do you actually believe in past lives? Or is it merely a trope?"

"No, not really. Trope, I guess. Well, I see that belief as an excuse not to live, or to find a seemingly logical explanation for ineffable shame or inexplicable good fortune similar to Original Sin or Calvinist Predestination, based upon the past actions of an unprovable actor."

"Or merely not taking full responsibility for this life?" Con added, "I think a design for the future, a hope for the future, in the form of a plan, or even a wish—that can be a way of not honoring the present, of living in denial. I mean, hope and fear, they're really just—"

"Bastard brothers?" Emer interrupted.

They locked eyes like there were two conversations happening simultaneously, one heard and one wordless. Emer was reminded of a line from Keats. Something like "heard melodies are sweet, but those unheard, sweeter." She wondered if she should say it out loud.

Izzy said, "Unprovable actor? What's an unprovable actor? You mean like Matthew McConaughey? Clearly this conversation requires more wine than I currently have in my possession."

"I believe," Emer elaborated, "more like all our lives are happening at the same time on different planes, a very, very deep present. And if that's not scientifically true, it is philosophically true in a pragmatic sense."

Con nodded. "No time like the present."

"Are you making fun?"

"Absofuckinglutely not," he said.

"Oh shit," Izzy deadpanned, "he means business."

"You have a way with adverbs, Con," Emer said.

They all smiled and fell silent and stared at one another for a moment or two.

"Is there something else you'd like to ask?" Emer asked Con. "I get the feeling there is."

Izzy wide-eyed stage-whispered loudly enough to stop conversations ten feet away. "She's single!"

"True story," Emer said.

"As am I," Con said.

Izzy blurted, "Case closed. He's a keeper."

Izzy backed away and went in search of more chardonnay.

Con asked his question. "Do you see this story, this love story, spinning out into infinite variations? Or are you saying that this one, the one that ends with the man making the ultimate, romantic sacrifice for the woman in the eternal struggle between perfection of the life or of the work—that that's the best of all possible worlds?"

"I'm a writer, I don't 'say' anything, I write around it."

"Touché."

"But I guess I'm 'saying' that, yes, there are infinite variations on a love story, but the best outcome, the best possible world is the one we are in right now. I have to believe that for my own sanity; and that this ending, the ending that's being written by Fate, negotiated tonight between my book and its audience, is the best ending."

"In other words, you don't know how it ends." He smiled.

"Not a clue."

"I was hoping you'd say that," he said.

"I think this is a longer conversation," she said.

"I think you're right. I'd like to have that conversation."

"Maybe we will. But not tonight. 'Cause I gotta go talk to these Hollywood peoples, Hollywoodians—about selling my soul to Tinseltown."

"Oh, I don't like that ending," he said.

"Then stay tuned," Emer said. "But it was nice to meet you, Cuchulain, CC, Con, I mean again, nice to meet you again. See you."

"Nice to see you again, too."

They shook hands, and Emer felt that electric surge of the novelty gag run up her arm and had the impulse to not let go.

Emer drifted to the other side of the room to continue with

some agents who had expressed interest in turning her vision into a series of movies about gods interbreeding hybrid powers in New World offspring. Con, feeling suddenly alone and awkward, moved away to grab his overcoat, but Izzy, materializing out of nowhere like an inebriated apparition, grabbed his arm and said, "Don't go anywhere, you idiot."

"What?"

"Dude, she'll be back."

And as if on cue, Emer turned again away from Hollywood and headed back to Izzy and Con, Izzy stage-muttering, "Whoa, sooner than I thought."

"Con?" Emer said.

"Yes, Emer."

"It's my birthday."

"Is it really?"

"Yes," she said as she shook her head no.

"Twenty-nine?"

"Something like that, yes."

"Well, if you'd given me a little more heads-up, I would've gotten you something," he said.

"That's very sweet," she said.

They stared at each other. Izzy said under her wine breath, "Not awkward at all."

Con smiled and asked, "Any wishes?"

Emer did not need to think. She made her wish. "Yes. A wish. I'd like to go somewhere right now, Con. With you."

"No time like the present," Con said.

JAMAICA 11.0

IT'S LONG PAST RUSH HOUR, so the train is not packed at all. Emer and Con enter the car and find a seat immediately. The conductor welcomes new riders to the train and rattles off the upcoming stops.

"You're a cheap date," Cuchulain says.

"That's what you think," Emer replies.

The conductor concludes the itinerary, "And the last stop will be Jamaica. Watch the closing doors."

The train shudders and moves forward, disappearing into the familiar unknown of a dark tunnel ahead. Emer takes Con's hand as the world outside swoons and fades away.

JAMAICA, OF THE MIND

AN OLD COUPLE WALKS DOWN THE BEACH hand in hand. They might be in their eighties, if they're lucky. Maybe the beach is in Costa Rica, maybe it's Jamaica. Or some other Jamaica of the mind. We don't know. The beach is pretty deserted, but there's a young kid who sits there every day with a Polaroid camera and some glass bottles. His name is Ruggerio or Sylvester or Sidney. We're never sure. He's figured out a little racket.

The old couple, they call themselves Con and Emer, passes the boy and he aggressively asks them to pose for a photo. They have a few bucks on them so they give them to him. He takes their photo and retrieves a light green glass bottle and cork from his weatherworn backpack, and he tells them to make a wish, put the photo inside, cork it, and send it adrift on the ocean—let fate take it, he says; he actually says, "Let fate take it."

The old couple likes that idea. They like the idea of living in a bottle together, they like the idea of letting fate take it. They insert the photo through the neck of the green bottle and cork it up tight. The old man, Cuchulain Constance, like the virtue, but his friends call him Con, like the man—his shoulders hurt, but he winds up like the ballplayer he used to be and throws the bottle as far out into the sea as he can. It lands way short of where he'd hoped, and he shrugs, like: I ain't the man I used to be. Emer looks at him with eyes that say: That's okay, I remember the man you used to be.

Nevertheless, the bottle makes it past the small breakers and, rather than being brought back to shore immediately by a wave, starts to bob out to sea.

Cuchulain and Emer sit on the sand and watch until the bottle is no longer visible. Sometimes they think it's lost only to find it a moment later popping up again. Their eyes are not so good. A couple of times, the bottle flaps its wings and flies off, and they realize they've been looking at a gull. They laugh at the magic of misperception.

After an hour or so, there are no specks or whitecaps to interrogate; the bottle is sunken to the bottom, or in the belly of a whale, or floating out to new lands, new times, finding a future they will never know, entering new parallels and parallel lives.

They won't be alive much longer, but one day, someone will find that bottle and wonder who the strangers in the photograph were. Someone may make up stories about the strangers and what they did. And some of it will be true.

All of it will be true.

AN END

ACKNOWLEDGMENTS

So much gratitude for my editor, Jonathan Galassi, whose continued belief and encouragement and steady hand quietly teach me more about being an author each time we persevere. Three novels with you, and without you, zero. My agent, Andrew Blauner, who somehow sees me and somehow still believes. And to Eleanor Chai, who long ago, when I pitched this story as being about a woman named Maudey, told me there was something in it. I would've given up on it if not for that. Thank you to Chris Carter for twenty-five years of showing me—a too heady, word-besotted AWOL graduate student/actor—the glories and importance of plot and the structure of the unbelievable. And to the Collegiate high school faculty of the 1970s, who introduced me to Yeats and taught me to write—Jim Shields, Dr. Stone, Boss Breimer, et al. And Maria DiBattista, who taught me Woolf and Beckett when I was nineteen and continues to teach me to this day. My sister, Laurie, a master teacher, who gave me a wealth of pedagogic stories to pull from. To Chantal Clarke for her judiciously fascinating research assist. And finally, to Rachel Chapman and those brilliant Yale undergraduates (you know who you are, I do not) who staged Yeats's *The Only Jealousy of Emer* back in 1985 or so and showed me a weird romance that stayed in my mind all these years, waiting, like the gods, their turn, waiting . . .